JUST ONE KISS

It wasn't the photographer's lights that were making Bridget warm and turning her cheeks pink. It was Jonas, standing under the mistletoe . . . waiting for her. In the cream-colored fisherman's sweater and those worn jeans, he looked utterly masculine and sexier than any man had a right to be. Bridget was grateful that her daughter had left for a few minutes. If the photographer asked her to kiss Jonas, she didn't know what she would do.

"Go for it!" Gil said loudly. "Give the man a kiss. How can you resist?"

She couldn't. She couldn't even think of a reason to refuse.

W9-BRX-510

BOOK YOUR PLACE ON OUR WEBSITE
AND MAKE THE
READING CONNECTION!

We've created a customized website just for our very special readers, where you can get the inside scoop on everything that's going on with Zebra, Pinnacle and Kensington books.

When you come online, you'll have the exciting opportunity to:

- View covers of upcoming books
- Read sample chapters
- Learn about our future publishing schedule (listed by publication month *and author*)
- Find out when your favorite authors will be visiting a city near you
- Search for and order backlist books from our online catalog
- Check out author bios and background information
- Send e-mail to your favorite authors
- Meet the Kensington staff online
- Join us in weekly chats with authors, readers and other guests
- Get writing guidelines
- AND MUCH MORE!

Visit our website at
http://www.kensingtonbooks.com

Mistletoe And Molly

JANET DAILEY

ZEBRA BOOKS

KENSINGTON PUBLISHING CORP.

http://www.kensingtonbooks.com

ZEBRA BOOKS are published by

Kensington Publishing Corp.
850 Third Avenue
New York, NY 10022

Copyright © 2007 by Kensington Publishing Corp.
"Green Mountain Man" Copyright © 1978, 2007 by Janet Dailey

All rights reserved. No part of this book may be reproduced
in any form or by any means without the prior written con-
sent of the Publisher, excepting brief quotes used in reviews.

If you purchased this book without a cover you should be
aware that this book is stolen property. It was reported as
"unsold and destroyed" to the Publisher and neither the
Author nor the Publisher has received any payment for this
"stripped book."

All Kensington titles, imprints, and distributed lines are
available at special quantity discounts for bulk purchases for
sales promotion, premiums, fund-raising, educational, or
institutional use.

Special book excerpts or customized printings can also be
created to fit specific needs. For details, write or phone the
office of the Kensington Special Sales Manager: Attn. Special
Sales Department. Kensington Publishing Corp., 850 Third
Avenue, New York, NY 10022. Phone: 1-800-221-2647.

Zebra and the Z logo Reg. U.S. Pat. & TM Off.

ISBN-13: 978-1-4201-0041-9
ISBN-10: 1-4201-0041-6

This novella was originally published under the title "Green
Mountain Man."

First Printing: October 2007
10 9 8 7 6 5 4 3 2 1

Printed in the United States of America

Chapter One

The tires made a crunching sound in the crusty, packed snow along the edge of the plowed road. Crossing the highway overpass, Jonas Concannon felt the grip of nostalgia at the sight of the picturesque village nestled in the valley. A patchwork of roofs rose ahead of him, the snow melting where the chimneys were perched.

The white church spire was almost lost against the backdrop of snow-covered mountains and fields. Garlands of snow draped the trees, the full evergreens and the bare branches of the maples alike.

At the top of the small hill just before the center of town, the traffic light turned red. The car protested the forced stop on the slope of the icy street. Jonas frowned.

The light changed to green and the tires spun uselessly for several seconds. He couldn't go forward, couldn't go back. He put the car in first gear and gained enough traction to get over the top of the hill. There was a touch of cynicism in his half-curved smile.

Nothing had changed. At least on the surface it seemed that way. Vermont had been covered with snow when he had left it ten years earlier. Everything in the village of Randolph appeared exactly as it had then.

But it couldn't be the same, Jonas thought. Not after ten years, no matter how much it looked like a picture postcard.

Turning onto the main street of downtown, he drove slowly across the bridge into the business district, glimpsing a few familiar faces among the bundled figures on the sidewalks.

He wondered why he'd come back, then mentally answered the question. Because he needed a respite from city life and the demands of the hospital clinic where he was completing his residency and working the longest shifts. He'd known that would happen when he'd signed on, and he was sure as hell giving it his all—but he was on the verge of burnout. Maybe it was obvious. He'd been granted time off without anyone asking too many questions.

Jonas saw an empty parking space and maneuvered the car into it. He'd told Bob and Evelyn Tyler that he would drive up on Friday, and had made good time. They wouldn't be expecting him until late afternoon. He had plenty of time to walk around the town.

Snow was shoveled in a mound near the curb. He had to force the door into it to get out, stretching his long legs for a minute, which were cramped from hours of driving. His breath formed a vapory cloud as he stepped into the chilly air and he reached back into the car for the fleece-lined jacket lying on the passenger seat.

Shrugging into it, Jonas slammed the car door and stepped over the snow pile to the sidewalk. He didn't bother to button the jacket. Instead he shoved his hands deep in the pockets to hold the front shut and began walking down the street.

Impervious to the freezing temperature and the overcast skies, he wandered aimlessly past the stores, gazing into shop windows and at the people he met. Several people he recognized, but he made no attempt to renew acquaintances.

A snowflake floated in the air before him, large and crystalline, and his hand reached out to catch it, triggered by a long-forgotten habit, something he used to do with Bridget. He stopped abruptly, the muscles working along his jawline as he stared at the white flake melting in his palm.

Face it, he told himself sternly, she's why you've come back. You're wandering the streets on the off chance that you'll see her. His hand closed into a tight fist, as if to crush the snowflake and the memories it evoked.

He began walking again, more slowly, hands clenched in irritation within the pockets of his jacket. During the ten years he'd been away from Randolph, he hadn't tried to keep in touch, not after Bob had written him that first year with the unwelcome news that Bridget was married.

It was purely by accident that he'd run into Bob and his wife in Manhattan shortly before Christmas. The giant tree at Rockefeller Center had been found and cut down in Vermont that year, then transported to New York on a flatbed trailer, arriving with the usual fanfare and news coverage. The Tylers had decided to be there for the great moment when it was lit up, officially marking the beginning of the holiday season. Jonas had been hurrying past the windswept plaza, but he'd had to squeeze through the crowds lining the sidewalk. Then a gloved hand caught him and Evelyn's pleased squeal of recognition stopped him in his tracks. The three of them had gone out for dinner in midtown afterwards, taking in the dazzling holiday windows of the Fifth Avenue stores first.

It had been a brief reunion, with Jonas insincerely promising to come for a visit. He had never intended to come. December, January, and February passed in a blur of patients and problems . . . then March arrived, and his resolve weakened. The pressures of work had gotten to him in a big way. A senior physician had tactfully recommended that he take time off and Jonas hadn't argued.

Couldn't go forward, couldn't go back. The line of his

mouth thinned at the way he had deluded himself into believing the only reason he was returning to Randolph was for rest and relaxation. This past week when he had contacted Bob to let him know he was accepting his invitation, Jonas had carried the self-deception further by insisting no one know of his visit. And he'd specifically asked that there be no welcome-home party.

"Damn!" Jonas muttered beneath his breath. He had nothing against parties, but he hadn't wanted to take a chance of meeting Bridget amidst a crowd of people, especially not with a few of Bob's famously stiff drinks clouding his mind. But that *was* why he was here—to see Bridget again. He cursed silently in frustration, hating the inner weakness that had brought him back.

Pausing in front of a shop window, Jonas stared at his reflection framed in a pane partially steamed over. What was the saying? That you never quite get over your first love? Maybe he had returned to deal with his disappointment at last, he reasoned, or at least to find out what had happened to her. He shouldn't even care by now.

Since he had learned she'd married within a year of his leaving, he'd tried to imagine her with three or four kids hanging on her, twenty pounds heavier, with a husband . . . but Jonas didn't know the man she had married. He had even blocked the man's name from his memory. The mere thought of that stranger lying next to Bridget, touching her silky skin, totally depressed him. A wintry frost entered his gray-green eyes.

A hand touched his shoulder. "Excuse me, but aren't you—"

Jonas turned around. "You must be mistaken," he snapped without sparing a second to identify the elderly woman.

Ashamed of his rudeness, he walked quickly away. Long, impatient strides carried him to the end of the block. Instead of crossing the street, he turned up the side street, wanting to avoid the traffic and people and the risk that someone else might recognize him.

Slowing his steps, Jonas raked a hand through his thick, tobacco-brown hair. He breathed in deeply, filling his lungs with the cold air while trying to check the tide of emotion flowing through him. His nerves and muscles were stretched taut.

Looking around to get his bearings, he glanced at the shop nearest to him. Magnetically his gaze was drawn, caught by the gleam of chestnut hair on the other side of the plate glass window. For a moment his breath was stolen by the shock of recognition.

Bridget.

He'd know her face, her profile, anywhere, even blurred by the foggy shop window. He had expected that when he saw her again after ten years, he would feel curiosity and, perhaps, the pangs of long-ago desire. Actually seeing her, he felt shaken. He hadn't anticipated such an intensely physical response or this fiery leaping of his senses. Just one glimpse of her brought back memories that were tender, sexual, and overwhelming.

She moved, disappearing from his view. Jonas knew he had to see her more closely without the distortion of the fogged glass. Through it, she had seemed unchanged, no different than when he had left ten years ago. He didn't want that. He wanted to see her changed into someone he no longer loved.

A bell tinkled above his head as he opened the door and walked in. Bridget's back was to the door, but she didn't turn around. Jonas paused inside, staring at her and feeling the years roll away.

A bulky pullover in forest green gave an initial impression of shapelessness until his gaze slid to the tailored wool pants of winter white she wore. He couldn't help but

admire the slenderness of her hips and the rounded firm-
ness of her buttocks.

Her figure hadn't changed more than an inch in ten
years. She turned slightly at an angle and Jonas corrected
his assessment. Not even the bulky sweater could conceal
the sensual fullness of her breasts under the heavy knit.

Fire spread through his veins and he swore inwardly at
the desire the sight of her was arousing. It wasn't what he
wanted to feel. He wanted to be indifferent, distantly
amused that he had once been attracted to her. He lifted
his gaze to her oval face, hardening himself against its
classic beauty.

Her complexion seemed paler, the innocence gone, only
the freshness remaining. There was a strained look to her
mouth, a forced curve to her lips as she smiled at the
woman standing in front of her. Jonas remembered the
way her hazel eyes used to sparkle. When he looked at
them, he found them luminous and bright but lacking that
certain something.

It was a full second before he realized Bridget wasn't
looking at the woman before her but staring beyond at
something else. His gaze shifted to locate the object of her
intense interest and encountered her image in a mirror
placed in a corner so the shopkeeper could always see who
entered the store.

Jonas realized that she had seen him almost from the instant he walked in. While he saw her reflection, Bridget
saw his, the mirror locking their eyes until she sharply
averted her head.

He waited for her to acknowledge him, to voice the
recognition that had been in her eyes. But she gave not the
slightest indication that she was even aware he was in the
shop. All her attention was directed at the woman with her.
The low, vibrant pitch of her voice that he remembered so
well was not for him.

The impulse to force the moment of confrontation surged through him, but he checked it, steeling himself to wait. A frown creased his forehead when Bridget walked behind the cash register counter, entering the sale and packaging several skeins of yarn for the woman. It struck him only then that she worked in the shop.

"Don't forget to call me when that dazzle yarn comes in, Bridget," the woman reminded her as she picked up her sack and turned toward the door.

"I won't."

At the last minute, Jonas realized he was blocking the exit and stepped to one side, nodding at the woman when she walked past him. She gave him a curious look and he wondered why, until it occurred to him that a yarn shop didn't get a whole lot of men coming in. The bell above the door dinged briefly and the woman was gone.

All thought about Bridget working in the store vanished at the knowledge that there were only the two of them. There were no other customers. They were alone and Bridget couldn't ignore him any longer.

"Hello, Jonas."

So cool, so composed. Jonas seethed at her calmness. She could have been greeting a casual acquaintance instead of a man she had once sworn she would never stop loving. But, of course, she had stopped loving him.

That was evident by the gold wedding band she wore on her ring finger. A cold feeling seized Jonas, though he didn't even know the man who had put it there. But that unknown someone was entitled to certain rights from Bridget that Jonas couldn't claim.

"Hello, Bridget." He walked to the counter where she stood.

"You're looking well," she offered politely without extending a hand in friendly greeting.

On second thought, Jonas decided that was best. A

handshake would have been a farcical gesture considering their previous relationship. He kept his hands in his pockets, an elemental tension crackling through his body.

"So are you." He returned the compliment, letting his gaze skim over her face and figure. Alert to what she might be thinking—was this encounter affecting her as much as it affected him?—he saw her stiffen slightly under his deliberately intimate inspection. Just as quickly she relaxed, tipping her head to a vaguely inquiring angle.

"What brings you back to Randolph?"

He watched her lips form the words and their final curve into a courteous smile of interest at his expected answer. He remembered their softness, their responsiveness beneath the pressure of his. Passion lurked beneath her calm exterior and he knew how to arouse it.

Hadn't he been the one to awaken Bridget in that way? And hadn't she responded like the woman she was? It was on the tip of his tongue to admit that she was the reason he had returned. Just in time, he remembered that another man was first in her life.

"I'm here visiting Bob over the weekend," he explained.

"Bob Tyler? Yes, he mentioned that he saw you before Christmas." Bridget nodded, her chestnut hair gleaming with a golden sheen from the overhead light. "He said that you'd promised to come for a visit, but I didn't think you really would."

"Didn't you? Why?" challenged Jonas, not liking the insinuation he sensed behind the remark. Regardless of the doubt he had felt at the time, events had proved he'd been right to leave ten years ago.

The bell above the door chimed loudly a second before someone slammed it shut with a force that rattled its glass. Jonas pivoted toward the sound, startled by the interruption, but the two little girls paid no attention as they raced breathlessly past him.

"Mom, is it all right if I go over to Vicki's house?" The request was issued by the smaller of the two.

Jonas froze, his gaze narrowing on the rosy-cheeked girl looking earnestly at Bridget. A wisp of sandy brown hair had escaped the striped stocking cap on her head, the trailing end wrapped around her neck.

It looked handknit, probably by Bridget, from warm brown yarn that matched her daughter's hair. Jonas understood in that instant how strong the bond between them must be—and felt guilty for coming back into his lost love's life. He wasn't entitled to be here. He wasn't entitled to anything. She had a child, maybe more than one, and a whole life he knew nothing about. He looked again at her daughter.

The girl's brown hair was a shade lighter than Bridget's, but she had the same classic features and the same hazel eyes, the same slenderness. She was Bridget's child, not necessarily a miniature of her mother, but the resemblance was obvious just the same.

"Oh, Molly. Don't you have homework?"

"No. I finished it."

"Well, then if you're sure it's okay with Vicki's mother, it's okay with me." Bridget's permission was met with gleeful giggles and hurried assurances from the second girl that her mother didn't mind. "I'll pick you up at Vicki's house a little after five. You watch for me."

"I will, Mom." The promise was blithely made, the girl's bubbling excitement centered on now and not later.

As the two girls turned to leave, they simultaneously noticed Jonas and paused. Molly's bright hazel eyes studied him, not looking away. Jonas looked right back, searching for a resemblance to someone else . . . her father. Finally the girl glanced hesitantly at Bridget.

"Molly, I'd like you to meet an old friend of mine, Jonas Concannon." Reluctantly the introduction was made. "Jonas, this is my daughter, Molly, and her friend Vicki Smith."

"Hello, Molly, Vicki." He nodded curtly, for some reason not trusting himself to say more.

"Hello." The breathless greeting from Molly was shyly echoed by the second girl.

"Run along, you two." Bridget smiled, and the pair darted past Jonas and out of the door with the same exuberance that marked their entrance.

Jonas watched Molly disappear before slowly bringing his gaze back to Bridget. "She looks very much like you," he commented stiffly.

"I'll—" There was a breathless catch to her voice, which Bridget self-consciously laughed off. "I'll take that as a compliment."

"I meant it as one," he confirmed. "How old is she?"

"Eight. Of course, Molly would insist that she's almost nine. It's funny how when you're young, you always want to be older."

Bridget lifted a hand to flip her shoulder-length hair away from the rolled collar of her sweater, the first gesture of nervousness Jonas had seen her make. There was a measure of satisfaction in knowing she wasn't as poised and nonchalant as she appeared.

He hoped he was making her uncomfortable. He knew what she was doing to him. God, how he knew! He thrust his hands deeper in his pockets.

"Do you have any more children?" The question was what he might be expected to say, but over and over his mind kept repeating that Molly could have been theirs.

"Only Molly. She's happy and healthy, and I'm satisfied with that." Bridget forced a smile, the corners of her mouth trembling with the effort.

Jonas wondered if she, too, was thinking that Molly could have been their child, but she wasn't. Another man had fathered her, and Jonas felt the unmistakable sting of jealousy.

"How are your parents?" He changed the subject abruptly.

"They're doing great." Her hazel eyes didn't quite meet his look as she answered. "It's coming into the busy time for them with sap starting to run. You wouldn't recognize the sugar bush. Dad has pipes running all over now. It's much more efficient than bucketing it out in sleds the way they used to. But it took him a while to install a state-of-the-art system. Now he wonders why he waited so long."

"Genuine Vermont maple syrup." That was a safe enough subject. Jonas tipped his head back, remembering. "It's been years since I've had any."

Not in ten years. But it was eleven years ago that Jonas was recalling. He had volunteered to help Bridget and her father gather the sap one weekend. Once the sap started running it was a daily chore and he had taken part on that one occasion.

Jonas remembered tramping through the wet snow to the large grove of maple trees on the farm with Bridget at his side, her gloved hand clasped in his. Her father had walked behind the sled pulled by the Morgan mare, the bells on the harness jingling in the crisp air.

The sky was sharply blue, the sun brilliant and the barren branches of the maple trees had cast cobwebby shadows on the snow. It was all so fresh in his mind that it could have been yesterday.

"Let's see if I remember right. The maple trees have to be about forty years old, then it takes four of them to make a barrel of sap." Jonas began reciting the lecture Bridget's father had given him back then, as if he'd been a city boy. "And it takes a barrel of sap to make one gallon of maple syrup. You don't make it into syrup by snapping your fingers. No, sir, you have to boil it down to a thick consistency, testing until you get it to the exact density. Then it has to be filtered and graded, packed and labeled. It's a science."

"You sound just like my dad."

"Is that a good thing or a bad thing?"

"I don't know," she murmured. "Takes me back, though."

He gazed at Bridget, a gentle smile softening the hard line of his mouth. "Do you remember that day?"

"How could I forget?" The firelights were back in her eyes, dancing and laughing, caught in the magic spell of memory. "You bombarded me with snowballs."

"Strictly in self-defense. You kept shoving snow down my collar," Jonas reminded her.

Her lips parted in a ruefully acknowledging smile at the way she had provoked him all those years ago. The snowballs had only been a part of his retaliation. The rest had come when Bridget lost her footing in the snow and fell while trying to run from him.

She'd lain there laughing, too breathless to move, and he had joined her in the bed of snow, intending only to silence her with a kiss. No, that wasn't true. He had wanted to make love to her, well out of sight of her father and everyone else. He'd settled for a kiss. One incredible kiss.

But it had been innocent enough until Bridget had seen the veiled look in his eyes and had made an almost inaudible moan of surrender. He'd met her later, in a cabin well away from her parents' house, after she'd sneaked out to be with him. There had been nothing innocent in the second kiss, nor the third or fourth. Jonas remembered fighting through her heavy winter outer garments to find the slender, feminine body they hid.

Only there hadn't been any satisfaction in that. He had wanted to feel the warm softness of her flesh, and she had let him go as far as he'd wanted . . . as far as they'd both wanted to go. Jonas had almost wanted to stop, had hoped her father would come looking for them, the mare's jingling harness warning them of his approach.

Even then Jonas was afraid of loving her too much. But he couldn't help himself, couldn't believe how much he wanted her. After that night, he'd had the feeling her father had known what had happened, known they had gone further than a playful romp in the snow, but he had said nothing.

Their rendezvous in the cabin had been the first of many times that Bridget had driven Jonas slowly and pleasurably out of his mind. There had been moments when he was certain she enjoyed making him crazy with wanting her.

It had been the beginning. But where there is a beginning, there must also be an end. Jonas thought it had ended, until now, this moment, when he wanted her more than he ever had in the past.

Tearing his gaze from her trembling lips, he saw that Bridget felt it, too. It was there in the darkening of her hazel eyes, the sweet torment of physical wanting.

"Bridget." His low, husky voice said her name in urgent demand.

She looked away, drawing a deep breath and releasing it in a shuddering sigh. "That was a long time ago, Jonas."

"Was it?" he said tautly, wondering how in hell she could control her emotions when he had so little control over his.

"I . . . Oh, excuse me, someone's at the door." Thank heavens for Dorothy Pomfret, Bridget thought. Dotty popped in whenever the mood took her and someone offered her a ride. "One of my yarn suppliers. Excuse me." Except for that second's hesitation, Bridget was again cool and composed.

Flicking an impatient glance toward the door, Jonas saw an older woman with thick gray braids, dressed in a colorful, flowing coat paired with work boots and carrying canvas bags brimming over with spun wool. She was a step away from the entrance. He turned instantly back to Bridget, his look hard and demanding. "Send her away," he ordered. "Tell her you're closing early today."

The stubborn set of her chin gave him his answer before

she spoke. "I won't do that, Jonas," she said quietly. "Not can't, but won't."

The shop door opened and closed to the tinkling of the overhead bell.

"Hello, Dotty," Bridget said.

"Hiya." The older woman glanced at Jonas, then turned her attention to Bridget.

As brief as her look had been, he had the feeling that he'd been assessed in an instant. Jonas sensed a shrewd intelligence in Dotty that was at odds with her eccentric attire.

"Have you heard the weather report?" Dotty asked Bridget.

"No, I haven't."

"Well, I can't stay long. It's going to snow," the woman insisted, then looked absent-mindedly around the store. "My sheep can tell. They won't leave the fold."

Jonas sighed inwardly. His big moment had been interrupted by someone who talked to sheep. Vermont was still full of oddballs and old hippies. He glanced back at Bridget, who was giving the woman in braids her full attention.

"Here you go," Dotty said, holding up a canvas bag bulging with skeins of wool. "All the same dye lot, so the color matches perfectly."

"That's great, Dotty. Thanks so much." Bridget took the bag by the handles and looked inside. "Ooh, gorgeous. You're using the natural dyes, right?"

"Yep."

"I'll be able to sell all of this right away."

"Good. I need the money," Dotty said briskly. "Who's the customer? From around here?"

It took Jonas a second to realize that she didn't mean him. She just wanted to know where her handcrafted wool was going, was all. He had forgotten how small a Vermont town could seem. The sense of community was still strong up here, unlike the impersonality of Manhattan.

"No," Bridget was saying. "A lady up north in Stowe. She wants to make an afghan to go with her new drapes and she sent me a swatch. A subtle celadon green like this would be perfect."

Dotty Pomfret frowned. "I would call that moss myself. Or maybe jade."

"Whatever. As long as she buys it."

The other woman nodded. "Oh, by the way, I need some jute. Where do you keep that?"

Jonas shifted in irritation, wishing the woman would hurry up and leave. He studied Bridget's face while she pointedly ignored him. Did she own this place or did she just work here? Something about her capable, in-charge manner suggested ownership. He looked around at the custom-built shelving. A skilled carpenter—her husband?—had done that. The attractive displays were undoubtedly her handiwork. He happened to glance at the business cards in a small holder by the cash register and saw her name on one. She did own it. He would have liked to learn more, but the older woman with gray braids seemed happy to monopolize Bridget's attention.

"It's on the shelf next to the display of knitting needles. But there are different kinds. What exactly are you look-ing for?" Bridget inquired.

Jonas gritted his teeth. This kind of female back-and-forth could go on forever. The cozy store had shelves and bins full of yarn, fabrics, and other materials for projects to while away the endless winters.

"I don't know." The woman shrugged, reaching in her pocket for a slip of paper. "I'm picking it up for my sister. Elizabeth wrote down what she wanted. Hey, if it didn't come from a sheep, I don't know what it is. Wool is my thing. She's into macramé."

Jonas wanted to roll his eyes but he didn't. Crafting just wasn't his thing.

"I'll help you." Bridget stepped from behind the counter as the woman headed toward the shelf she'd indicated.

One last chance. Dotty couldn't see them. Jonas turned to block her path, catching her by the shoulders to stop her when she would have pushed her way past him. Bridget stiffened in resistance, flashing him a resentful look.

"Have dinner with me tonight." The invitation was halfway between a command and a plea. His fingers began to caress her shoulders. "For old times' sake."

The impulse was there to draw her against his chest and kiss her into a submissive mood of acceptance, but Jonas couldn't do that, not after ten years, and not after the circumstances of his leaving, regardless of what had happened in the interim.

"It isn't possible, Jonas." Bridget firmly removed his hands from her shoulders. Aloof, she added, "Have a good time this weekend. I know Bob and Evelyn will enjoy your visit."

In final dismissal, she brushed past him. The gold of her wedding band flashed on her left hand and Jonas cursed himself for forgetting its presence. He watched her disappear behind the aisle without a backward glance.

He was making a fool of himself. He shouldn't have come back. It had been too many years since he'd left, and the ashes were cold. It was too late to breathe fire into them now. She was married. Another man had taken his place.

Jonas stormed out of the shop without a backward glance. He was halfway to his car before the mountain air cooled his temper and slowed his stride. The ignition keys were in his hand and he was reaching for the door when he glanced at the skis on top of his car.

Making a split-second decision, he turned away to enter the drugstore. He didn't have Bob Tyler's number on his cell phone, but he'd bet anything the Tylers were listed in the local directory. The old booth and its folding door were at the back of the store. How quaint. The phone even had a rotary dial. Jonas hoped the damn thing worked. He thumbed through the thin book until he found the number he was looking for. Dropping coins in the slot, he dialed the number and waited.

A man answered and Jonas spoke briskly. "Hello, Bob, this is Jonas."

"Jonas! Where are you? Evie has the spare room all ready for you and dinner in the oven." There was a brief pause before he added, "Evie said if your car has broken down, she doesn't want to hear about it. No excuse will be accepted for missing dinner tonight."

"Look, I'm sorry, Bob," Jonas broke in impatiently, "but something's come up. I can't make it."

"You don't expect me to believe that, do you?" Bob laughed. "What is she? Blond or brunette?"

Jonas neither confirmed nor denied that there was a woman involved in his decision. "Let me take a raincheck on your invitation, Bob, and I'll visit another time," he lied.

"You're always welcome, you know that."

"I gave you my cell number in New York, right? And my office number?"

"You sure did."

"So, uh, if you ever get back to Manhattan, call me," he offered politely.

"Maybe next month. Evie has been talking about going back ever since our December trip. She wants to do some serious shopping."

"New York's the right place for that."

Bob groaned. "Don't I know it. Okay, Jonas. Sorry we won't be seeing you. Take care and don't do anything I wouldn't do."

A few minutes later, Jonas was behind the wheel driving

out of town. Maybe I'll call Eileen when I get back, he thought disinterestedly. He hadn't seen her for a while, not since before Christmas. Running into the Tylers in New York meant Bridget's memory had been working on him as early as then.

"Damn!" He slugged the steering wheel in frustration, and winced.

Once Dotty got to talking, she didn't stop, Bridget thought. She listened absent-mindedly while she flipped through a catalog of craft supplies. Coming into town in winter was something Dotty did only when her neighbors gave her a ride. Her ancient pickup seldom started when the temperature dropped.

The Pomfret sisters lived by themselves on a ramshackle farm they couldn't afford to fix up. Now and then they sold off some acres to people from away who were looking to build a second home in scenic Vermont, surviving on that and Dotty's income from spinning and dying the wool from her flock of cantankerous sheep. The older woman was a real character, but the shop's customers were willing to pay a premium for her skeins.

Bridget had sent up a silent prayer of thanks when Dotty's unexpected arrival cut Jonas's visit short.

Jonas Concannon. Of all people to show up out of nowhere. Why and how he had, she didn't even want to speculate. He'd looked at her so intensely, like he was drinking her in after all these years. Staying calm had taken a huge effort—Bridget hoped she'd seemed nonchalant. It wouldn't do to let him know that seeing him made her heart race the way it had when she was only nineteen and he'd kissed her for the first time. Everything that happened after that . . . she wasn't going to go there. That was then. This was now. She was on her own, she had a daughter, Jonas was definitely not a part of her life.

Had he looked her up on the Net, found her website, and decided to stroll in? She hadn't asked and there was no way of telling. Bridget looked around her beloved shop, which she'd built into a thriving business that garnered orders from around the country.

Specialty knitters had spread the word about the wools she offered, and the custom quilt design business she'd added had boosted profits to the point where she was actually making a living and didn't have to depend on her parents. This year she'd even hired an assistant. Although Mrs. Dutton was nowhere to be seen at the moment.

Probably over at To Go, lingering over coffee and a cruller. Bridget couldn't blame her. The long winter was winding down and Vermonters were coming out of hibernation. She sighed, still thinking about Jonas. With Dotty around, Bridget didn't want to explain who he was or reveal how much his appearance had affected her emotionally.

And having Molly walk in and seeing the two of them together—that had been almost too much. Bridget would have sent her daughter over to Vicki's house even if Molly hadn't asked. That moment of their meeting had been mercifully brief.

Bridget glanced at the older woman, who was wandering the aisles by this point, just for something to do, the impending snow forgotten. A few more people came in and distracted Bridget from the whirlwind of her thoughts about Jonas for a while.

If not for the long winters, she never would have made a go of this business, Bridget reflected as she helped the customers. Of course, with everybody being online these days, they were doing even better than she expected. In fact, she felt sometimes like she wanted to cut back, but she couldn't. She made a point of being e-free on weekends—

the hypnotic power of a computer screen kept her rooted in her swivel chair more often than she liked, and Bridget would just as soon be outdoors with Molly, hiking or riding through the woods that surrounded their own land. Her daughter was growing up so fast.

Maybe that was a side effect of not having a father around. But the shop meant Bridget had time for Molly, who often stopped in after school and liked to create projects of her own. They were sewing a mother-daughter quilt together, one block for each month of the year, and Bridget did the designs from Molly's drawings. So far they had completed three blocks: a simple snowflake for January, a heart for February, and pastel crocuses for March. She looked out the window, reassuring herself that there were flowers under the snow, just waiting for the meltdown . . . and the inevitable muddiness of a New England spring.

Bridget looked at the clock. Five minutes to five. Almost time for her to go get Molly. Mrs. Dutton bustled in, grocery bags in her gloved hands.

"Sorry, honey. They were having a sale on tomato soup and you know how Elwood loves tomato soup . . ." She bubbled on as she stashed the bags behind the counter, taking off her warm things and waving to the customers. "Ohmigosh, is that Dotty?"

The woman with gray braids heard her name and came over, flowing coat swishing and workboots clomping. Bridget slid off her stool and found her own coat, happy to let Mrs. Dutton chat with Dotty for a while. If whoever had driven Dotty to town didn't show up, Mrs. Dutton would eventually drive the older woman home. Around here, people looked out for each other.

She left to collect Molly from her little friend's house, thinking about Jonas as she drove. A quick cell phone call from the curb saved her the trouble of stomping through the snow and ringing the bell. Molly raced out and got in, planting a kiss that smelled like watermelon candy on her mother's cheek.

"Hi, honey." She didn't put the car in drive, wanting to make sure her daughter was safely buckled in before she pulled the car away from the curb. Molly tended to forget about things like that, but Bridget didn't. She had only one child and she wasn't likely to have more.

There was no sound of latch meeting catch, no click. "I'm waiting," Bridget said sternly.

"Oh, Mom," Molly said. But she complied, folding her hands in her lap when her seatbelt was buckled. "Me and Vicki finished sewing the crocuses."

"Vicki and I," Bridget corrected.

Molly nodded. "That's what I said. Me and Vicki. But some of the stitches look lumpy."

"You can do them over. That's how you learn, by making mistakes." She'd certainly made a few in her life and she'd been a lot older than Molly at the time, Bridget thought. She permitted herself a rueful smile that Molly couldn't see in the semidark.

"I don't want to. It looks good enough. Can we start another block for April?"

"Sure. What do you want to put on it?"

Molly thought it over. "Mud. April is mostly mud."

Bridget laughed as she drove away from Vicki's house. "What about colored eggs and chocolate bunnies and pompom chicks?

"Oh yeah. I forgot about Easter."

Bridget ruffled her hair. "I didn't. Spring is coming, little girl. Wait and see."

Chapter Two

Toweling drops of bath water from her skin, Bridget paused uncertainly, listening. Someone was moving around in the living room. Draping the towel over a hook, she reached for the cotton robe hanging on the bathroom door. The material clung to her damp skin, interfering with her efforts to pull it around her.

She ventured into the small hallway, tying the sash as she walked. The living room was empty when she peered around the corner, but she heard movement in the kitchen. Pushing the hair away from her forehead, she frowned.

"Who's there?" she called, moving hesitantly toward the open archway to the kitchen.

A dark-haired woman moved into her view, smiling and waving to her from the area near the kitchen sink. "It's just me."

"Mother!" Bridget sighed in exasperation. "What are you doing?"

"I brought over some scallions and lettuce from the garden. It really makes a difference to start the plants in the greenhouse first. Do you know we might have tomatoes ripe enough to eat in a couple of months? I do enjoy fresh vegetables and your father just loves working with plants."

She began opening cupboard doors. "I brought some tulips too."

"I guess it really is spring."

"Where do you keep your vases, Bridget? I think you should start locking your door. Living alone the way you do in the country and with new people moving in all the time, you just never know who might walk in."

"That's true," Bridget said, stating the obvious. She walked to the cupboard above the stove to get the vase.

"Oh! You were taking a bath!" Margaret Harrison declared, only that moment noticing the robe her daughter wore and the damp tendrils of chestnut hair around her neck.

"Yes." Bridget was accustomed to her mother's lack of observation. "Long day at the shop. I just wanted to wash it all away."

"Oh. Is running a business still what you want to do?"

Her mother could go from zero to sixty with a loaded question like that. Bridget knew she shouldn't let it get to her, but it still did. "Of course. I have Mrs. Dutton to help and Dotty keeps me supplied with premium wool. The quilt-kit concept is taking off and the business is growing. Would you like to see a profit-and-loss statement?"

As she expected, her self-absorbed mother wasn't interested in the facts. Margaret only sniffed. "Dotty Pomfret really is dotty. I can't believe she still dresses like a hippie. Work boots and that weird cape."

"It's a coat. She wove the material herself."

"Someone should tell her the Sixties are over."

Bridget put her hands on her hips. "She manages to support herself and her sister Elizabeth. Anything wrong with that?"

"No. She's just so—so eccentric."

"That's not a crime. And you know as well as I do that

the Pomfrets have been in Vermont for generations. A lot longer than the Harrisons, come to think of it."

"And they don't have much to show for it," her mother said smugly.

Nettled, Bridget decided to tell her mother something she'd been keeping to herself. "I don't know about that. *Good Living* is featuring Dotty in a story on Vermont. Sheep and all."

Margaret's carefully groomed eyebrows shot up. "Really?"

"Yes. It's a Christmas crafts feature. They're going to photograph the shop too."

"Oh, my. *Good Living* . . . that's better than Martha Stewart." Instinctively, Margaret patted her hair, as if photographers were about to break down the door for a candid shot of her with a head of lettuce.

"It's going to be good for business."

"Of course it will. Just wait'll I tell your dad. He'll be thrilled for you," she said. "When is that going to happen? What do you have to do to get ready?"

"In a month or two. And I don't have to do a thing. They know what they need. A crew comes in and decorates the shop with a ton of Christmas stuff and we get photographed looking picturesque under the mistletoe and whatnot."

Margaret stifled a cough. "Well, Dotty is certainly picturesque. But I don't think any man wants to kiss her."

"Be nice," Bridget said in a level tone. "It won't kill you."

"If you say so, dear. Tell me more. Where are they going to get mistletoe in spring?"

Bridget shrugged. "Magazines shoot holiday features months ahead. I'm going to let them figure out the details."

"Will Molly be in the photographs?"

Bridget permitted herself a proud smile. "Yes. If I can wrestle her into a velvet dress and hair ribbons."

"I see. Well, congratulations. That is exciting news. Why didn't you tell me before?"

"Aarghh! I can't win with you!"

"Well, why didn't you? Any mother would want to know."

"Because I just found out myself. Now can we talk about something else?"

"Of course," Margaret said. "Are you going out tonight?" She began arranging the tulips in the vase Bridget had handed her.

"Yes, with Jim," Bridget replied. "I can arrange the flowers."

"Okay," her mother agreed, "I'll wash the lettuce and the scallions."

"There's no need for you to do that, Mother." Bridget was determined to stay calm. "I will."

"But you're going out this evening, you can't have your hands smelling like scallions." She turned on the cold water tap at the sink. "Where do you keep your knives, Bridget?"

Counting to ten, Bridget opened the silverware drawer and handed a paring knife to her mother. "Here you go."

"Wouldn't it be easier if you kept the knives in a separate drawer? There's too much risk of accidentally cutting yourself when they're with other utensils. Of course, it is your house and you're entitled to keep them where you please."

"Right. Thanks for helping." The faintly caustic remark sailed right over her mother's head.

"Jim is a good man. I like him," Margaret Harrison continued, not missing a beat. "He'd make an excellent father for Molly. Nice-looking man, even if he is short. Dependable, and intelligent, too. He isn't still working on that highway crew during the summers, is he?"

"Actually, he is." Bridget tried to concentrate on the tulips. Just opened, the colorful blooms nodded on stalks that curved a little. There wasn't anything she could do to make them prettier than they were.

"That's such a shame. He should spend the summers furthering his education instead of doing manual labor," was the sighing reply.

"Jim is still trying to pay for the cost of his first education," Bridget pointed out dryly.

"Of course, I understand that," her mother said, but Bridget doubted that she did. "But I just know that he could do so much better than teaching in our little college. I—"

"The Technical College in Randolph Center is an excellent school," Bridget said, annoyed enough to defend him.

"Yes, but Jim could do better. With an advanced degree, I'm sure he could be a professor some day in some Ivy League college. Hmm . . . maybe Princeton or Dartmouth. It would be so much better for you and Molly."

Just what it took to make a career move like that, not to mention the difficulty of getting academic tenure, wasn't worth explaining to someone who wouldn't listen anyway. "Isn't anybody good enough for me as they are?" Bridget demanded, thoroughly irritated by her mother's constant meddling. "Do you have to keep trying to change people and mold them into what you think they should be?"

"I am not trying to interfere." Margaret Harrison looked sincerely stunned by the accusation. "Your father and I only want what's best for you."

"Don't bring Dad into it," Bridget protested, "I have a feeling he only thinks and says what you tell him." She regretted the words the moment she said them, but her mother could be impossible.

Sure enough, Margaret Harrison fixed her with a steely glare. "Bridget, you know very well we talk things over—"

"Until he finally agrees with what you decide." Bridget turned away. She was losing her temper, and it was pointless.

"We always think about what would be best for you. And that includes the men you see. We want you to have the best, and there's nothing wrong with that." Her mother smiled. "Molly is going to be a teenager soon enough. Kids grow up so quickly these days—too quickly."

Bridget braced herself for a lecture on that subject. Fortunately or not, her mother returned to the general subject of ingratitude. "You'll find out for yourself what your father and I went through with you. Speaking of Molly, where is she? Out riding?"

"No, she's been wanting to spend the night with Vicki ever since spring break started. Since I was going out with Jim, tonight seemed the perfect opportunity."

"Vicki? The Smith girl? Really, Bridget, she could do better—"

"Mother!" Bridget pressed a hand to her forehead, rubbing at the throbbing pain of tension. "molly is my daughter and Vicki's a perfectly nice kid. As far as I'm concerned, she can pick her friends."

"But—"

"You can't control her the way you controlled me!"

Her mother stared at her for a silent moment, a hurt look in her brown eyes. "Why in heaven's name would you bring that up?"

"I don't know." Bridget shrugged impatiently. Her hand was shaking as she reached to adjust the tulips in the vase. She felt a familiar, hollow pain in her chest. "It doesn't matter."

Her mother turned back to the sink, rinsing the lettuce under the tap. "Your father and I were right to do what we did. After all—"

"But maybe I didn't want you to be right." Bridget fought back the emotions that gave her voice a telltale catch. "Maybe I loved him. Maybe that's all I cared about."

She ran her fingers through her hair. "Didn't you ever think of that?"

"That's all in the past, Bridget. You shouldn't let it upset you anymore. You have Jim now and—"

"I don't happen to love Jim," she said quietly. "He's very nice and we have fun sometimes, but that's about all there is to it. So don't go planning any wedding in the future. One was enough."

"You surely can't be feeling bitter about that," her mother protested with a disbelieving frown.

"That's enough. Please go home." Bridget reached over and turned off the cold water. "I don't mean to hurt your feelings, but I would like you to leave before I lose my temper."

"If that's what you want—" Margaret Harrison's chin elevated in stiff acceptance, wounded dignity in her proud smile. "Of course I'll leave."

She carefully dried her hands on a dishtowel near the sink and Bridget felt blindsided by emotional guilt.

"Damn it," she sighed, "it's not that I don't understand. I know you love me, but I'm twenty-eight years old. I have my own home and my own family now. I have to live my own life and make my own mistakes. You can't keep treating me like a child and trying to run my life."

"I am not trying to run your life, but I can't stop thinking of you as my daughter."

"I'm not asking you to. And I will always be your daughter," Bridget said patiently. "The only difference is that I'm an adult. Please give me some credit for having a little common sense and intelligence."

"I do—I always have," her mother insisted.

"Have you? Is that why ten years ago—"

"You were incredibly naïve then. And ridiculously romantic," Margaret said sharply. "I think I proved once and for all that Jonas Concannon wasn't the man for you. I don't understand why you keep harping on the same subject."

Bridget turned away. It was not something she could discuss with her mother. "I have to get dressed. Jim will be here in a few minutes."

As she started toward the bedroom, her mother asked, "Where are the two of you going tonight? Didn't you say something about seeing a movie in Montpelier?"

"That's where we were going originally, but Jim called this afternoon to change it." Her tone was neutral, but she could guess that her mother's next question wouldn't be.

"Then where are you going?"

Bridget stopped, her mouth opening in a silent laugh born of anger and disbelief. "Didn't you hear a word I said earlier, Mother?" she asked. "I don't have to account to you for my whereabouts."

"Someone should know where you'll be in case something happens to Molly. Is that too much to ask? We might need to reach you," Margaret reasoned.

For once, her mother had made a halfway reasonable point, although Mrs. Smith would be taking care of Molly tonight and not the Harrisons. It was all the unreasonableness that made Bridget more stubborn than she needed to be. Which only made her seem childish in her mother's eyes. She couldn't win. Shaking her head, Bridget didn't argue. Sometimes it was easier to give in than to fight for every scrap of her independence.

"Bob and Evelyn Tyler are having a party tonight. We're going there," she sighed. "Mrs. Smith knows where she can reach me."

"The Tylers?" Her mother's mouth curved in an expression of distaste. "Their parties are so rowdy."

"They're good clean fun. Noisy sometimes," Bridget admitted, "but remember, mother, we live in Vermont where the trees are close together and the people are far apart. Please go home. Dad will be wondering where you are."

"What's the occasion? For the party, I mean."

Margaret typically ignored what she didn't want to hear.

"Nothing special. It's just some friends getting together on a Saturday night. Now I have to get dressed." Again she started toward the bedroom.

"What time will you be home?"

Bridget stopped, angry sparks flashing in her eyes. "I have no idea." She looked over her shoulder in challenge. "Maybe I won't come home," she said dramatically. "Maybe I'll find an orgy going on somewhere and have Jim take me to it instead!"

"Bridget!" her mother breathed in shocked astonishment. She found nothing funny about the false threat.

"You'd better leave. Because, so help me, if you're still here when Jim comes, I'll start locking the door and I'll make sure you don't have a key!"

"I don't know what's the matter with you, Bridget, but you've certainly been short-tempered lately," Margaret declared indignantly, her voice fading away as Bridget went out of the kitchen.

The bedroom door banged against its frame as Bridget shut it behind her. Immediately she stopped, breathing a silent laugh. The bedroom-door-slamming scene happened too often, a part of her adolescence she hadn't left behind. It was a meaningless display of temper that wasn't going to get her anywhere. At twenty-eight, Bridget had become convinced that her parents were unable to see her as a grownup. She would just have to learn how to fake self-control, that was all.

As for the shortness of her temper, she knew the reason for that, too, and her preoccupation with the past. It was a direct result of that Friday in March when Jonas had visited her store. When she'd seen him standing outside, the years had melted away and she'd morphed into a nineteen-year-old ninny as if by magic. When he'd walked into the store, she couldn't make up her mind whether to run to him or from him. She had done neither, fortunately. And dear old Dotty's unexpected arrival had saved Bridget from doing or saying something stupid.

All in all, Bridget thought she had handled the meeting fairly well, appearing calm and poised regardless of the emotional turmoil that had been going on inside. There had been a couple of bad moments. In the end, she had kept her pride intact and brushed him off.

Previously she had been convinced that, although she hadn't forgotten him, he had become just an unpleasant memory. Bridget had long since willed herself to believe she could have a happy and rewarding life without Jonas.

But seeing him again had brought back all the love and passion she had once felt, and all the searing hurt she had known ten years ago. It wasn't easy reliving it again and going through the agony of getting over him a second time. She would, of course, and maybe this time it wouldn't take as long.

In the meantime, Jim would be arriving any second. Vermont's merry widow, he called her. The word widow sounded so old and she was so young. She let out a sigh. Right now she *felt* old. Bridget was determined that tonight she would just have a good time and ignore any memories of the past that tried to haunt her.

The merriest person at the party would definitely be her. Bridget O'Shea, widow of the late Brian O'Shea. Walking to her closet, she began to search for an outfit that would match her new mood. Hmm. She picked out pants and a top that would get her past her mother, should Margaret Harrison venture back to make small talk with Jim.

Twenty minutes later a male voice called out, "Hello? Anybody home?"

"I'll be right out, Jim," Bridget answered, taking a last-minute look in the mirror, fluffing the sides of her hair with her fingers before leaving the bedroom. "How do I look?"

She made a brief pirouette before the man standing in front of the sliding glass doors. Medium height, on the stocky side, with dark hair, Jim studied her appreciatively through his horn-rimmed glasses.

"Like a blast of sunshine." A lazy grin spread across his face, the ready smile one of the most appealing things about him, as he ran an appraising eye over her.

"Too bright, huh?" Bridget laughed, glancing down at her outfit.

The plaid of her slacks was in shades of yellow, predominantly canary, with a thin red stripe for outline contrast. The short-sleeved knit top with a scooped neckline was white with a large flower of the plaid material appliqued in the front.

Matchy-watchy, to the max. Her mother had picked out the set and boy, did it look it. But Jim was too nice to make unfavorable comments about a woman's clothes and too tactful to ever answer any does-this-make-me-look-fat questions.

"You look great," Jim assured her.

She hesitated. "Should I wear my warm coat or a jacket?"

"That depends on whether or not you were planning to take a moonlight stroll with me around midnight." His fingers curled an imaginary moustache.

"Seriously, Jim." Bridget smiled with affectionate exasperation.

"I was serious." He lifted his shoulders in an expressive shrug and sighed. "But you're not."

"Come on"—she refused to let the conversation shift to their personal relationship—"should I take a coat or jacket?"

"Coat," Jim answered at last. "No telling how much of

the party will be outside and how much in. April in Vermont? It's going to get chilly after the sun goes down."

"Okay then," Bridget decided. "I think it's in the kitchen."

"Hurry up," he prompted as she started toward the kitchen. "I volunteered to bring a keg of beer and I don't want it to get warm before we get to Bob's."

The coat was hanging from a hook by the back door. "Here it is." Bridget folded it over her arm and turned to rejoin Jim.

Her attention was caught by the spotless sink. There wasn't a trace of lettuce or scallions in sight. She looked for the tulips and saw the vase sitting on the coffee table in the living room, rearranged into a more attractive grouping than she had done.

"Of all the—" She pressed her lips together for a second. "I don't believe it."

"Don't believe what?" Jim asked curiously. "Why the frown? What's wrong?"

"Nothing," she said tartly. "It's just my mother, tidying up after me."

"My mother is the same way. Irritating, isn't it?" he agreed with a smile. "Ready?" He opened the sliding glass door onto the porch for her. "It can't be easy living across the road from your parents, still under their thumb, so to speak."

Bridget flicked a brief glance at the big white house opposite her small A-frame chalet. "That's putting it mildly," she replied and walked beside Jim to his Subaru station wagon. "I think my mother spends as much time taking care of my house as she does her own."

"Look on the bright side. Not everybody can have free maid service," Jim said as he opened the passenger door of the car for Bridget.

She smiled in rueful acceptance of his attempt to cheer her up. "True. I guess it really isn't too bad. And I can't say that I didn't know what my neighbors would be like before I moved in here."

"Now you have the idea." He smiled and walked around the car to the driver's side.

"It was really convenient when Molly was younger," Bridget enlarged on the statement. "I didn't have to worry about her coming home from school and not having anyone here because I was working. All she had to do was walk across the road to grandma's until I came."

"Molly's a bright kid," Jim commented idly as he reversed out of the driveway. "Is she staying over there tonight?"

"No, she's spending the night with a girlfriend, much to my mother's dismay," she sighed. "She's such a snob."

"Your mother wants to do the right thing. She's a lot like mine," he said. "Always knows what's right and proper for somebody else, regardless of that somebody else's opinion. It's a great way to make enemies and keep everyone walking on eggshells."

"Did you say you were a psychology professor?" Bridget laughed.

"No, I just know my mother. And from what you've told me about yours, they could be related," he grinned.

"You're very good for me, Jim." She leaned back in the seat, relaxing, no longer upset by her mother's interference.

"I could be better, but we won't go into that," he added quickly when his sliding glance saw Bridget tense. "Patience is one of my main virtues, as you'll discover."

"And perception," she added thoughtfully.

Jim shrugged. "Well, it doesn't take much to see that you were deeply hurt when you lost your husband."

She looked out the window at the verdant landscape. Her reply was carefully phrased—she hoped it didn't sound rehearsed. "Brian was a good man, compassionate and understanding. You're like him in many ways."

"Is that why you're so wary? The good don't always die young, Bridget," he teased, but with a note of compassion.

"I know," she agreed, nodding faintly without letting her gaze wander from the countryside. "Gee, it's all so green, isn't it?"

Jim studied her profile for a second, knowing she had deliberately changed the subject, but as he had said, he was patient. Six months ago, she had refused to go out with him. He had made progress since then.

"Yeah, Vermont really is, once spring makes up its mind," he commented.

It was only a few minutes' drive to the Tyler house. Of course, any place in Vermont seemed to be only a short drive away through unspoiled countryside. Rolling hills and jutting mountains were covered with trees just beginning to turn a fresh new green—hickories, maples, and birches, interspersed with dark green pines. Lush meadows and carefully tended fields dotted the valleys, rustic and beautiful with occasional stone fences meandering through them.

A stand of white birch marked the front lawn of the Tyler house. There were already several cars in the driveway when Jim pulled in. The sounds of laughing voices and music indicated the party had begun.

"I think everyone's in the backyard," Jim observed. "You go ahead and I'll get the keg of beer from the back."

"All right." Bridget smiled, stepping out of the car when he switched off the engine.

She had barely rounded the corner of the house when she was hailed with a chorus of greetings. A half a dozen couples, some wearing jackets and some wearing coats, had already arrived. Hamburgers were sizzling on the grills set up near the picnic tables in the backyard. It wasn't really warm enough to eat outdoors, but their hosts couldn't very well set up the big grill inside. One table was already laden with an assortment of other foods for a buffet.

"It's about time you came. We were going to eat without you," Bob threatened laughingly.

"No, you wouldn't," Bridget countered, "Jim is bringing the beer."

At that moment, Jim rounded the corner, toting the keg of beer on his shoulder. Thirsty volunteers gave him a hand in setting it down and breaking it open. With good-natured jostling, they argued over who would draw the first draft.

Evelyn emerged from the rear entrance of the house, pot holders offering a protective grip for the handles of the hot dish she was carrying. She started to greet Bridget, but she coughed at the smoke hanging in the air and didn't complete it.

"Bob!" she wailed in protest. "You were supposed to be watching the hamburgers!"

"Sorry." Bob, tall and dark with a waistline that was beginning to thicken, raced to the smoking grills. "I hope everybody wants their hamburgers well-done," he joked as he began the rescue efforts.

"He's worse than a child," Evelyn murmured to Bridget with a rueful shake of her head. "You can't turn your back on him for a minute."

"Can I help with something?" Bridget asked.

"You can fix the relish tray. Everything is in the refrigerator and the dish is on the counter," her hostess suggested.

The barbecue parties the Tylers gave were always informal gatherings with everyone lending a hand. It was almost a family affair. Most of the couples had known each other since school days.

"Consider it done." Bridget started toward the house.

"I just unmolded the jello salad to end all jello salads. Keep the cat away from it, okay?" Evelyn called after her. "I don't know what he thinks it is, but he's fascinated by it."

"Will do." She laughed the promise.

The pumpkin-colored tomcat was crouched on a kitchen chair when Bridget entered the house. A gleaming jellied salad, the object of the cat's interest, was sitting on the table. His tail swished in resentment as she shooed him from the chair before walking to the refrigerator.

Humming softly to herself, she began setting out the celery, carrot sticks, and various other ingredients she found and began arranging them on the partitioned plate. As she was spooning olives from the jar, she heard footsteps enter the kitchen from another room of the house. Anticipating one of the three Tyler children, she didn't bother to look.

"Hello, Bridget."

The spoon of olives halted in midair. For an instant she couldn't breathe. Her gaze darted to the man pausing beside her to lean a shoulder against the refrigerator door. First searing fire, then ice ran through her veins.

"Hello, Jonas." Was that her voice responding so calmly? "I see you've finally managed to accept Bob's invitation for a visit."

Her hand was amazingly steady as it carried the spoon to the relish tray, but she was painfully aware of him standing beside her. The clean male scent of him filled her senses.

His hair glistened damply as if he had recently stepped from the shower, darkening its normal dark brown shade. A white shirt was opened at the throat, its long sleeves rolled halfway up his forearms. A pair of crisp new Levi's covered his long legs.

"Yes. I canceled my March visit." Jonas reached past her to steal an olive. "But I imagine you know that," he added dryly.

"Evelyn mentioned you'd called at the last minute to

postpone it," Bridget admitted. It would have been useless to deny it.

"And you didn't say anything about seeing me." It was a statement, not really needing any confirmation.

"I didn't see the point." She added more olives to the tray. "They were already disappointed that you hadn't come. I know they must be delighted to have you here now."

"I guess that woman—was her name Dotty?—didn't talk about seeing me in the store."

"Oh right. Dotty Pomfret." Bridget shrugged. "I don't think she knew who you were. Maybe she took you for a lost tourist or something. We didn't discuss it."

"Guess I'm just not that important."

Bridget didn't want to take that bait. She kept her eyes on the relish platter. There was room for radishes, but she didn't bother with them. She wanted to get out of the house and mingle with the crowd outside. There was safety in numbers.

"You aren't," Jonas stated.

"Huh? Aren't what? I'm not following you." She screwed the lid on the olive jar, avoiding his gaze as she had since he had appeared.

"You aren't delighted that I'm here now," he mocked.

"Of course I am," she lied brightly.

"That's funny. You don't look it," Jonas observed, tipping his head to get a better view of her expression.

"I'm sorry you think that." Bridget shrugged and picked up the relish tray. As she turned to leave, Jonas moved as if intending to keep her from going. "Would you bring the jello salad from the table when you come? I think we're just about ready to eat."

His brooding gray-green eyes studied her seemingly composed features for a disturbing second before he walked to the table. Bridget knew he was right behind her when she left the house.

"Hey, the guest of honor has arrived!" Bob declared when he saw Jonas following her. He lifted his glass of beer in a toast. "Welcome home, Jonas!"

Evidently this was Jonas's first appearance at the party, Bridget guessed, as the other couples gathered around to greet him. Placing the relish tray with the other food dishes, Bridget walked to the charcoal grills where Evelyn had replaced Bob as the chef.

"Let me hold the platter," she offered, taking the oblong flat dish that Evelyn was trying to balance while lifting the patties from the grill with a long-handled spatula.

It was surrendered willingly. "Jonas is getting a hero's welcome, isn't he?" Evelyn spared a brief glance in the direction of the main group.

"He certainly is!"

The hint of sharpness in Bridget's voice didn't go unnoticed. She realized it when she saw the flicker of concern in Evelyn's eyes.

"You don't mind about Jonas being here, do you?" she asked. "After Bob asked you and Jim, I wondered if it would bother you. I know it was ages ago, but the two of you broke up so suddenly. None of us ever knew exactly what went wrong. You left so soon after Jonas did."

"No, I don't mind," Bridget was quick to assure her. "And you're right, it was ages ago. When we were all young and stupid."

Her hostess grinned. "Speak for yourself!"

The truth was that it seemed like only yesterday. Bridget's gaze wandered to Jonas, memories rushing back. The first time she'd seen him eleven years ago she thought he looked like a mountain man, tall and rugged, standing an inch over six feet.

Well muscled despite his youth, without an ounce of spare flesh, he already had a wide chest and broad shoulders that tapered to a slim waist and hips. He had an earthy maleness that women noticed—especially one as innocent as she had been.

The years hadn't made many changes in his appearance, except that he seemed somewhat aloof, without the open warmth in his smile that had melted her teenage heart. He was more sophisticated now—the city had left its mark. But Jonas was still a heartbreaker. Any woman would confirm that.

Watching him, Bridget saw him laugh, the slashed lines deepening around his mouth, his eyes crinkling at the corners. She remembered the potency of that smile. He was quite capable of disarming any female, herself included. Nothing could change that.

"Ah, food!" Jim was standing beside her, sniffing hungrily at the platter of meat. Possessively he curved an arm around her waist. "You and I are going to be first in line to eat."

Bridget was about to make some idle response when Jonas swung a harsh, narrowed look at her. That was another thing about him that hadn't changed. His alert gaze never missed anything.

He still possessed an uncanny knack of connecting with her emotionally even when he seemed not to be aware of her. It was disconcerting to learn that this invisible link hadn't weakened.

More than ever, she knew Jonas still wanted her. But she wasn't going to fall into that trap a second time. She'd managed to keep him at arm's length in her shop; she could do it here. Deliberately she beamed an adoring and happy smile at Jim, knowing Jonas would see it and draw his own conclusions. She was sorry if Jim mistook her meaning, but more than ever before she needed him to stay close to her tonight, a shield to ward off trouble.

Jonas could think whatever he wanted. She didn't have to answer to him either.

Chapter Three

Jonas didn't make any attempt to test her, not even approaching Bridget while she was in Jim's company. The setting of the sun made it too cold out even for hardy Vermonters and the party was forced to continue inside.

The open-plan layout of the living room and dining room meant it was impossible for Bridget to avoid Jonas indefinitely. When she saw him wandering toward the sofa where she and Jim were seated, she braced herself for the inevitable conversation. Unfortunately, Bob chose that moment to refill his beer glass, leaving a chair vacant beside the sofa.

"Mind if I sit down?" By the time the entire question was spoken, Jonas was already sitting in the empty chair.

"I don't," Bridget lied, trying to sound casual, "but Bob might when he comes back. He was sitting there."

"I'll fight with him over it." Jonas smiled lazily, the glittering light in his eyes mocking her denial before sliding to Jim. His arm was draped over the back of the sofa near Bridget's shoulders.

"Have you met Jim Spencer?" An introduction seemed necessary. "He teaches at the college."

"And survives the summers doing road construction,"

Jim inserted before Bridget could say any more. He offered a hand to Jonas. "Saw you outside. Nice to meet you."

"Same here." Jonas nodded in apparent friendliness.

But Bridget saw the assessing gleam that measured his opponent, a suggestion of male rivalry in the look. Muscles flexed in his tanned forearm as Jonas briefly gripped Jim's hand. Then he leaned back, relaxing in the chair. Yet Bridget guessed that he was no more relaxed than she was, her nerves jumping, alert to every move he made or didn't make.

A sound system was playing in the far corner of the room. The couples had scattered into clusters in various parts of the room, milling around in changing groups, laughing and talking, enjoying themselves as Bridget wished she could.

"Bob's parties haven't changed since we went to them together, right, Bridget?" Jonas seemed to casually toss out the observation.

Bridget tensed. She hadn't mentioned anything to Jim about Jonas. Prior to the party, she hadn't known he would be here. Once he'd surprised her in the kitchen, she hadn't wanted to call attention to the fact that she had an old boyfriend present.

"You two used to know each other?" The possibility hadn't seemed to occur to Jim until that moment.

Her gaze ricocheted from his curious look and was encountered and caught by the cynically amused light in Jonas's eyes. The hard line of his mouth twitched slightly.

"Bridget and I knew each other very well," Jonas answered.

Her cheeks flamed at his dry, suggestive tone, the heat spreading through every inch of her body. Jim's arm slid down to her shoulders, firmly staking the claim he hadn't thought necessary at first.

"That was a long time ago, Jonas," she breathed in resentment, flashing him an angry look.

"So you said before," he returned with a glint of skepticism that said time had no bearing on the matter.

Considering the havoc he was raising with her senses, Bridget was afraid he was right and she didn't want him to be. His gaze flicked to the empty glass in her hand.

"Would you like me to refill that for you?" Jonas offered.

"Yes, please," Bridget answered. She would have said anything to have him gone.

"I'll get it for you." Jim reached for the glass she had started to hand to Jonas. His air was definitely possessive, making it clear that *he* took care of Bridget's needs, not Jonas.

Shrugging, Jonas seemed to accept Jim's claim and didn't argue. Bridget couldn't protest. Only when Jim was walking away did she notice the satisfied curve to his mouth that indicated Jonas had guessed what Jim's reaction would be. He had been left alone with her the way he had planned. Bridget felt suddenly vulnerable.

"Afraid?" Jonas challenged in a treacherously low voice.

"Of what?" Her hazel eyes were deliberately blank and innocent.

"Of being alone with me," he explained.

"Don't be silly, Jonas," she said, angered that he could sense her reaction.

His jaw tightened, a mask stealing over his face to make his expression unreadable. He lowered his gaze to the amber liquid in the glass in his hand.

"Why didn't you tell me your husband was dead, Bridget?" he demanded.

Unconsciously, she turned the plain gold band on her finger, a nervous, protective reaction to his sudden change of the subject.

"I assumed you knew," she answered truthfully. "Everyone here does."

"I didn't know until Bob mentioned it." There was an impatient snap to his answer, followed by an equally sharp glance. "You seem so matter-of-fact about it."

"Brian has been dead a long time. Life goes on," Bridget defended herself, bridling at his implied censure.

"Why do you still wear a wedding ring?"

"That's none of your business."

Again he let his gaze concentrate on the beer in his glass. "Did you love him?"

"That really doesn't deserve an answer," she hissed in pain and anger, nearly choking from the tightness in her throat, "not if you think I would let a man father my child without loving him."

Jonas glanced at her but seemed otherwise unaffected by her indignant outburst. If anything, he seemed a little dubious.

"Oh. I suppose you loved him as much as you claimed to love me." Although it was spoken smoothly, there was a sarcastic bite to the statement.

"No," Bridget retorted in kind. "I didn't make the same mistake twice."

"Where did you meet this Brian—" Jonas waited for her to fill in the blank.

"O'Shea, Brian O'Shea," she obliged and hesitated. There was no reason not to answer his question. Anyone in the room could tell him the story. "After you—left, mother thought I should get away for a while, so I went to stay with her sister in Pittsburgh. Brian was her husband's nephew."

"Ah, yes, your mother." His tone was cold. "I suppose she approved of Brian."

"Yes. He was a good man, gentle and understanding, two things I needed very desperately at the time." Without realizing it, Bridget got up, unable to continue the conversation.

Fluidly, Jonas rose to stop her, his fingers circling her wrist. "I figured you were hurt when I left," he admitted, "but it couldn't have meant all that much."

Didn't it? Look at my heart, she wanted to cry. But Bridget kept silent, preferring to let him believe that she had gotten over him whether it was true or not.

"So what happened? How did—Brian die?" He almost growled the other man's name.

"In a car crash. Instantly." Her words were clipped and to the point.

"And you went running home to mama," Jonas concluded.

"Within a few months, yes." Her chin lifted to a proud angle, but she didn't let her gaze rise to meet his. "It isn't easy to cope when you're young and alone and have a small child. And I was homesick for Vermont. I didn't like the city."

"And what about Jim? What is he to you?" His fingers tightened ever so slightly around her wrist, then relaxed.

"Does it matter?" Bridget protested, darting him an angry look.

"It shouldn't but it does." He let her go as if he regretted admitting it. At the wary light in her eyes, he gave a little groan and swore beneath his breath. "And I shouldn't have said anything."

"You're right about that. My entire life is none of your business."

"Got it. No more questions. Pretend we're strangers then. Let's dance."

"No."

But he was already propelling her to an empty space in the living room and turning her into his arms. Bridget couldn't object without creating a scene. Besides, if she protested too strongly Jonas might suspect how vulnerable she still was where he was concerned.

The firm hand at the back of her waist forced her to dance close to him, the muscular hardness of his thighs brushing against hers. Bridget stared at the open collar of his shirt, fighting the dizzying sensation of being in his arms again.

Her hand rested lightly on his shoulder as she tried not

to feel the warmth of his flesh burning through the white of his shirt. His hand began to roam slowly over her lower back and spine, melting her resistance. His touch felt so familiar . . . and it felt so good to be near him. It felt *right*. When Jonas bent his head, she had to close her eyes as his breath stirred the hair along her neck.

"We'll start fresh, Bridget," he said softly. But she could hear the determination in his voice.

"No." She shook her head, trying to sound as determined as he did.

"Why not? You want to—I can feel it." There was no mistaking the confidence in his tone.

"No, I don't, Jonas," she said tightly. "If—If I've given you that impression, then it's only because I'm susceptible to memories, too, remembering the way it used to be."

"It doesn't have to be just memories. I still want you, you know."

"No," she breathed, "you only want a weekend fling with an old flame."

His mouth moved against her hair, sending tremors quaking through her all too willing body.

"Honey, I want more than that. Much more."

"You . . . you can't come waltzing back into my life and expect to take up where you left off," Bridget protested.

"Can't I?" Jonas asked, his head bending lower as he searched for the sensitive area along the curve of her neck.

His self-assurance bordered on arrogance. Hearing him talk to her like that was what Bridget needed to remember more than her love. It reminded her of why he had left so long ago. She had been a different person then—a girl, really. Her hands strained against his chest, wedging a space between them.

"No, Jonas." Her voice was cold and self-assured. That, more than her physical resistance, stopped him. "Ten years ago you said good-bye to me. Now it's my turn. I don't care if I ever see you again. So when you leave for New York, don't bother to come back to Vermont because of me."

His rough features grew hard and there was an icy look in his eyes. But his voice was soft, so soft the words weren't altogether clear. "I'm sorry to disappoint you, Bridget, but I'm not going back to New York."

"What?" She stiffened, uncertain if she'd heard him right.

"The reason I was late getting ready for tonight's party is because I'd spent the afternoon in town." A look of amusement she didn't understand glittered in his eyes. "I had to meet with the realtor to sign all the papers for my new home."

"Where?" Bridget drew back and he released her, letting her stand freely in front of him.

"I bought the old Hanson farm. We're neighbors now. Isn't that a pleasant surprise?"

Too startled to reply, she just gaped at him. No matter what, she didn't want him to know that he'd done something guaranteed to turn her life upside down and inside out.

"I'm glad," she lied bravely. "Mr. Hanson had been trying to sell that place for years. Now he'll be able to move into town. It's a beautiful piece of property, Jonas, I'm sure you'll like it. Congratulations."

He was puzzled by her calm response, maybe even angry. Bridget could see it in the muscle leaping along his jaw. Abruptly he turned away to stride into the kitchen. The victory, temporarily, was Bridget's. But she didn't feel like a winner. The sensation was more like that of a survivor.

No one appeared to have noticed that Jonas had left her standing in the middle of a song. Bridget joined the nearest group, letting their voices and laughter hide her shaky composure. Soon Jim was at her side, handing her the glass of beer he had left to get.

After nearly an hour, what Bridget thought was a decent interval, she suggested to Jim that they leave, pleading a headache. He agreed without hesitation, although his gaze swung to Jonas at the far side of the room, guessing the cause of her headache. Not once did he ask any awkward questions that she would have been reluctant to answer.

Twice in the two weeks after the party, Bridget saw Jonas in town, always at a distance. He didn't enter the shop or try to talk to her. She wasn't certain that he had given up, though, but then she had never pretended to totally understand him. At the age of nineteen she had sometimes believed she could, until that long-ago day when he had told her he was leaving, ignoring her declarations of love.

Her mother was incensed when she learned Jonas was moving back to Vermont, and positively livid when she discovered he had bought the Hanson farm that abutted their rear property line. Bridget hadn't told her, but Margaret found out. The local grapevine was pretty efficient.

"Bridget, he's up to no good," Margaret Harrison had warned her daughter, having raced over to the chalet the minute she had heard. "And don't you go getting involved with him again. I don't care if he is a doctor—"

"He is? Who told you that?"

"Suzy Briggs looked him up online for me. She's quite thorough. It's amazing what you can find out."

So Jonas had done that well for himself. That must really stick in her mother's craw. Bridget didn't know what to think and she didn't quite know why she hadn't ever looked him up online herself. She wondered why he hadn't told her anything specific about himself—and why he wasn't married. A tall, good-looking doctor with a New York City practice? Women must be throwing themselves at his feet. She snapped out of it when her mother's voice rose to an unpleasantly high pitch.

"You learned your lesson as far as Jonas Concannon is

concerned, and you learned it the hard way. You have to accept that he hasn't changed. I know once you realized what kind of a man he was—"

"Don't worry, Mother," Bridget had interrupted her but her tone was patient, almost weary. "It isn't a lesson I'm likely to forget."

That wasn't enough. Despite Bridget's assurance, Margaret Harrison seemed to believe it was her duty to remind her daughter of her warning every time they met. She was constantly cross-examined as to whether she had seen or talked to Jonas just about every day for the following two weeks. Margaret was invariably skeptical of Bridget's answers, which was just as upsetting as Jonas's return to Randolph.

Bridget wasn't always going to be able to avoid him, but right now it was her mother she wanted to avoid, though. Bridget was dreading another interrogation as her parents' large white house came into view around the road's curve. Her own small A-frame was hidden briefly by the thick leaves of the trees. Slowing the car, she saw Molly in the garden with her grandfather and honked the horn, relieved that she wouldn't have to go to the house to get Molly.

Glancing up, Molly waved and began sprinting to meet her, tawny chestnut hair tied in pigtails flying behind her. Instead of turning into the driveway of the big house, Bridget turned the car into her own. A breathless Molly reached her as she stepped out of the car.

"You're late," Molly panted. "What happened?" She answered her own question. "I guess someone came in the shop five minutes before you were going to close."

"I stopped for groceries." Bridget took one of the bags from the back seat. "You can help me carry them in."

"I'm not strong enough."

"Don't give me that."

Molly made a face, but obligingly gathered the bag in her arms.

"What did you do today?" Balancing a second sack, Bridget reached for a third.

"I worked on my quilt blocks. I finished April and May."

A bunny and a somewhat crooked maypole, respectively. The little girl was proud of every stitch and was turning into quite a quilter.

"What's next, Mom? Can I design something on your computer?"

"Sure. We'll think of something good for June, sweetie. I've just been so busy—"

"We could do a watermelon. Or a bullfrog. There's a big one in the pond. I want to catch him for a present for Grandma."

Bridget smiled. Molly was still a tomboy at heart. "I don't think your grandma would be happy if you gave her a frog."

"She says I drive her up a tree sometimes." Molly grinned impishly.

"Oh, Molly!" Bridget couldn't help laughing as she shook her head. "Let me guess. Today you kept on saying you wished you had something in-ter-est-ing to do."

"You sound just like me," Molly crowed.

"I was trying to."

Molly sighed. "Grandma has just been in a bad mood lately. What's wrong, Mom? Why is she so upset?"

Pushing the car door shut with her hip, Bridget tried to avoid the true reason. "Everyone has bad days now and then."

"But she keeps talking about the same thing. It's boring."

"Oh? And what would that be?" Bridget blew out her breath, wishing her mother had the self-discipline to watch what she said around an impressionable kid. Apparently not.

"That man, that man, that man. Why did that man have to come back? Over and over. She bugs Grandpa about it and asks him if there isn't some way to make that man go away." Molly frowned, glancing up at her mother for an explanation as they crossed the driveway to the steps leading up to the chalet's porch. "What man?"

"Walk ahead and open the screen door for me, will you?" Bridget requested, stalling for more time while she tried to think of a reply.

Molly shifted the bag of groceries to one arm as she put her foot on the bottom step, looking at her mother and almost knocking over a flowerpot on the near side. "Do you know who Grandma means?"

"I—" The sentence was never finished. *That man* was standing on the porch. Even though she'd anticipated such a meeting eventually, it took Bridget a minute to recover from the shock of seeing him. She took a deep breath. There was no sense in scaring Molly or even making her nervous. "What are you doing here, Jonas?"

"I decided it was time to visit my neighbors," he replied calmly. "The porch seemed like a good place to wait." His gaze drifted lazily around him. "Nice place."

"Thank you." Her tone was crisp. She didn't invite him in.

"Are we neighbors?" Molly studied him curiously, not recognizing Jonas as the stranger she had seen so briefly weeks ago in her mother's shop. "Oh—you must be the person who bought Mr. Hanson's farm."

"That's me." Jonas inclined his head in acknowledgement, giving the pigtailed girl standing beside Bridget a curious look of his own.

"Put the groceries in the kitchen, Molly. There's one more bag in the car. Would you get it for me? Then take it inside too." It was an order, not a suggestion, issued to keep Jonas at a distance she was comfortable with. Bridget didn't care if he thought she was rude. She wasn't going to invite him in until she was ready.

"Sure, Mom." Molly breezed through the outside door,

heading for the kitchen, smiling at Jonas as she went by him. He seemed amused by her self-assurance.

"You'll have to excuse me, Jonas, but I can't stop to have a neighborly chat with you now. I bought ice cream and—and other frozen stuff that has to be put away," Bridget explained with false pleasantness. Okay, that was going to take her exactly one minute and then she would simply tell him to scram. She followed her daughter inside, closing the screen door and leaving him on the porch side of it. That was a hint.

He didn't seem to get it. "I don't mind waiting until you're through." He deliberately ignored her hint that she wanted him to leave. "Go ahead, I'm in no rush."

Aware of his alert gaze watching her unload the grocery bags through the mesh of the screen door, Bridget waited until Molly scampered off to her bedroom before talking to him again. "Why did you come, Jonas?"

"I wanted to see you," he returned evenly.

The hopeful look on his face pretty much dissolved her wariness. And if her mother happened to come by, she'd see Jonas on the porch and probably try to pick an unnecessary fight.

Bridget decided against keeping him outside for the rest of this conversation. She walked back and let him in, taking care to stand as far away from the door she held open as she possibly could. He entered, looking around.

"I thought I'd made it plain that I wasn't interested." She returned to the kitchen, trying to keep her voice neutral as she set the canned goods from the bags onto the counter.

Jonas didn't acknowledge the comment. She looked up to see him examining the pictures on the mantel and the bookshelves.

Molly as a baby. Molly as a toddler. Molly at Mommy-and-Me aerobics classes, being lifted on Bridget's legs and giggling with glee. Molly's first day of school. And every other magic moment involving Molly when Bridget had happened to have a camera on hand or a friend with a camera to capture it.

"You're proud of her," Jonas said softly.

"Yes, I am."

"I couldn't help noticing that there aren't any pictures of your late husband."

"So?" Bridget flashed.

"Whoa." He held up his hands in a peacemaking gesture. "Sorry. Don't bite my head off. I was just curious."

"I don't have many," she snapped. "He didn't like having his picture taken and he didn't photograph well. Does that answer your question?"

Jonas's mouth tightened. "I actually didn't ask any questions. I was just stating a fact. I really am sorry. Obviously it's a sensitive subject." Turning away, he stared out the window, his hands in his pockets.

At that moment Molly returned with her finished quilt blocks for her mother's approval.

"Those look great," she said warmly, welcoming the distraction. "We can take them to the Vermont Quilter's Fair in Norwich at the end of June. Maybe you can meet some other kids who like to quilt."

"Okay," Molly said happily. She beamed up at her mother. When Bridget noticed the way Jonas was studying both of them, she realized the reason for his curiosity.

It hadn't been because he doubted her husband's existence. It was more like masculine egotism. He had wanted to know what Brian looked like probably because he wanted to know if Bridget had married someone who resembled him.

Men were so predictable. She wasn't going to enlighten Jonas now or later. No matter what, it wasn't his business.

Bridget couldn't quite read the expression on his face. There was something poignant in it and something lonely. Well, she could tell him a lot about what that felt like.

"Okay, honey, run along," she said to Molly.

"It's going to be dark soon."

Bridget glanced at the window behind Jonas. The summer shadows were lengthening and the sky was a deeper blue, streaked with pink-tinted clouds. Sunset in Vermont was always worth slowing down for. She was half-tempted to invite him to stay for dinner . . . but no.

Just because he was giving her a puppy-dog look didn't mean she had to feed him. "You could play with your dolls, Molly."

"I'm too old for dolls," Molly declared, giving her mother a haughty look. "That's kid stuff."

"You weren't last week," Bridget pointed out.

"That was a million billion years ago."

Jonas laughed in a friendly way at the ridiculous statement, but it seemed to encourage the little girl's contrariness. She pouted and Bridget felt a flash of annoyance.

"Molly, I don't think you've fed the horses yet," Bridget said pointedly.

"I'll do it after dinner."

"Do it now," Bridget ordered with forced calm.

The small mouth was pressed tightly closed, rebellion gleaming briefly in Molly's hazel eyes before she stalked to the door leading outside. She yanked it open, then glared over her shoulder.

"He's 'that man' Grandma was talking about, isn't he?" she said suddenly. Bridget didn't want to meet Jonas's eyes for a few embarrassed seconds, but she did when Molly ran out of the house without waiting for an answer.

"I know what your mother thinks of me," Jonas said calmly.

"I wish Molly hadn't overheard whatever was said. But there's nothing I can do about it." Bridget crossed her arms over her chest. "My mother has a knack for making a difficult situation worse."

"That was then. This is now. Does it have to be difficult?" he asked stiffly. "The past can't be changed."

"I'm well aware of that," she admitted. "And the last thing I want is for Molly to be hurt by what happened between you and me ten—no—eleven years ago."

"Ten years, four months, and fourteen days ago," he corrected her.

"Am I supposed to be impressed that you kept track?" Bridget said bitterly. She rubbed her arms with her hands, feeling suddenly cold despite the gentle warmth of the spring evening. "While you're remembering everything so accurately, Jonas, don't forget that you were the one to walk out on me. I haven't forgotten that and I never will."

"I haven't either. And there are a few other things that both of us need to remember."

Before Bridget could dodge him, Jonas was pulling her into his arms, overpowering her struggling resistance. The familiar pressure of his hard mouth covering hers evoked a storm of memories. Lightning flashed through her veins to kindle the banked fires of the passion they had shared.

Her lips parted willingly under the expert persuasion of his demanding kiss. Pleasure took over as she once again experienced the wild excitement of his embrace. The frightening explosion of her senses was more awesomely wonderful than she remembered. Every fiber of her being quivered in reaction to the hard, male contour of his body pressed roughly against hers.

She was lost to the emotional upheaval, at the mercy of the arousing caress of his hands intimately roaming over her curves. There was satisfaction in feeling him shudder with ultimate longing when he buried his face in the curve of her neck.

"This is what we both want. Ten years apart hasn't made the feeling go away," Jonas declared huskily. His hand rested along her throat, his thumb on her pulsing vein. "I can feel your heart racing the same as mine."

Breathing shakily, Bridget slowly pushed herself away from him. Jonas didn't try to stop her, certain now of his power over her. Her fingers raked through her hair, hesitating for a second at the back of her head in an effort to regain some of her equilibrium.

"I don't deny that you can make me want you, Jonas," she admitted, "but it's strictly chemistry."

"You don't believe that." He shook his head complacently, the flames of desire still smoldering in the gray-green depths of his eyes.

"I do," Bridget insisted. "You walked out of my life ten years ago and you aren't going to walk back into it."

"Is that an order?" he asked.

"Listen to me, Jonas," she returned sharply. "I got along just fine without you and it's going to stay that way. There isn't any room for you in my life. I have Molly and my business and—Jim." She added the last deliberately, knowing that it would anger him.

It didn't seem to. "You feel safe standing behind him, don't you?" Jonas said quietly.

"I'm only stating the way things are," Bridget lied. "You can interpret what I say any way you want to."

"I understand what you're saying." His jaw clenched tightly and he fought for a measure of self-control. "You aren't going to give our relationship a chance to develop into something more."

"I'm giving it the same chance you did, Jonas, when you left. None." Her voice was cold. "Please leave my house."

"I don't get any credit for coming back, is that it?" His voice was bleak, the hopeful look in his eyes gone.

"Not after ten years, Jonas. You waited too long."

He stared at her for several harrowing seconds before he turned and walked out the door. Not for a minute did Bridget think she had seen the last of him, but she leaned weakly against the counter, grateful for the momentary respite.

So he was going to be living right next door—it would take all the strength she had to keep him at a distance. She'd really been lonely too long. Dating Jim took the edge off that for now, she liked and trusted the guy, but somehow . . . he seemed more like the brother she'd never had than a lover. She ought to be honest and tell him the truth: he really wasn't the man for her.

But right now, she needed someone by her side. The whirlwind of conflicting emotions that Jonas set in motion was just too much for her to handle. All he had to do was get close to her to make her heart beat faster. One kiss and her pulse raced—he'd interpreted it correctly. How long would it take before his persistence wore her down, she wondered. Already she was beginning to have twinges of doubt. He sounded so sincere. But he had a lot to prove to her before she truly believed anything he said. An awful lot.

Jonas had made a fool of her once. Bridget refused to let him do it again. She turned around when the outer door opened.

"He's gone," Molly declared with satisfaction. "I hope you told him off, Mom. He is the man Grandma was talking about, isn't he?" This time she wanted a definite answer.

"I believe so," Bridget admitted.

"What's his name?"

"Jonas Concannon."

Molly took an apple from the pottery bowl on the counter and bit into it. "Maybe Grandpa can make him leave."

"You shouldn't say things like that," Bridget reprimanded, but only half-heartedly.

"Why not?"

"Because Jonas is our neighbor, whether we like it or not." But Bridget wasn't certain how Molly really felt about Jonas. Her mother's indiscreet chatter didn't help matters. "You have to remember that your grandma doesn't always think before she speaks," she said carefully. "But I don't want you repeating that to her. She would be upset if she knew what you'd heard. I hope you aren't listening at doors—are you?"

"No. May I have a cookie?" Molly rattled the package that hadn't been opened yet. "There's a couple of broken ones. I'll eat those first. You said they don't have so many calories."

"You don't have to worry about calories yet," Bridget replied. "But it's true that a broken piece has less calories than a whole cookie."

Just one of a thousand little strategies to not eat the whole damn package in one sitting, as she was sometimes tempted to do. She opened the package and gave Molly three, then put the rest in the cookie jar.

The little girl ate them between bites of the apple.

"Want some milk?"

"I won't be hungry for dinner if I drink milk."

Bridget thought it over. "I'm going to be a bad mother and let you have cookies and milk for dinner, how about that? Plus the apple."

"I love you," Molly mumbled with her mouth full.

"And I love you." She poured a glass of milk and let her daughter finish eating while she stared out the kitchen window, lost in thought, her chin in her hand.

"Do you like him, Mom?"

That was an impossible question to answer.

"I don't know. Would you hand me the milk?"

"Did you know him before he came here?" Molly lifted the milk container from the kitchen counter and gave it to Bridget.

"He used to live not too far from Randolph."

"When?"

"Before you were born." Bridget wished the questions

would end, but Molly rarely left a subject alone until her curiosity was satisfied.

"Did you know him then?"

"Yes, I did."

"Very well?"

If she didn't answer the question, Molly would simply ask someone else, probably her mother. And Bridget didn't want her mother discussing Jonas with Molly.

"I used to go out with him."

"On dates?" Molly made a face. "You mean he was your boyfriend?"

"Yes." Bridget began rolling up the plastic grocery bags and put them in a drawer to reuse.

"Did you love him?"

Bridget turned sharply. "Don't you think your questions are becoming a little too personal?"

Hearing those words from her daughter struck a raw nerve. For a moment they stared silently at each other, hazel eyes meeting hazel eyes. Molly didn't demand an answer, but her curiosity gleamed brighter than before.

With a sigh, Bridget relented, wishing she had answered it before rather than risk having the importance of her response magnified out of proportion. "I thought I loved him."

"What about my father?"

"There are many kinds of love, Molly," Bridget explained patiently. "You don't love your grandmother in the same way you love me. That's the way it always is. I loved your father very much, or I would never have had you."

Apparently satisfied, Molly chomped a final bite from the apple and sauntered to the window overlooking the valley pasture. Bridget released a deep silent sigh of relief.

"Still and all," Molly spoke absently, "I wish that man would go away."

"Everything can't always be the way you want it. Jonas has the right to live anywhere he wants to live." Silently

Bridget wished that he hadn't chosen Vermont, or the Hanson farm. Outside of the fact that he was too close for her comfort, it would mean changes in her routine. For one thing, she liked to birdwatch in the woods that bordered his farm and take a shortcut home through what was now his property. And both she and Molly rode all over that land. Mr. Hanson hadn't minded.

Molly turned from the window, a perplexed and thoughtful frown on her face, chestnut pigtails trailing down her back. "I heard Grandma say that they'd paid him a lot of money to leave once and asked Grandpa if they shouldn't do it again. Do you suppose they will?"

Unbelievable. Margaret Harrison just couldn't shut up about the most private things, apparently. Motionless, Bridget tried to find the breath to speak. She would have to have a very serious talk with her mother. What if Molly started saying things like that in school?

"What did your grandfather say?" she asked, dodging a direct answer to the question.

Molly nibbled at the corner of her lip, then sighed, "He said he didn't think it would work a second time."

"You know what? I'm beginning to think you heard things wrong. If they didn't want you to hear, it would be easy to get mixed up and what you're saying doesn't make a whole lot of sense. I want you to put it all out of your mind, okay?"

Molly yawned. "Okay."

Bridget had to admit, if only to herself, it was remotely possible Jonas had returned for reasons having to do with the conversation her daughter had overheard. "Did you dust the furniture today?"

"Yes. Can I go into town with you tomorrow to see Vicki?" Molly tossed the apple core into the wastebasket.

"We'll see."

"Please," she coaxed. "It's boring all by myself after school."

"You aren't by yourself, Molly. You have—"

"Grandpa and Grandma," she declared with a disgruntled groan.

Bridget felt a flash of guilt for leaving Molly with them so often. But the little girl hadn't wanted to go to the after-school program this year and she did understand that her mother had to work. "Maybe you can come in tomorrow afternoon."

"Great!" The frown disappeared in a burst of exuberance. "When do we eat?"

"Cookies and milk didn't do it, huh?"

"No. Now I want some real food."

"Coming up. In the meantime, why don't you wash your hands and start fixing a salad?"

"Okay," Molly agreed readily and moved toward the hallway to the bathroom. She paused at the hall entrance, her hand resting against the wall. Glancing over her shoulder, she said to Bridget, "I really don't play with dolls any more, Mom." There was a funny expression of disdain on her youthful face.

"Imagine that," Bridget murmured dryly to herself as her daughter disappeared.

Bridget was forced to postpone the discussion with her mother until the weekend. The evenings when she was home Molly was naturally nearby, and since the object of the discussion was to warn her mother not to talk about Jonas when Molly was around, Bridget would have been disregarding her own advice.

She waited until Molly had saddled her Morgan mare, a daughter of the mare her grandfather owned, and gone for a ride. Then she walked across the road to the big house.

As usual the house was immaculate, a reflection of its fastidious mistress. The woodwork and furniture were polished to a glowing sheen. Not a speck of dust lurked anywhere. Sunlight gleamed through clean windows, accenting the pristine whiteness of the curtains.

Brightly colored throw pillows were plumped and artfully arranged on the plush sofa, seeming to deny that an elbow had ever rested against them. Books were orderly and arranged on the shelves with not a single magazine or newspaper on any of the tables. Bridget always had the impression she was looking at a room about to be photographed for a magazine, regardless of which room of the house she was in.

Her mother's initial delight at Bridget's unexpected visit didn't last long. She had launched immediately into the usual unthinking chatter until Bridget interrupted to explain the reason for her visit. Margaret Harrison's indignation was immediate.

"Your father and I were talking privately. Bill kept his voice down. I had no idea at all that Molly was listening," she said defensively. "I certainly wouldn't even have mentioned that man if I had."

"I know that, Mother," Bridget replied. "I'm only saying that if you must mention Jonas, don't do it when Molly is around. She's at an impressionable age. I tried to convince her that she didn't get the story straight and I told her not to think about it any more."

"Well," Margaret said huffily. "Facts are still facts. I wasn't lying. You certainly don't expect me to encourage her to like him, do you?" Her mother stiffened visibly. "After the way he treated you. I would think you would want to make sure Molly had nothing to do with him."

"You misunderstand my reason. I don't see any reason for Molly to know about what happened ten years ago. Thanks to your big mouth—"

"Bridget!"

"Sorry. I have to admit I'm really teed off about this, Mom. Anyway, thanks to you she now has a general idea, and that's where I want it to end." Bridget lifted the delicate china cup from its saucer and inhaled the aroma of freshly brewed tea, hot and strong the way she liked it. "Jonas is our neighbor and there's nothing you or I can do about that."

"I think Molly shouldn't see him at all," her mother sniffed, her dark head regally erect, not a brunette hair out of place. "If he's returned to Randolph with the thought of winning you back—and I think he has—then he very well might try to win her over first. What better way of getting to you and persuading you to forgive him?"

It was a somewhat plausible theory, especially coming from someone who watched a lot of soap operas like her mother, and it might have eroded Bridget's resolve not to be taken in by Jonas again. Except the theory had a weak point.

"I think you're wrong, Mother," she insisted.

"I doubt it. The man would do anything to get what he wanted. He's proved that as far as I'm concerned," was the emphatic response.

"I know what you mean, but . . ." Bridget hesitated, trying to put into words something she only sensed. "Jonas thinks that Molly is Brian's child. It was obvious the other day when—" Bridget stopped. She hadn't meant to tell her mother of Jonas's visit.

"When he was looking at the family pictures and you told Molly to go play with her dolls," her mother said with a faint air of superiority, as if nothing could be hidden from her for long. At Bridget's startled glance, she smiled complacently. "Molly told me all about it. Or have you seen him since then?"

"No, I haven't." Bridget resented the way her mother

could make her feel guilty for something she hadn't even done—and make her feel as if she was still a child.

"It's a shame when my own granddaughter gets sent out of the room. What's going on? Why wasn't she allowed to stay when Jonas was there?"

"I think you're encouraging her to be a tattletale," Bridget snapped. "And that's going to stop right now. I won't allow it, Mother. I'll take her to work with me every day if I have to."

Her mother glared at her without replying. Bridget felt obliged to say more, if only to put a few suspicions to rest. "Anyway, I asked Jonas to leave and he did."

"The next time he comes over, I wouldn't even open the door to him if I were you."

Obviously Molly hadn't told her grandmother that Jonas had been made to stay out on the porch or that it had been a while before Bridget had invited him in. But her decision to do so had been impulsive and not something Bridget understood even now, so she wasn't going to try to explain it. She was deeply upset by the behavior that her mother was encouraging, and at a loss as to how to stop it, despite her vow to take Molly to work. Yes, she could do that, but her mother would find some other way to get information out of her granddaughter. Margaret's controlling behavior wasn't healthy for any of them. Bridget sipped at her tea, making no comment at all.

"I saw him in town the other day," Margaret Harrison spoke absently. "Of course, he didn't see me," she added hastily. "But I noticed the way the women seemed to gravitate to him, staring at him whether he looked their way or not. Tell me the truth, Bridget. Are you still attracted to him?"

"You know the old saying, Mother. Once bitten, twice shy." But she was attracted to him. All the wariness in the world didn't alter that. Bridget replaced her cup in its saucer and straightened from the wing-backed chair. "I have a lot to do. I'd better be getting back to the house."

"Must you?" her mother sighed ruefully.

"Yes," Bridget insisted.

"You and Molly come over for dinner this evening then."

Bridget opened her mouth to refuse, then thought better of it. She might get a chance to talk to her father alone and get his take on the situation. "What time?"

"Is six too early?"

"That's fine. See you later." She walked quickly to the front door before her mother could succeed in delaying her a few more minutes.

Chapter Four

It was a perfect spring day, just right for aimless strolling, which was what Bridget was doing. She needed to clear her head before the crew from *Good Living* arrived and turned her shop upside down.

She turned the corner and saw that they were already there. There was a supersize van parked at the curb, engine running for no good reason she could think of, and people she didn't know coming and going with photographer's lights, reflectors, and a bunch of other unfamiliar equipment. She looked into the window from the street before she went inside her shop. The airy space was crowded with more lights on stands, a couple of assistants switching them on and off, and adjusting reflectors set here and there. Mrs. Dutton was blinking in the middle of it all.

Dotty Pomfret came out, giving Bridget a weary nod. "The invaders have arrived."

"Oh, my."

"They are manhandling my wools, Bridget. I find it upsetting."

Bridget patted Dotty's arm. "They have to put everything back the way it was."

The older woman gave a gloomy sigh. "They make me

nervous. And they're supposed to come and photograph the farm tomorrow, which means the sheep will be nervous. I am not looking forward to this."

"I'm sure everything will be fine, Dotty. Don't you worry."

Dotty humphed. "My dear, you have never tried to reassure sheep. Once they are worried, they stay worried."

Bridget peered through the window. She recognized some of the invaders from the Our Contributors page in *Good Living* magazine—the ponytailed young guy had to be Gil Blanding, the art director. Tall, wearing a black T-shirt and jeans, Gil was moving the stock around the shelves, plumping up the skeins of yarn and creating artful disarray with what had been carefully folded, color-coordinated fabrics. He stepped back to take in the result, frowning, and picked up a skein, looking at it thoughtfully.

Bridget said good-bye to Dotty and went in, tapping Gil on the shoulder.

His gaze moved from the yarn to her. "Oh, hello. You must be Bridget. Mrs. Dutton showed me all the pictures on the bulletin board. Lovely store." He pulled out a few inches of yarn from the skein and let it dangle when he put the skein back on the shelf. "There. The perfect imperfection, don't you think?"

"Sure. Whatever you say." She wasn't going to argue. Free publicity was worth letting someone fool around with her shelving system.

Gil clapped his hands and addressed his crew. "Okay, people, let's get a move on. We don't have all day. Where's our model? Come out, come out, wherever you are."

Going to the counter where she and the shop employees had lunch, Bridget rolled her eyes for Mrs. Dutton's benefit, and set down the bag of homemade cinnamon-sugar doughnuts she'd picked up on her stroll. The crew and assistants would probably devour them, but the model wouldn't. Oh well. Whoever it was had probably packed enough carrot sticks and celery stalks for the weekend.

She'd set aside several items handknit by local artisans for Gil's approval, hoping he would choose one or two to feature in the photographs for the article—and hey, he had. A skinny, leggy blonde in an unusual tunic made from Dotty's best wool came out of the back room, followed by a makeup artist waving a fluffy sable brush tipped with face powder.

"Mara, I'm not done. Hold still."

Mara shot the makeup artist an annoyed look. "Okay, okay. But I'm so itchy. When I can take this thing off?" She rolled up the sleeves and struck a pose, one lean hip jutting out and her arms akimbo.

"Fabulous, Mara," the art director crooned. "But then you were born fabulous."

Mara smirked. Bridget wanted to throw a doughnut at her.

"You can't take the sweater off, though," Gil was saying. "Mr. Photographer is not happy with the light."

An older man with cropped salt-and-pepper hair, changing settings on a state-of-the-art digital camera, looked up but not at Mara. Instead, he caught Bridget's eye and winked at her. She smiled back, surprised at the friendliness in his expression. He didn't seem quite as New York-y as Gil, and his worn chambray shirt and shabby sneakers sent the message that he didn't care all that much about fashion or fabulousness.

"Do you have to call me Mr. Photographer?" he asked Gil, an amused undertone in his voice.

"What would you like me to call you?" the art director inquired.

"Harry."

"Sorry, Harry." Gil nodded absent-mindedly, moving to stand in back of Mara and tightening the tunic around her waist. "Clothespins, please!" he called. An assistant and a stylist rushed over with a bag of supplies and clipped the sweater all along the model's spine, fitting it to her slender body. Gil came around in front to inspect the effect, obviously pleased with it. "There. Better, don't you think, Mara?" He took the model by the shoulders and positioned her in front of a long mirror.

Mara pouted. "It still itches."

Bridget didn't care. The sweater looked great. These people did know what they were doing, and Gil was a hoot. The art director tapped the tip of the model's nose. "Shiny, shiny." He beckoned to the makeup artist. "Felicia, please finish her face so we can get started."

Felicia hurried over and powdered away, making the model sneeze. Bridget stood next to Mrs. Dutton as the crew got the gear in position, ready for the first round of photos. An assistant was posted at the door to ask customers to come back later, but no one stopped by.

News of the photo shoot would have been all over town in five minutes if anyone had. The process was interesting, even if the model wasn't the most pleasant person on earth. But Mara waited patiently enough while her hair was fussed over one last time. A crew member turned on a fan and tilted it up to keep her cool under the lights and lift her hair a little. Mara, looking professional but bored, struck a few poses in front of the shelves while Harry kneeled in front of her, taking pictures one after another.

Gil gave directions and Mara followed them. Bridget took a doughnut out of the paper bag and munched on it while she watched. She would have sworn that the model's eyes lit up at the sight.

"Great," Gil said with satisfaction. "We want that sparkle. Keep going."

More handknits were featured in the ensuing shots, to Bridget's happiness. She wondered if there was a way to get the artisans who'd made them featured in the article too. She grabbed a pad of paper and a pencil, and noted down the names as the different articles of clothing were donned by Mara, aided by the stylist.

"Okay, let's break for lunch," Gil said at last. He disappeared to the back of the store while the crew got busy with the equipment. Mara yanked off the last of the handknits, revealing the tiny tank top she'd been wearing under all of them. She handed the sweater to the stylist and scratched her arms blissfully.

Bridget softened. Mara must be allergic to wool. And she had to be starving. The thin cotton of the tank top showed her ribs.

"Don't scratch your arms," the stylist whispered. "What if you have to wear a sleeveless top?"

"Not likely," Mara replied. "This is for the Christmas issue, remember?"

Wearing a Santa hat, Gil returned from wherever he'd been. It was an incongruous addition to his stylish ponytail. "Ho ho ho. Winter wonderland time, everybody. Albert, break out the candy canes and fake snow."

The props guy, who seemed to be Albert, followed Gil into the front of the store, holding two bushel-basket-size containers of Christmas decorations tipped down so the contents were visible, including a beribboned ball of artificial mistletoe. Bridget and Mrs. Dutton exchanged a smile. Seeing things like that in May was just plain odd.

"Okay to hang this stuff?" he asked her politely.

"Of course," Bridget said. "I'd love to help."

"Fine with me," Albert said. He went to the back and came out with a ladder, setting it up in front of the shop window.

Gil studied the window display, ignoring a few passersby on the sidewalk, who were studying him and the equipment inside the store curiously. Big doings for this little town, Bridget thought with an inward smile. She waved to a woman she recognized, who shaded her eyes with one hand and peered inside for a few seconds, then moved on.

"Maybe you'd better lock the door for now," Gil said. "Looks like street traffic is picking up a little. We don't want just anybody wandering in, do we?"

"Guess not." Bridget locked the glass-paned door and turned the sign on it to CLOSED.

Head tilted up, Albert was looking up at the beams that framed the shop window. "Easy enough. We'll use thin nails and you won't see a thing when we take it all down."

"Thanks," Bridget said.

The props man went up the ladder, a heavyset elf in a plaid shirt and chinos, holding a compartmented box of nails and a hammer. He gestured to Bridget to hand him one of the containers of Christmas decorations and set it on the flip-down shelf of the ladder. The large container was narrower at its bottom but the shelf was barely wide enough to hold it. However, nothing in it was heavy, as far as Bridget knew. Albert looked into it and then down at his boss.

"Whaddya want, Gil?"

"Country charm. Keep it real."

Albert pulled out a long garland of plastic cranberries and papier-mache popcorn, interspersed with cardboard gingerbread cookies.

"Real enough for me," Gil said cheerfully. "Have at, you two. I trust you and I'm hungry. Bridget, is there anyplace in Randolph that serves sushi?"

"Not yet," Bridget replied with a smile. "You can get great burgers, though."

The art director looked faintly appalled. "I don't eat cows. Albert, do you want a sandwich?"

"Not right now."

Gil left, going out the back way. Mara skittered after him, followed by Harry and whoever else hadn't left yet.

Mrs. Dutton accepted the stylist's invitation to accompany her and the makeup artist, launching into a breathless description of the apple pie at To Go, the luncheonette three blocks away.

Bridget was alone with Albert, glad of the chance to decorate the way she wanted. Models and whatnot were not her area of expertise, but she had a very definite idea of how she wanted her store to look, considering the article was going to appear in a national magazine.

Albert hammered in several nails and she handed up the garland, which actually did look real when it was up, hanging in graceful half-circles that moved slightly in the breeze created by the fan.

They went through the box and he let her pick the things she wanted. For a final touch, Bridget selected a pair of white-painted pinecone angels and positioned them on either side of a small shelf that held red-and-white striped baby sweaters. Very Christmassy.

"Nice," Albert said approvingly. "And now for the mistletoe." He reached down into the box and straightened up a little too fast, dropping the ribboned ball of gray-green mistletoe back in. "Ow!" He put a hand on his back and rubbed it. "I gotta get down off this ladder. My back is killing me."

"I'll hang it," Bridget offered. "You should take a break. If you don't want a sandwich, you could have a little something, just to sit down. To Go usually sells out of apple pie by two o'clock, by the way."

Albert climbed down a little stiffly. "That gives me half an hour. You want anything?"

Just being in the presence of an ultrathin model was enough to kill Bridget's appetite. And she'd had two doughnuts. "No, thanks. See you in a bit."

Albert handed her the hammer and lumbered away. She heard the back door of the shop close and then creak

open—she would have to fix that latch one of these days—
as she dragged the ladder under the Victorian light fixture,
being careful not to tip over the box of decorations on the
flip-down shelf. The finial would be a perfect place to
hang the ribboned ball.

She went up the steps and wound its thin wire around
the finial, climbing down and dragging the ladder to one
side when she was done.

Bridget folded her arms over her chest, thinking that
mistletoe in May was silly and wonderful at the same time.
Like the cranberry-and-popcorn garland, the ball moved
slightly in the breeze from the fan. Its faint humming filled
the quiet store and she didn't hear the footsteps at first.
Looking up at the ball, she assumed it was Albert coming
back for his wallet or something, or one of the crew, and
she nearly jumped out of her skin when she saw Jonas
come into the front part of the store.

"What are you doing here?" She realized that the question didn't sound very friendly but he had startled her.

"I looked in the window and saw you hard at work." He
smiled. "The door was locked and I didn't want to knock.
Not while you were up on a ladder."

She nodded, feeling a little foolish. "Right."

Jonas shoved his hands in the pockets of his jeans and
looked around. "What's going on?"

"We're being featured in the *Good Living* Christmas
issue. So's Dotty. They're shooting at her farm tomorrow."

"How about that. The place looks nice."

"Thanks."

She kept her eyes on his face, unwilling to look up at the
mistletoe and hoping he hadn't noticed it. No way would
she let him kiss her under it. The kiss wouldn't count if he
did, anyway. The ball was totally fake.

Jonas glanced up at it without saying anything, then took

in the rest of the décor with an amused glint in his eyes. "Decking the halls must be fun. So where is everybody?"

"Out to lunch. They'll be back soon."

"Oh."

She had a feeling he wanted to make a move—on her—but he just stood there. His nearness made her breath catch and her heart beat faster. Okay, her shop was open to the public and there was no reason he couldn't come in, but she wished that he hadn't. Feeling like he could sweep her off her feet all over again wasn't helping. Bridget looked around for something that would distract him and saw the paper bakery bag. She should wave it under his nose and make a mad dash to safety. Men were simple creatures, her mother liked to say, adding that food or sex usually did the trick.

"Have you eaten?" he asked suddenly.

"Yes." She was not going to go out with him. Someone had to hold down the fort.

"Too bad. I haven't."

He could have whatever was left in the bakery bag and spare her the calories. "There's doughnuts." She pointed at the bag. "I picked up enough for everybody."

Jonas nodded. "Sure, I'll have a doughnut. Got any coffee?"

"Coming up." Eager to do something—anything—that would keep both of them out of trouble, Bridget went to the counter and got the coffeemaker going, kneeling to look in the small fridge where they kept their lunches for the fresh pint of half-and-half.

The smell of brewing coffee made her lingering reverie disappear, for which she was grateful. Bridget rose, pint container in hand, and set it on the counter, next to the sugar-packet holder. She took out two. "Half-and-half. Two sugars."

He nodded, a smile turning up the corners of his mouth. "Just how I like it. You remembered."

For some reason, Bridget found that last remark unnerving. "Yes, I did. Not that it means anything."

"I didn't say it did. I just said you remembered."

Not forgetting her manners, no matter what he said, she found a cup and set it in front of him. "Don't go getting ideas, Jonas."

His smile got wider. "Don't worry."

He poured himself a cup and for the first time, she noticed what he had on. A plain white T-shirt, with a faded medical school logo on the right side of the chest. What a chest. She had forgotten how good he looked in something as ordinary as a T-shirt. He had on faded jeans with worn areas of white that defined the musculature of his legs. Her gaze moved over him from head to toe. He looked ready for summer, and younger than he usually did, his brown hair a bit shaggy.

His stance was relaxed as he found a cup and poured himself a cup of coffee, adding a wickedly large shot of half-and-half, then tapping the two sugar packets on the side edge of the counter. He ripped them open and poured them into his cup.

"You're a doctor. Don't you know sugar and cream are bad for you?"

Jonas shrugged, grinning. "Hey, I like to walk on the wild side."

He sipped his coffee, looking at her over the rim until she had to smile back. Almost imperceptibly, she felt herself relax.

"Aren't you going to have some?"

"I guess I will." She moved toward the counter and he stepped sideways. Bridget kept her tone of voice brisk and businesslike as she fixed her cup. "It's going to be a long day and I want to stay on top of things until the shoot's done."

"I can understand that. Looks like they kind of took over."

Bridget nodded. "The good part is, they featured the

items I wanted. I'm hoping to get the knitters' names featured in the article. Every little bit helps. The Randolph economy isn't exactly booming."

"No? You seem to be doing well."

Bridget sugared up her coffee and clinkety-clinked the spoon as she stirred. "That's because a lot of my business is online."

"Smart."

She felt a flash of defensive irritation, even though she was sure he hadn't meant to sound patronizing. Granted, she hadn't gone away to college, hadn't even had a chance to think about it with a little girl to raise—but that wasn't anything she was going to discuss with him.

"Once the website was up, the orders started coming in from knitters and quilters all over the country. I run sidebar ads in sewing and crafts magazines, but word of mouth is what really brings in new customers."

Jonas nodded, motioning with his free hand to a display of quilting brochures not too far away. "Those are for customized kits, right?"

He must have walked by them on his way in. Bridget couldn't help but feel relieved that he was sticking to safe questions. "Right. The brochures have a quiz on hobbies, color preferences, pets, things like that—and the online brochure is the same. They fill it out and then I e-mail each interested customer a mini-version of a quilt she could make, using her preferences and design templates I created."

"Hmm. Clever idea. Did you think up that concept yourself?"

"Yup." Bridget picked up her cup of coffee and nodded at her computer. "I'll show you how I do it." She walked over and sat down, waiting a minute for the screen to come to life as Jonas looked over her shoulder.

Bridget pulled up a file and filled in its boxed blanks, typing with one hand. "Let's say a customer's hobby is gardening. And she likes pastel colors. And cats." Bridget clicked back and forth between her graphics program and the form she was filling out, picking out stylized flowers and cats in pink, blue, and yellow.

"All I have to do is put those elements together using standard blocks I create for each category—it takes me about five minutes. Then I e-mail her a couple of different versions. The design is personalized but it relies on standard elements that don't have to be redesigned each time."

"Very cool. And very smart. But what if you get a request from someone who likes motorcycles, ripped denim, and bulldogs?"

Bridget laughed. "I can handle special orders. It takes a little longer to come up with the images, so I charge more, that's all."

She opened a folder on the computer and an assortment of art popped up, from tattoo-style mermaids to geometric glyphs. Jonas looked genuinely interested and she warmed to her subject. "These are hard to do. Most people prefer the easy stuff like daisies and stars. If they like the mini-version and place an order for a kit, I graph the blocks for the design they choose, add the instructions, print it all up, and send it out. They sew it from their own fabrics, which means no inventory to speak of."

"That's a business for the new millennium."

"Yeah, well, thank God for PayPal."

Jonas laughed. "You really are ingenious. I'm impressed."

Bridget blushed a little. "I get more orders every month. Which means I can set my own hours and stay here in Randolph with Molly—"

She stopped, feeling his thoughtful gaze on her.

"That makes sense."

"Living up here, there aren't many great jobs," she pointed out. Jonas had to know that, even if he'd been living in New York for so long. "I couldn't make a go of a shop like this just selling to local people. As for tourists—well, they're seasonal. The design-your-own-quilt concept really took off online, and I feature our handknits on the website too. Okay, nobody's getting rich but everybody's doing all right."

He looked at her as if she was somebody new to him. "You're amazing, you know that?"

"Oh, shut up." Bridget smiled at him all the same as she shut down her computer. Somehow here in the store she felt a lot more confident than she had in her house. And talking about her business meant the conversation never got too personal. But she was glad to hear the back door bang repeatedly as the crew returned from lunch and began to fill the store again.

Mara sauntered in last, casting an interested look at Jonas, who hardly seemed to notice her. All the same, Bridget was annoyed. Gil was finishing up a small takeout container of plain rice from the Chinese restaurant, scooping it up with a plastic spoon. He waved the spoon in Bridget's direction, his mouth too full to say hello, while he looked over the decorations that had been put up in his absence, nodding approvingly.

"You've been busy," he said after the last bite went down and he tossed the container and spoon into a wastebasket. "Looks good. I can work with that. Mara, go put on that wonderful nubby sweater. I want to get going."

"All the sweaters are nubby," the model complained, swaying what she had in the way of hips as she went by Jonas. "The whole damn state is nubby. I'm tired of nubby."

Bridget frowned. Whether it was because of Mara's remark or her attempt to catch Jonas's eye, she couldn't say.

"Oh, hush," Gil said a trifle impatiently. He looked at Jonas carefully. "Hm. We could use you. Is this a friend of yours, Bridget?"

Nonplussed, she didn't answer for a few seconds. "He's my new neighbor," she replied at last.

"I'm Jonas Concannon," Jonas said. "And you are—?"

Gil stuck out his hand. "Gil Blanding, the art director for *Good Living*. Have you ever modeled before?"

It was Jonas's turn to look nonplussed. "Uh, no."

Gil didn't seem the least bit interested in finding out what Jonas actually did. He took a man-size ribbed sweater from one of the shelves and held it up against Jonas. "Wow. You have a great look. Rugged but intellectual. Harry, come here. Put on that sweater, would you, Jonas?"

Smirking at Bridget, Jonas pulled on the sweater, running a hand through his messed-up hair in a vain attempt to straighten it afterwards.

"Hey, Harry, we could put him and Mara under the kissing ball . . ."

The rest of the art director's big idea didn't register with Bridget. She was steamed, really steamed, but there wasn't much she could do. Mara had come back out from the screened-off area that was serving as a dressing room, and the nubby sweater actually made her look curvy. But it didn't seem to meet her high standards, because Mara was still sulking.

Her expression brightened considerably when she saw Jonas standing there in the ribbed sweater, playing the role of male model for all he was worth.

Gil reached out a hand to Mara to bring her closer—and positioned her next to Jonas. "What do you think, Harry?"

Harry, it seemed, viewed the world mostly through a viewfinder. He peered into his and waited a minute before answering. "Works for me, Gil. The guy doesn't even need makeup. Great skin."

Jonas faced the camera with a great big smile that made Bridget want to kick him.

"Pearly whites to die for," Gil murmured. "Mara, cuddle up."

The pouty model was happy to oblige. Bridget could only seethe while she reminded herself that the publicity would be great for the store and bring in extra income for her knitters.

Mara pressed her nubby side against Jonas's rugged ribs, and Harry began to take quick shots of them. "Huh. These two might have chemistry," Bridget heard him say under his breath.

Still and all, when she looked at Jonas, she noticed he was looking at her, not at the blond model hanging all over him. Mara might as well have been an inanimate object.

"Okay, action!" Gil said loudly. "Take two steps back so you're right under the mistletoe. Mara, I want you to get your fingers in his hair and try to plant a big smooch on his cheek. But don't make contact and don't mess up your lipstick. We're running late."

Bridget was thankful for that. Mara puckered up. With an inward sigh of satisfaction, Bridget noticed that Jonas looked uncomfortable when Mara's squishy, sticky, much-too-pink lips got close to his face.

Harry, staring into his viewfinder, shook his head. "Oops. We lost the magic. Jonas, try not to look like you're facing a firing squad, okay?"

Jonas straightened and Mara's expression got a little sour.

Harry shook his head again. "Mara, you can do better than that."

"My lips are tired," she whined, no longer interested in wowing Jonas.

Just as Bridget had thought. A kiss under fake mistletoe couldn't possibly be real. But maybe it would look real when the article was printed. Arms folded over her chest, she watched as Gil fussed on the sidelines, and the stylist made some last-minute adjustments to the fit of Mara's sweater. The painstaking rigmarole began again.

At last Harry said he had a few shots he didn't hate, and Jonas moved out of Mara's clutches, looking relieved.

"That wasn't as much fun as I thought it would be," he murmured out of the side of his mouth to Bridget.

Serves you right, she wanted to say.

"Can I take this off?" he asked Gil.

"Of course," the art director said indulgently. "But stick around. We could use you in the background."

Jonas looked a little chagrined.

The assistants began heaping up colorfully wrapped presents under Gil's direction. Bridget figured out that Mara was supposed to open one or two, or at least tug on a ribbon like she was going to, because there was nothing at all inside the boxes.

Gil clapped a hand to his forehead. "Oh no. We forgot the tree!"

The assistants looked at each other. Bridget doubted that any of them knew what to do next.

"We need a symmetrical pine about six feet tall—I think I saw one on the village green." Gil's voice was agitated and there was a gleam in his eye. "No one will miss it if we—"

Bridget stepped forward to intervene. "That tree belongs to the town. The Girl Scouts planted it. Besides, you can't just go around cutting trees when and where you feel like it."

The art director directed a scornful look at her. "Do you have a better solution?"

"Yes," Bridget said quickly. "Make our own. I could cut one out of extra-long green paper—I have some—and stick a big yellow star on the top. It'll look like a kid did it. Bold but charming."

Gil pondered that for a moment. "I like it," he said at last.

Bridget half-expected him to snap his fingers and yell "Cut!" at her. But he didn't.

"I'll get the paper." She went over to her work area for

scissors and found the extra-long paper she'd been saving for no particular reason, letting it unroll on her worktable and weighting the corners with smooth stones that Molly had gathered from the creek last summer. Bridget quickly sketched the outline of a simple Christmas tree, and began to cut it out, trying not to think about what she was doing. She really did want it to look like a kid had cut it out.

Creativity was all about just letting things happen, she thought. Her scissors moved as swiftly as her pencil had, until a cut-out section curled up again and got in her way. Jonas's big, strong hand smoothed out the curl and he left it there, resting lightly on the paper. Bridget glanced up, right into his eyes.

There it was . . . that warmth that melted her. With just one look he could take her back to a time when she had been a lot more innocent—a time when she only wanted to be in his arms, forever. It was odd how remembering it didn't hurt. Bridget's jealousy of Mara, her irritation with the ridiculous business of modeling and at the annoying invasion of her shop, vanished at that moment.

"Wait a minute," Gil said, coming over to the worktable and breaking the spell. "This could be a great shot. Mara and Jonas really didn't click, but these two do. Do you see what I'm saying, Harry?"

The photographer came over and framed Jonas and Bridget in his viewfinder, studying them intently. "Yeah. I do."

"I'm thinking . . . a young couple, first Christmas, having fun. . . . What are you thinking?"

"Same thing," Harry said. "Get a sweater on her, somebody. We have to finish today so we can get out to the Pomfret farm tomorrow."

Gil snapped his fingers for the stylist, who selected a lightweight knit that matched Bridget's eyes. She raised her arms to allow it to be slipped on her, just catching

Jonas's appreciative downward look at her breasts. The stylist chose a cream-colored cable knit for him.

In less than two minutes, Bridget was powdered, blushed, lipglossed, and mascara'ed, and her hair was fluffed.

"Look at you," Gil said. "An all-American girl if ever there was one. With a couple of adorable teeny-tiny freckles."

Bridget hoped that description would make Mara mad. Of course, she lacked Mara's glamorous cheekbones, but she had two perfect freckles she hadn't even known she possessed.

Gil pretended he had a pair of scissors in his hand. "Snip, snip. Go back to what you were doing, you two. Harry can work around you, that's not a problem."

Blushing for real under her light makeup, Bridget got back to cutting out the paper tree. Harry's camera clicked softly and repeatedly. Occasionally he asked one or both of them to lift up their chin or look at each other or whatever he thought made the pose look right. Jonas didn't say a word. He seemed almost embarrassed, as if they had been caught doing something naughty.

"Now for the star," Gil prompted. An assistant got the tall tree off the table and affixed it to the wall with hidden gobs of duct tape. "You can take turns putting it on the tree. We'll see which pose looks best."

Bridget cut out a star from yellow paper and handed it to Jonas. "You first," she said under her breath.

Jonas took her hand and walked over to the tree, not stretching to hold it over the narrow point at the top.

"Yes indeed," Gil said. "Smile down at her."

Jonas already was. Bridget smiled back, until Mara's voice broke into their Moment of connection.

"Awww," the model said sarcastically. "Doesn't she look radiant?"

Harry looked up from his viewfinder. "Mara, we don't need your comments."

Even though the photographer only wanted to keep the peace, Bridget was grateful to him. The stylist tactfully distracted the model by waving a dress on a hanger. Mara took the bait and headed for the dressing area.

"You're young and in love," Gil crooned. "This is your first Christmas. Tra la la."

Jonas smiled down at her more warmly still, as if he'd forgotten that he was holding up a paper star. As artificial as the pose was, there was very real emotion in his eyes. She knew he remembered their real first Christmas—she certainly did. Gil hadn't meant to be tactless and the art director had no way of knowing how special that long-ago holiday had been.

Jonas had given her a beautiful antique pin he'd saved up to buy and something much more meaningful than that: her first kiss. If only that memory would fade away forever . . . Even with so many people around, Bridget felt tears rise in her eyes and prayed she wouldn't cry.

"Beautiful. Your eyes are really shining, Bridget," Harry said.

Jonas let go of the star and touched a hand to Bridget's cheek. She *was* going to cry. She had to look away. He did too when the star fluttered down but he caught it before it landed on the floor.

His eyes were suspiciously bright and he covered his emotions by humming a few notes. "Catch a falling star— what's that old song?"

"You're supposed to save it for a rainy day," she whispered.

"I will," he whispered back.

Gil was barking orders again. The assistants scurried around. "Okay, it's Bridget's turn to hold the star in place," Gil said. "I'm happy with this concept. Harry, are you happy?"

The photographer only grunted.

"Jonas . . ." Gil looked at him expectantly and he handed over the star to Bridget.

She began to pose per the instructions she was given. Stand this way. That way. Look at Jonas. Look at the tree. Bridget had never realized how heavy a paper star could be if you had to hold it against a wall for almost an hour. Her arm ached. But what they were doing gave her an excuse to be close to him.

She heard the doorknob rattle and remembered that she'd locked the door to the shop.

"Mo-om!"

Molly was on the other side of the glass.

"Can I put this down?" Bridget asked, talking through her teeth.

Gil looked around. "Is that your daughter?"

"Yes, that's Molly."

"Harry, are you done with this set-up?"

"I'm done. Bridget, Jonas, at ease." Harry brought his camera over to Gil to scroll through the photos in the memory as Bridget went to the door. Making a comical face, Molly smushed her nose against the glass and splayed out her hands. Bridget had to laugh.

She let Molly in and waved to her mother, who was in the car at the curb, on her way to meet a friend in town as planned. Bridget hadn't known that Jonas was going to show up, but she was glad she didn't have to explain that to her mother.

Molly had a garment bag draped over one arm, dragging on the floor. "I brought my velvet dress and some other things," she explained.

Bridget took the bag. "Great. Let's show them to the stylist and see what she thinks."

"Okay." Molly studied her mother's face. "You look pretty, Mommy. Who did your makeup?"

"A nice lady called Felicia. Would you like to meet her?"

"Sure! Can I wear makeup?" Molly asked eagerly.

"A little," Bridget said.

"I want to look famous," Molly said dreamily.

Bridget smiled and headed with her daughter to the back of the store. "I'm not sure what that means, but maybe Felicia will know."

Molly noticed Jonas and raised her eyebrows at her mother, as if she was about to ask some pesky questions.

"Not now," Bridget said very softly but firmly. "Just say hello."

Jonas grinned when he saw them coming toward him hand in hand. "Hello, Molly."

Molly tipped her nose up in an absurdly haughty way. "Hello." She swept past him, not really thinking about anything but the prospect of being glamorous.

Bridget winked at Jonas. It was all she could do, considering Molly's behavior. What little girl wouldn't want to star in a magazine photo shoot and get all prettied up?

An hour or so later, Molly wasn't quite so impressed with it all. She'd posed demurely in a plaid taffeta dress with a velvet bodice, not complaining once about the tightness of the matching velvet ribbon in her hair. But she had protested the thorough hairbrushing she'd had to endure, until Bridget reminded her that it was no different from getting her mare, Satin, ready for a show.

Mrs. Dutton had volunteered her five-year-old nephew, who owned a velvet suit, to pose with Molly under the mistletoe. Even though her lips never touched his cheek, the little boy, a real ham, scrunched his eyes shut and screwed his face into a priceless scowl.

Then it was Bridget and Jonas's turn. The makeup artist retouched her lipstick as Molly watched, brushing shimmering, berry-bright gloss over Bridget's parted lips.

Molly wasn't the only one watching. Bridget was aware of Jonas nearby, talking casually with Harry. But his eyes were on her. She could feel it.

"Stay still," Felicia said. "Oh, where's the blusher—" She scrabbled through her compartmented bag, not finding it, and happened to look up at Bridget. "Wait a minute. You don't need it. Your cheeks are really pink. No wonder." She fanned herself with one hand. "Those lights are much too hot—c'mon, Molly. Let's grab a cold soda and sit in the van. It has pretty good air-conditioning."

It wasn't the lights that were making Bridget warm and turning her cheeks pink. It was Jonas. Harry had told him to stand under the mistletoe to get a light reading and there he was . . . waiting for her. In the cream-colored fisherman's sweater and those worn jeans, he looked utterly masculine and sexier than any man had a right to be. He was getting to her. Bridget was grateful that her daughter had left with Felicia for a few minutes. If Harry asked her to kiss Jonas, she didn't know what she would do.

"Go for it!" Gil said loudly.

"Wh-what?" Bridget stammered. "What do you mean?"

"Give the man a kiss. How can you resist?"

She couldn't. She couldn't even think of a reason to refuse. So she went over and kissed him carefully, mindful of her lipstick.

Breathless, a little surprised, Jonas put his hands around her waist and returned the kiss just as carefully.

Harry clicked away, murmuring encouragement. "That's good. Fine. Another one. Okay. Turn a little to the left, Jonas. Great. That oughta do it." He paused.

Bridget had a feeling the photographer was looking up from the viewfinder, but she wasn't looking at him. Her eyes were closed. Jonas was kissing for her for real.

"Hey, you two," Harry said in an amused voice. "Stop already."

Two days later . . .

As far as Jonas could see, the old Hanson house had no major problems, except for a porch that sloped. Jonas stepped back, hands on his jeans-clad hips, and made a mental list of the various things that needed fixing. He would have to prop up the porch roof with a couple of house jacks, rip out the rotting supports, replace the foundation, floorboards, and railings . . . and add a swing for two.

The blazing kisses he'd shared with Bridget were something he intended to repeat, and not with her daughter nearby or a photographer and crew standing around. Mrs. Harrison would pitch a fit if Gil Blanding decided to use the last few photos Harry had taken in the upcoming article. But Jonas doubted it. *Good Living* was a family magazine.

Bridget had been skittish at first, but that was understandable. He'd come over to her house uninvited and walked into her store when she wasn't expecting. But once she'd warmed up, she'd responded, body and soul, in a way that let him know she wanted him.

He didn't know when he would get that lucky again, but he could wait. And there was a limit to what he could accomplish, so to speak, with Molly around. At least that was one reason to be nice to Margaret Harrison. She took care of her granddaughter and that meant Bridget had more freedom than a lot of single moms. Not that he'd ever dated any others.

He'd gone out with a few of the female residents who rotated at the clinic, as busy and sleep-deprived and overwhelmed as he was. But not often, and the interaction was physical, not emotional. None had been interested in a time-consuming real relationship. Medical school, internship, and clinical training didn't leave room for a social life.

But he'd never stopped thinking about Bridget. She'd claimed his heart long ago—that hadn't changed. He'd known that the second he'd seen her in the shop in town. They were meant to be together. Buying a place down the road from hers was a statement she couldn't ignore or brush off. It said that he was back and he wasn't going to go away.

Patience and persistence would win her over, no matter what.

As Jonas walked around the rest of the farm, assessing the condition of the outbuildings, he began to wonder what the hell he'd been thinking. Some of the ramshackle structures had been put together by gosh and by gum, and some had been built to last by master carpenters. But nothing could withstand the rigors of Vermont winters forever.

The barn needed a new roof—he saw daylight when he looked up. The biggest holes probably were convenient for the owls that undoubtedly nested up there, allowing them to exit and enter to do their hunting in the surrounding fields. Soft hoots and an occasional screech had kept him up last night.

He'd been so eager to close on the deal, he hadn't paid much attention to the building inspector, a conscientious old coot with a marked New England twang, who wasn't all that easy to understand as he explained what needed fixing and what could wait.

Jonas made a rough estimate of the cost of repairs and then he mentally kicked himself for not thinking about any of that until now. It was probably cheaper to burn it all down and start over. But he never would, not in a million years. The farm had been here a long time and he wanted to make sure it would still be here a hundred years from now. He headed down a path that bordered an overgrown field. The tractor-capped yard guy who was supposed to keep the wilderness at bay hadn't gotten this far yet. Mr. Hanson, who'd lost his wife some years ago after his two sons moved to California, could no longer keep up with the maintenance on a big place. Jonas had gotten it—house, barn, fields, and outbuildings—for a fair price.

Good thing, too. He didn't need to add a huge mortgage on top of the med school loans he was still paying off. And he planned to open his own practice in the Randolph vicinity—that wasn't going to be cheap. As a family-practice physician, especially in a rural area, he wasn't ever going to be rich. But Jonas had never cared much about that. He'd enjoyed the variety of people he'd treated at the New York clinic, and he liked the idea of practicing in a medically underserved area. All over the US, so many older, small town doctors were retiring that communities were having a tough time finding replacements. He figured he had as good a chance as anyone else of making a living.

But . . . one thing at a time, starting with the roof over his head. When the necessary repairs had been finished, this old house would be perfect for raising a family. With the only woman he'd ever wanted.

Jonas looked at the decrepit porch again and sighed. Before he carried anyone over the threshold, he was going to have to replace it.

That afternoon found him at the edge of his property, inspecting a shed and a sadly diminished woodpile that had been used to supply the firewood holder on the porch without being restocked. Fortunately, someone had tossed a heap of logs into the shed to season and stay dry over the winter—maybe the yard guy. They were ready for split-ting, sawn into two-foot lengths.

He could get started on those, Jonas thought. He could use the exercise, but it had been a long time since he'd chopped wood. He stepped inside the shed, looking for an axe, and saw several hung on a low beam. The dull metal blades gleamed in the darkness and he tested the edge on one with a finger.

Ouch. It was sharp. Old Mr. Hanson took care of his tools, evidently, even if he hadn't used them for a while. Jonas took that as a sign. He picked an axe at random and propped it outside on the chopping stump, then went back into the shed for as many logs as he could carry.

He balanced the first on its end, hefted the axe and swung, splitting the log cleanly in half with a well-placed strike that made a sharp, satisfying crack. Hah. He grinned, pleased with himself. Paul Bunyan had nothing on him.

Halved and then quartered, the wood smelled clean and light, like the Vermont air. He tossed the split wood into a rough pile to stack later, enjoying the rhythm of manual labor and getting sweaty.

Jonas paused to pull his shirt out of his jeans and unbutton it. Too bad he didn't have a handkerchief. But the shirt would do to mop his face if he took it off. He'd be warm enough if he kept working.

He slid out of it, wiped the sweat from his face, and hung it on a nearby tree. Then he returned to his task, energized, working faster and harder than before. He had no idea he was being watched.

Bridget put down her binoculars, feeling awfully guilty. She was a hundred yards away, but even so—she knew Jonas didn't know she was there.

She'd ignored the sound at first, assuming it was the handyman or the yard guy the realtor hired to look after the place, hard at work. But the steady chopping interrupted her concentration and made birdcalls hard to hear. Once she'd turned around and trained her binoculars in the direction of the noise, she'd seen Jonas . . . and she hadn't been able to look away. A fallen tree had created a clear line of sight to the property line and the spot where he was chopping wood.

Bare chested, he was gorgeous, with a lot of hard, sinewy muscle. His arms were pumped from swinging the axe and all she could think about was how good it had felt to be held in them when he had kissed her. She'd sensed the power of his clothed body, even ventured a tentative caress or two both times, but seeing him like this was almost overwhelming.

Jonas put down the axe and walked over to the tree where he'd hung his shirt, using it to wipe his face. He pressed his sweat-dampened hair back with both hands, bringing out the rugged contours of his face, and propped his hands on his hips, catching his breath.

Bridget shivered and not because she was cold. Truth be told, the sight of him like this was a thrill and then some.

He walked back to the stump, picked up the axe, and got back to work. *Thunk*. Chop. *Thunk*. Chop. He tossed the split wood into the ever-growing pile near the stump. Every time he raised the axe over his head and his muscles tightened for a split second before the downward swing, her heart skipped a beat.

It wasn't as if she'd never seen a man chop wood. But Jonas looked incredibly sexy doing it. She could see that he was getting tired—his taut belly, ridged with muscle, drew in and away from the waistband of his jeans as he took deeper breaths. His skin gleamed with sweat in the fading afternoon light. The chilly spring air made his flat male nipples tighten—and eventually the chill won out.

Jonas selected one last log—a big one—and cleaved it with a mighty blow that sent both halves tumbling to the ground.

He sat down on the stump, blew out his breath in a sigh she could almost hear, then rose and went to get his shirt.

Bridget watched him button it, feeling tenderness well inside her at the simple action. It was easy to imagine him buttoning up in just that way after . . . after an afternoon of lovemaking. Oh, how she wanted that. She dropped the binoculars but the strap caught them. The sudden pressure against the back of her neck brought her back to reality.

She didn't raise them to her eyes again, embarrassed by her own shamelessness. Okay, no one had seen her, but if they had . . . Bridget turned and headed home, creating a roundabout shortcut that involved a little bushwhacking. A few minutes and a few scratches later, she was on the main road and a healthy distance from the Hanson farm.

Bridget went into the crafts room where she and Molly did projects, making a huge, happy mess whenever they felt like it. She spotted the quilt blocks Molly had been working on thumbtacked to a corkboard. The one in progress, the bullfrog, looked pretty good, except that the legs were too long, dangling past the bottom edge of the twelve-inch-square block. Bridget folded one skinny green leg at the knee and pinned it into a bent shape, then did the same with the other one. There. Now the frog fit.

She sighed, unsure of what to do next as far as Molly was concerned. Or herself. The brief and beautiful spring was almost over—it was near the end of May. Soon it would be summer, bringing scads of tourists. The shop would certainly benefit, but she wouldn't mind letting Mrs. Dutton run it for her while she took a trip somewhere else, with or without Molly.

No—she couldn't just up and leave. She'd promised to volunteer at Molly's school, and the kitchen needed painting, and it was high time she straightened out her financial paperwork and started a college account for Molly—*and, and, and*, Bridget told herself. She would never be done with all the *ands*. Her unsettled emotions made Bridget suspect that Jonas had a lot to do with her restlessness. Whoa, she told herself. You really don't want to be regretting anything when he gets fed up and goes back to Manhattan.

He couldn't have been thinking straight when he bought that house—he couldn't turn back into a Vermonter overnight. Had he forgotten how long winter was up here? Someone who was into downhill racing or cross-country skiing would be happy: the slopes and trails were less than an hour's drive from Randolph, and, as she remembered, Jonas did like to ski. But he would have to do without nightlife and the other sophisticated distractions that Manhattan offered. She felt a little bit envious that he had the option of going back to the city if he got cabin fever— she didn't and she never would.

Hmm. He did seem to be making the right preparations— he'd been chopping wood like one possessed. Only a real Green Mountain man got started on the woodpile six months before the weather turned cold. He hadn't strayed so far from his roots after all. Or from her. Wishful thinking, Bridget warned herself. For all his lumberjack skills, Jonas just wasn't likely to adjust to living up here, not once winter hit.

Jonas finished stacking the wood he'd cut and sat on the stump, his shirt slung over his shoulders. The work had been hard, but it was satisfying. He wasn't used to it, though, and he knew it would be wise to take a couple of ibuprofen so his muscles wouldn't be too sore tomorrow. But come to think of it, he didn't have any. Considering how much work there was to be done around here, he ought to buy a bottle—hell, he ought to stock up a first aid kit with everything he needed. He didn't want to run over to Bridget's if he needed a bandage or antibiotic cream, even though, like most mothers, she had undoubtedly had enough experience with minor emergencies and illnesses to qualify for a practical nursing certificate.

Physician, heal thyself, he thought. Jonas grinned as he got up, dusted the wood slivers from his jeans, and walked to the house. He slid his arms into his shirt sleeves and buttoned up the shirt, breezing through the back door to look for his car keys.

He decided to take a back road into town he hadn't driven over yet—it had only recently been paved. The realtor had told him that it connected a number of outlying farms, so it was a good way to check out the scenery. He wasn't likely to run into anyone.

How wrong he was. Fifteen minutes later, Jonas sat behind the wheel of his car, surveying a sea of woolly backs that surrounded him. The flock of sheep had come around the bend, parted ranks around his car, and then stopped in their tracks. They didn't seem to want to move, except for one really dirty sheep by the driver's side of the car, who was rubbing its burr-laden, matted wool against the smooth enamel surface of the front fender and favoring Jonas with a blissful but remarkably stupid look.

He considered honking but he knew better. The only thing worse than a flock of motionless sheep was a flock of scared sheep. Maybe they were waiting for a command. What did you say to sheep to get them to move?

Jonas had grown up two towns away from Randolph but not on a farm, although he did know how to ride. He had no clue about sheep, however. He gave the matter some thought, finding his predicament more funny than not. Hmm. Wasn't it gee for oxen and mush for sled dogs?

He leaned out the window. "Gee. Mush."

The dirty sheep rubbing itself on the fender didn't budge. Jonas did attract the attention of a few of the others, though, who baa-ed and blinked at him and pressed in more, making it impossible for him to open his door.

He was stuck. Jonas reached for his cell phone. He might as well amuse himself by taking a picture of them and sending it to his buddy Del Anzalone, a new resident at the clinic. The closest Del, a Brooklynite through and through, had ever gotten to actual sheep was a lamb chop, medium rare.

"Hold still," Jonas instructed the nearest sheep. He flipped open the phone and snapped just as the critter moved toward him. The photo was blurred and mostly nose. He deleted it and took another. "Perfect. Thank you, Miss Sheep." Jonas punched in Del's number and added a text message. *Getting wild 'n woolly in Vermont.* He hit send and waited for a reply, drumming his fingers on the steering wheel while the sheep milled around.

None came. Del must be busy—the clinic always was.

Jonas swore under his breath. Who was in charge here? The sheep had to belong to someone. Biblical-size flocks like this couldn't run around unsupervised, even in rural Vermont.

As if in answer to his unspoken question, an odd but familiar figure came around the bend, carrying a shepherd's crook in one hand. A colorfully dressed older woman with long gray braids—someone he remembered but not from where—oh, right. Dotty Pomfret. Bridget's wool supplier.

"Hey!" Jonas waved out the window.

"Hey yourself," Dotty called without enthusiasm. She was in no hurry to get to him, he noticed, feeling a little annoyed. He heard her whistle and then his eyes widened at the sight of a black-and-white dog that jumped up . . . and walked effortlessly on the backs of the sheep.

At her whistled commands, the dog got the flock to move away from Jonas's car and down a low rise into a pasture, where the sheep stood huddled, looking nervously at the dog. One baa-ed disconsolately and the dog stared it down until it shut up. Satisfied with the job, the dog sat down and kept them where they were by sheer force of personality.

Jonas got out of his car, laughing loudly. "I've never seen anything like that. Where'd you get that dog?"

"He was born on my farm. But his mother was from New Zealand. His name is Kiwi."

She gave Jonas a look that seemed to say *and you are*?

So he did, putting out his hand to shake hers. "I'm Jonas Concannon. Pleased to meet you. Actually, we've met before, but very briefly."

She raised a quizzical eyebrow. "We did?"

"At Bridget O'Shea's store. In March."

"Do you . . . knit?" she inquired.

"Ah, no. I just happened to stop in. Bridget and I—well, we knew each other a while ago."

"I see." She peered at him, fiddling with the end of one of her long braids. "Oh, now I remember you. I'm Dotty Pomfret. My farm is that way." She pointed, not in the direction he was going.

"Need anything from town? I was just heading in."

"How neighborly of you." She beamed at him. "Do you have a pen? I'll make a list. Actually, there are quite a few things I need. You can charge everything to my name. Would you mind? My old truck isn't running and I would very much appreciate it if you—"

"Not a problem," Jonas said quickly. He had the feeling that Dotty Pomfret could ask him to do anything and he would do it, in somewhat the same way that the sheep obeyed the dog.

He found a pen and pad of paper in the glove compartment and jotted down what she said, relieved that he could get a lot of it at the drugstore.

"My sister and I don't get into town that often," Dotty

was saying, "so this really is very nice of you. Tell you what. I'll make you a sweater."

She looked him up and down in a way that disconcerted him, but Jonas didn't think she was ogling him. Still, he was being measured and not just in a physical way.

"I'll cast the first rows when I get home and it'll be done by fall."

For the first time, Jonas noticed the details of what Dotty was wearing: a baggy, misshapen sweater that hung down almost to her knees made of loopy, speckled yarn in a riot of colors. It didn't look like clothing—it looked like an art project.

"You don't have to do that," he said hastily. "I'm happy to help."

Later that evening, Dotty and Elizabeth went through the bags that Jonas had brought from town, taking out items one by one.

"He got everything on the list," Dotty said, pleased. "Very good."

Sitting on the floor between the sisters, Kiwi banged his tail.

"I didn't mean you," Dotty said. Kiwi gave her a disappointed look. "Silly. You are a good dog, though."

"What a nice young man he must be," Elizabeth replied. "And you say he's handsome. He's perfect for Bridget, don't you think?"

"It seems they knew each other back in the day."

Elizabeth raised an eyebrow. "Oh?"

"Now, now," Dotty said reprovingly. "We're not going to play Cupid."

"Could be fun."

"Could be a disaster. People have to figure things out for themselves. Otherwise they might as well be sheep."

Elizabeth chuckled. "I suppose you're right."

"Anyway, I don't know too much about him. He's from Vermont but he didn't grow up in Randolph."

Elizabeth nodded. "Bridget is a nice girl, I hear, but her mother is impossible. Margaret Harrison thinks very highly of herself. And the airs she puts on . . . good Lord."

"Well, I suppose she has some redeeming qualities. Most people do."

Elizabeth sighed. "I don't think she has anything nice to say about us."

"Can't be helped. You shouldn't listen to gossip. Shall I make tea?"

"Do we have any?"

Dotty rose from the checked-cloth-covered table and looked into a canister. "There's a few bags of cham-omile left."

Elizabeth sighed. "Okay. Put a little whisky in mine."

Dotty gave her sister a faintly shocked look. "Why?"

"To take away the taste," Elizabeth laughed. "I hate herb tea."

A few days later . . .

Outside, Bridget paused on the gray porch steps of the house, struck for an instant by the vivid hues of green painting the valley and the rolling hills. The green of the land brilliantly contrasted with the blue of the sky, the air startlingly clear and fresh with scents of summer.

Her gaze made an admiring sweep of the verdant scenery. It was a rejuvenating view that lightened her footsteps. She spied her father near the barn working on the farm tractor and smiled at the sight of him in denim coveralls, his hands covered with grease and a straw hat on top of his head.

He was still a farmer at heart, despite all the money he had made selling off acres of his land to wealthy out-of-staters who snapped up large tracts to preserve their unspoiled views. Earthy, easygoing, Bill Harrison was the complete opposite of his wife and was the steady anchor that had kept Margaret Harrison from becoming too puffed up with an inflated sense of her own importance.

"Hi, Dad!" Bridget waved.

He glanced up, surprised, wiping his hands on a snowy white kerchief. Bridget could hear her mother calling when she saw it. "Well, hello, princess," he smiled and looked to the white house. "Coming!" he shouted. He turned back to Bridget. "Molly was just here looking for you, you know."

"Did she say what she wanted?" She frowned curiously.

"No, I—there she is now." His gaze had made a searching swing, sighting his granddaughter on the other side of the road. "Just coming around the chalet."

Bridget saw Molly astride the bay horse at almost the same instant that Molly saw her and waved. "I'll go see what she wants. See you later, Dad."

Molly met her at the mailbox by the road. "I didn't know where you were."

"I saw your grandpa so I went over." More often than not, Bridget was glad that her parents lived so close. Yes, her mother drove her crazy sometimes, but Bridget was getting better about ignoring behavior she couldn't change. Besides, everybody felt that way about their mothers. "Dad said you were looking for me."

"Yes, I want you to come riding with me." She leaned forward in the saddle. "Please, Mom. I don't feel like riding alone."

"I'd like to, honey, but I have a lot of housework to do," she said, a touch of regret in her smile.

"You haven't gone riding with me for way too long," Molly argued. Bridget knew it was true. Not since she learned that Jonas had purchased the adjoining farm. "Please come with me and I'll help with the housework when we get back—I promise."

"Well . . ." Bridget hesitated and Molly knew she had won.

"You go change into your boots and I'll saddle Flash." She didn't wait for Bridget to agree as she reined the small bay around to ride to the horse shed behind the chalet.

Bridget glanced at the cloudless blue sky and the inviting green of the hills and shrugged. It was too beautiful a day for housework.

It took only a few minutes to change out of her sandals into a pair of boots and to tie the sleeves of a sweater around her neck in case it was cool. The usually difficult-to-catch sorrel mare was already tied to the fence, saddled and bridled, swishing her flaxen tail at the flies. Molly giggled at the look of surprise on Bridget's face.

"I had her all ready just in case you decided to come," she explained mischievously.

"Just don't you forget you promised to help with the housework." Bridget laughed, untied the reins from the post, and swung aboard the horse. "You lead the way. Flash and I will follow."

"We'll play follow the leader," Molly called over her shoulder and guided the bay through the gate.

At a canter, they wound through the green pasture dotted with wildflowers and splashed through a small stream to enter the sugar bush, thick with maple trees. A solid canopy of leaves intertwined overhead as Molly set a twisting course through the trees, dodging branches that threatened to whack the unwary.

As the trees began to thin out, a crumbling stone wall stood in their way. Bridget started to slow the sorrel, but Molly didn't check her mount, setting the bay at the low wall. Gracefully, the Morgan soared over the obstacle with easily a foot to spare. There was a lump of pride in Bridget's throat at her daughter's skilled horsemanship. She too urged her mount to the wall and jumped it cleanly.

Molly had reined in on the other side to wait, the bay mare snorting and blowing, still fresh to go many a mile more, but docilely waiting for the command. Bridget saw the breathless exhilaration on Molly's face and guessed that her own expression matched it.

Molly grinned. "Are you glad you came?"

"What do you think?" Bridget laughed, reining in the sorrel next to her daughter. "How long have you been jumping Satin?"

"Grandpa and I have been schooling her since early spring. I wanted to surprise you, though," Molly beamed.

"You sure did!" It had all happened too quickly for Bridget to feel more than brief alarm.

"Grandpa says she's a natural jumper, but then Satin can do anything." Molly stroked the mare's neck.

"Almost anything," Bridget cautioned.

"Almost," Molly conceded, wrinkling her nose as qualification. "I might start showing her next summer. Of course, we'll need a horse trailer."

"A minor, inexpensive item," Bridget teased.

"Can we afford it?" The little girl was suddenly serious.

"Oh, we might be able to buy a couple of wheels and a crate. We'll see."

"Honestly, Mom. Grandpa said—"

"So you had to mention it to your grandfather." Bridget sighed. She preferred to manage on her own without running to her parents for loans.

"I was talking about showing Satin," Molly said. "He said he might be able to find a used trailer that we could fix up."

"You mean that your grandfather would fix up." Bridget nudged the sorrel into a walk, trying to estimate how much a used horse van might cost and how much she could risk spending out of her savings.

"We really should buy it this summer so it could be all ready to go next year," Molly offered hesitantly.

"We'll have to see how much they cost first. I really don't know."

"Should I ask Grandpa to look for one on Craigslist or the ads in the paper?" Molly eyed her mother hopefully.

"I'll talk to him about it," Bridget promised.

"When?"

"We're going to have dinner with them tonight. Is that soon enough?" Her laughing hazel eyes gleamed brightly at the widened look of delight rounding Molly's eyes.

"Yeah," Molly breathed.

As they trotted their horses through a small stand of trees, sunlight streamed through the branches to dapple the ground. Last year's autumn leaves made a pleasant rustling sound beneath the horse's hooves. Overhead, a jay called raucously, flitting from limb to limb to follow them.

"He sure didn't waste any time," Molly muttered.

"What?" Bridget glanced blankly at her daughter.

"Putting up new signs to post his property." Molly gestured to a new white signboard nailed to a tree near the fence line. NO HUNTING AND NO TRESPASSING, the sign read.

Bridget paled, realizing that they were riding through Jonas's land. Boundary lines had never been observed in the past. They had always ridden this way since she was a young girl. The only difference this time had been that they had jumped the stone wall instead of using the gate.

Mr. Hanson had posted NO TRESPASSING signs too, but he'd let them weather over the years to the point where the paint was flaking off and he hadn't ever intended his neighbors to be intimidated. Bridget doubted if Jonas did, but the circumstances weren't the same.

"Yikes! There he is!" Molly exclaimed in a low hiss. "Come on, Mom. Let's go before he catches up to us."

Bridget barely had time to lift her gaze to the hill rising on their right and identify Jonas sitting tall on a rangy bay horse. A new acquisition, she figured, like his house. He hadn't been keeping a horse in New York City. Suddenly Molly was digging her heels into her horse. The eager mare bounded forward.

"Molly!" Bridget tried to call her back, for an instant checking the attempt of her own mount to follow.

She was more anxious than her daughter to avoid meeting Jonas, but it was silly to run, silly and childish. But Molly was gone. Despite her daughter's natural skill, Bridget couldn't let her ride headlong over the rolling terrain alone.

With the relaxing of the pressure holding it back, her sorrel needed no second urging to race after the other horse. The thunder of hooves pounding the grassy sod drowned out all other sounds.

There was no time to look back to see if Jonas was following. At this pace, Bridget had to focus her attention on what lay ahead. She was certain he had seen them, and she could guess his amusement at their flight.

A hundred yards from their starting point, a white board fence, the wood chipped and graying, blocked their access to the public road. As they neared it, Bridget turned her horse toward the gate only a few yards farther up from the point of approach, slowing the sorrel. But Molly didn't alter her course, only checking her mount to set it for the jump.

"No!" Bridget shouted. "Molly, no!"

It was too late. The horse and rider were already arching over the fence. They landed cleanly on the other side, only to have a road ditch yawn before them. Bridget heard an approaching truck and yelled a panicked warning.

She didn't think Molly had heard her. Either way it didn't matter because the mare's impetus would carry them

into the road, the Morgan gallantly collecting itself to leap
the ditch.

The horse landed on the graveled shoulder at the same
instant that the pickup truck topped the small knoll. Bridget saw Molly sawing frantically on the reins to stop the
horse and the driver swerving to the opposite ditch to avoid
hitting them.

The Morgan attempted a sharp turn, lost its footing in
the loose gravel and fell. Bridget heard her daughter's cry
of fear as she was thrown from the saddle and someone
screaming Molly's name over and over, unaware the
scream came from her own throat.

Driven by the desperate need to reach her daughter,
Bridget abandoned caution, jumping the sorrel over the
fence gate where a wide culvert covered with packed earth
topped the open ditch. Molly lay motionless along the
edge of the ditch as Bridget rode up, dismounting almost
before the sorrel had stopped.

The battered pickup had stopped several yards down the
road. The driver, gaunt and aging, came huffing up the
small incline, his fear showing in the graying color beneath his suntan.

"She just came out of nowhere. I couldn't stop. I'm
sorry—I'm so sorry," he said in a thin voice as Bridget
knelt beside her daughter. "Is she badly hurt?"

"I don't know." Her voice throbbed with fear. She
reached for the unconscious girl. "Molly?"

"Don't move her!" a familiar voice barked a second
before a pair of strong hands pushed Bridget out of the way.

Bridget was too shaken by the sight of Molly's white
face and closed eyes to protest as Jonas assumed control.
Dazed, she didn't question his right. Her hands were
clasped tightly together in a silent prayer that Molly was
not seriously hurt.

"Is there something I can do?" The elderly man hovered

above them, watching anxiously as Jonas examined Molly as best he could without lifting or turning her. His calm demeanor and professionalism impressed Bridget, despite her fear. If he hadn't been here . . . she didn't want to think about that.

"Call an ambulance." Jonas pulled his cell phone out of his shirt pocket and held it up, not looking at Bridget or the driver of the pickup truck. He was concentrating entirely on Molly, whose eyes were still closed. "She has a concussion at the very least—and she may also have a neck or spine injury. Internally, I don't know what's going on. She'll need to be stabilized on a backboard and we've got to get her to a good hospital with a trauma specialist."

Terrified, Bridget managed to think of the name of the nearest big hospital as the 911 operator came on the line, pinpointed their location through the cell phone, and said an ambulance was on the way.

Molly's eyelids fluttered open and she looked at her mother, then at Jonas. "What happened?" she murmured. "Where's Satin? Is she all right?" She made a move to sit up and then settled down again, breathing shallowly. "Did she break a leg? I don't think I did—Mom, don't cry."

"Oh my God—she's conscious—and she can talk. That's good, isn't it?" Bridget asked frantically as she took her daughter's hand. "Stay still, sweetie. Jonas, what do you think?"

He held Molly's small wrist and started taking her pulse, then ran his other hand lightly over her middle. "She still needs to go to a hospital. Head injuries are unpredictable and as I said, there may be other things going on. But she's not flinching. I don't think she broke any ribs." He looked into Molly's eyes. "Close your eyes, Molly. Now open them."

The little girl obeyed his calm commands without arguing.

"Her pupils are responding normally. Good."

Of course he knew what to do—he was a doctor—but

Bridget was overwhelmed by conflicting emotions. Gratitude. Fear. Above all, love for her daughter. You never knew how fragile—and how plucky—a child could be until one got hurt, Bridget thought miserably.

"I wish there was something I could do," the older man mumbled again.

Looking up from Molly for a moment, Jonas made a fast assessment of the pickup's driver, noting the man's shock and advanced age. The hard line of his mouth curved briefly into an understanding smile.

"Is there someone who can come get you?" Jonas asked. "You shouldn't be driving."

"Yes. My niece."

"Give Bridget the number and she'll call for you." He looked down again at Molly, who gave him a weak smile. Did her little girl see him as a rescuer? Awash in emotion that was almost too strong to handle, Bridget felt a flash of jealousy and resentment, and told herself to get a grip. Jonas wasn't playing a hero—he was doing what had to be done, what was best for Molly. She made the call at the old man's direction, and did her best to reassure his worried niece when she reached her.

Trembling from the effort it took to sound calm, Bridget was startled when Jonas began to give her orders. "Catch the horses and get them off the road. Put them back in the stable."

"Leave Molly?" she gasped in angered astonishment.

"We don't need another accident," he said coolly and returned his attention to Molly, closing the discussion.

Although Bridget recognized the wisdom and logic behind his order, his tone of voice was a spark to her temper. She wanted to disobey even as she rose shakily to her feet to comply, her knees weak and her stomach churning.

The rangy bay Jonas had been riding stood, ground hitched, behind them. Bridget grabbed at the reins and walked across the road to where her sorrel was grazing along the shoulder. For once, the recalcitrant horse allowed Bridget to walk right up to her as if knowing this was not the time to play a game of tag. Molly's bay mare was standing by the board fence, a knee scraped and bloody but showing no other marks from the fall.

Leading the three horses, Bridget started back to Molly. She stopped short at the sight of her daughter's hand in Jonas's. Molly was talking to him quietly about nothing in particular. Bridget knew he was monitoring her daughter without seeming to do so, but she could not shake off an unwelcome resentment at his rapport with Molly. It was as if he had usurped her parental, protective role—and the thought made Bridget feel even more dazed, as if she and not Molly had taken the knock on the head.

She heard the distant wail of the ambulance's siren gradually grow louder and finally stop as the emergency vehicle came over the hill and stopped where Jonas pointed.

As she watched, feeling helpless and afraid, Jonas and the EMT crew got Molly on the backboard and took her vital signs under Jonas's close supervision.

Just seeing her daughter's small body strapped down and a thick cervical collar carefully placed around her neck was enough to make Bridget cry a river of tears. But she didn't. She signed the forms on a clipboard that a tech handed her without paying much attention, forcing herself to be strong for Molly, when all she wanted to do was puke—or shriek.

"Ma'am?" an EMT guy asked her. "Are you coming to the hospital?" The other two were carefully lifting the backboard into the ambulance, chatting with Molly, who managed to reply. Stricken, Bridget looked at Jonas.

"Your call," was all he said.

She took a deep breath and came to a decision. Like him, she would do what was best for her daughter. If he rode with her, Molly would have the benefit of a doctor and EMT personnel right at hand. If anything went wrong—anything at all—they would take care of her daughter in a way that she couldn't. And the horses couldn't be left to find their own way home.

"I'll be there as soon as I can. Jonas can ride with her."

"Take care of Satin, Mommy," she heard Molly say.

"I will, sweetie. See you as soon as I can."

Jonas nodded and climbed into the back of the ambulance, sitting next to Molly on the jumpseat that the EMT guy flipped down for him. The driver closed the doors and the ambulance left, seconds before the old man's niece pulled up to take him home.

To save time, Bridget got all three of the horses put away at Jonas's house and dashed over to hers. She left a note for her parents who'd gone off somewhere—her father didn't have a cell phone and her mother couldn't remember to keep hers charged. She would try to call them from the hospital if she got a chance.

Bridget ran to her car and drove to the hospital in less than an hour. She didn't remember too much about the journey besides a lot of praying to make amends for all past, present, and future sins, amen, just so long as Molly would be okay.

The ER intake clerk paged a nurse to lead Bridget through the maze of rooms to the one where her daughter was. Molly was sitting up in a railed hospital bed and talking.

Thank God.

Jonas was with her. Bridget felt the same uncomfortable mix of gratefulness and resentment surge up once more.

"Hello, you two," she said quietly.

Chapter Five

Molly didn't look any too happy. "Hi, Mom," she frowned. "I hurt."

She started to lift a hand to the bump on her forehead, but Jonas checked the attempt. "That's to be expected. You banged your head," he told her. "The ER doctor said most likely you'll be all right, though," Jonas added. "You're lucky that truck didn't hit you."

Molly didn't seem to care. "Mom, how's Satin?"

"She's fine," Bridget smiled, a fine mist of tears brightening her hazel eyes. "Like you, she has a few cuts and probably some bruises."

"I want to see her." Molly tried to ease off the bed but it was too high for her to get down without help. She gave up when Bridget shook her head.

"Not yet. First you have to get cleaned up, then you can worry about your horse."

Jonas nodded his agreement at Bridget. "The nurse said she'll be right back. They want to make sure her condition is stable first. Molly's scheduled for a CAT scan but she seems to be doing okay."

Bridget was happy to wait for the nurse. She had no

intention of leaving Molly's side. She moved closer, her smile slightly weak and tremulous.

"Are you sure you're all right, honey?" she murmured.

"I think so." Molly began to shake a little. "I was so scared, Mom."

"So was I," Bridget laughed softly. "Whatever made you do that?"

"I don't know," Molly shivered. "I just didn't think about there being any traffic."

Jonas and Bridget stepped to one side when the nurse returned.

"Your top is pretty well ruined, Molly. I'm going to cut the sleeve away. Sorry about that." She glanced briefly at Bridget. "Is that all right with you?"

"Of course."

"What's she going to do?" Molly eyed the nurse warily.

"I'm going to clean those scrapes on your arm and leg. The dirt and bacteria can cause infection," answered the nurse.

"I don't want you to." Molly drew back against the hospital bed, mutiny darkening her eyes as she glared at the nurse.

"Molly, you have to," Bridget said, trying to think of a way to placate her daughter.

"I don't care. I don't want anyone to touch me," Molly declared.

"She's as stubborn as you are, Bridget."

Bridget flushed. Maybe Jonas meant the remark as a joke, but she wasn't in the mood for a joke. The feeling of resentment came back, but Jonas didn't glance her way to see it. Bridget exhaled and focused on what needed to be done right now.

"You don't have any choice in the matter, Molly," she said firmly but reasonably. "There are other patients in the ER waiting to be seen, and you have to cooperate."

She glanced at the nurse's name badge. "Audrey has to clean those scrapes."

Molly only nodded. Gently, Audrey took hold of the torn sleeve of her blouse and began snipping the cloth to expose the wound, but Molly tried to twist away.

"Molly, please hold still," Audrey said patiently. "These scissors are sharp," she warned.

With a huge sigh, Molly submitted at last and the nurse began cleaning the abrasion that ran almost the length of her arm.

At the touch of the antiseptic against her skin, Molly flinched and Bridget winced sympathetically, knowing it had to burn.

"That *really* hurts," Molly protested.

A corner of Jonas's mouth quirked upward. "Sometimes it helps not to think about it."

"Huh?" She scowled at him so fiercely that Bridget almost smiled.

"Let's talk. What do you know about Morgan horses?"

As a distraction, that just might work. But Bridget had no idea how Molly would react. She held her breath until her daughter suddenly spoke.

"A lot," Molly declared. "Justin Morgan lived right here in Randolph—the man, not the horse."

"Where did the horse live?"

"The horse lived here, too, but his name wasn't Justin Morgan."

The nurse and Jonas exchanged a conspiratorial smile that Molly didn't see.

"What was he called?" Jonas asked.

Molly blew out an exasperated breath. "The horse was called Figure. Later on, when he got to be famous, they started to call him Morgan's horse."

"Why was he famous? What made him so special?"

Molly winced, but the effort of thinking distracted her

from the pain. "The Morgan horse was special because he could do everything. He could work in the woods all day hauling logs, sometimes pulling logs that other, bigger draft horses couldn't, and he could run faster than anything around."

Nothing wrong with her memory, Bridget thought, amazed by how readily her daughter responded.

"What else?" the nurse asked. "Now you've got me interested. You learn something new every day, isn't that right, Dr. Concannon?"

Bridget guessed he'd introduced himself. That shouldn't annoy her but it did. Audrey was pretty and very capable.

"He was as gentle as a kitten. And he was the first American breed of horse," Molly declared.

"I didn't know that," Jonas said.

The nurse shifted her attention to Molly's leg, cutting a slit up the pants leg.

"That isn't all." Molly sat up slightly. Now that she was beginning to impress him with her knowledge, she wanted to enlarge on it. "The other American breeds like the American saddle horse, the Standardbred and the Tennessee walking horse—all of them can be traced back to show a Morgan cross in their beginnings."

"I'm impressed. I didn't know Satin came from such a distinguished ancestor."

"Satin is awesome," Molly said stoutly.

The nurse looked over at Bridget. "Her knee is going to need a butterfly bandage. She has a fairly deep gash there." She turned to look through a drawer of medical supplies, and frowned. "Shoot. None here. I'll be right back."

When Audrey got up and left the room, Bridget hesitated only a second. Touching Molly's hand lightly, she said, "Lie still," and motioned Jonas out into the corridor.

"Do you think she'll need stitches on her knee?"

"I'm not the attending physician. I really can't say."

"But you could ask the nurse. She'd listen to you."

Jonas gave her an amused look. "Seems to me that Audrey knows what she's doing. Anyway, you're Molly's mother. You should ask questions like that."

Bridget just stared at him, struggling to control her temper. "Somehow I don't think you should be giving me parenting lessons, Jonas," she said. There was a distinct edge to her voice. "This isn't the time or the place. And you don't know what you're talking about when it comes to that." Her voice cracked and she wiped away a tired tear. "Not like you have a kid, right?"

"No, I don't. But doctors and nurses can make mistakes."

"Don't say that! Molly's never been seriously injured before! You're scaring me!" She wanted to bawl but she was damned if she was going to do it in front of him.

"Take it easy, Bridget. I'm sorry. I didn't mean to alarm you. All the indications are that Molly will be fine."

"Then why are they going to do a CAT scan?" she asked worriedly. "She wasn't bleeding."

"To rule out a skull fracture. She lost consciousness, Bridget. It's a possibility. A physical examination isn't enough. Better safe than sorry."

"Oh, Jonas. I wish I hadn't gone riding with her. This never would have happened."

"It was an accident," he said firmly. "Kids have them, especially active kids like Molly." He reached out and took her by the shoulders.

More than anything, Bridget just wanted to rest her head on his brawny chest and feel his arms wrap around her in a reassuring hug. But she didn't dare.

She had never seen him in doctor mode, and probably never would have if not for Molly's accident. It was disconcerting. There was so much about Jonas she didn't know. He was far from being the small town boy she'd loved so foolishly so long ago. Bridget looked up into his eyes and saw only cool professionalism.

"If you have questions about your child's treatment, you have to ask. I'm not on staff here and I can't do it for you."

She guessed he was trying to be supportive, but Bridget was too frazzled to think straight. "Hey, I'm not sure what to ask. You were with her during the examination. I wasn't. I haven't even spoken to the ER doctor yet."

"You will. He'll be back to explain the CAT scan to you and answer your questions. He'll do a write-up and your pediatrician can request a copy."

Calm. Collected. He was talking almost as if he thought she was about to get hysterical.

She wasn't going to. It wasn't her style and it wouldn't do Molly one bit of good. "Okay. I'll ask the questions," she said dully. "Thanks for distracting her, by the way. It worked."

"If you want reassurance, Bridget," he replied in a level voice, "I can give you that. Your daughter doesn't show the signs of a serious concussion, although she had a mild one. Her abrasions have been treated and the cut is about to be bandaged." He raised his hand to wave to the returning nurse. "I'm going to get a cup of coffee. Want one?"

"No."

He rubbed her arms in a way that wasn't quite professional but it sure was comforting. She felt a little better. Just a little.

"I'll stay with you until they release Molly, how's that?"

She nodded and went back into the room to be with her daughter.

An orderly in scrubs showed up to wheel Molly down the hall for her CAT scan. Bridget accompanied her, holding her daughter's hand through the rails and chatting about nothing in particular. They passed Jonas, coffee in hand, talking to one of the residents. Bridget only caught a little of the conversation, and it made her curious. *Family practice. Doc Winston is selling.*

Maybe he was serious about staying. Still and all, he was bound to miss the excitement of New York and the prestige of a Park Avenue office. The thought was dispiriting. She turned her attention back to Molly and squeezed the small hand in hers.

They turned the corner. "What are they going to do?" Molly asked nervously.

"I don't know, honey, I've never had a CAT scan. I know it doesn't hurt."

The CAT technician appeared and began to explain, allaying the little girl's fears with his cheerful manner. "All you have to do is lie still and look up. Your mom's right, it doesn't hurt at all. It doesn't feel like anything. Basically, it's a picture of the inside of your head." He smiled at Molly. "So what's in there?"

Molly screwed up her face in a funny grin. "I'm not sure. My homework? My dreams?"

The technician laughed. "Well, those won't show up. But I tell you what. You think about something peaceful and it will be over before you know it. Your mom can stay right here with you."

"I'm going to think about riding my horse in the woods," Molly said immediately. "That's the most peaceful thing I know."

Bridget felt a wave of gladness. She didn't want Molly's love of riding to be affected by the accident, and she didn't want her daughter to be afraid of getting back in the saddle.

"Good idea, Molly," she said brightly. The technician helped Molly moved onto the table support that she would lie on, and Bridget gave her hand another reassuring squeeze.

"Ready?" the technician asked. Molly nodded. He

moved the table support back and positioned her head within the arch of the CAT scanner.

"Close your eyes and think about Satin," Bridget said softly.

"Okay."

A few clicks and the procedure was over before either of them knew it. The orderly had timed his return so Molly didn't have to wait, and she was rolled back through the corridors, sitting up in the railed bed and looking rather proud of herself.

"This is like being on a parade float," Molly said gleefully. The orderly and Bridget shared a laugh over that. When they came around a corner and saw Jonas, Molly gave him a beauty-queen wave.

He waved back. "How'd it go?"

"It was easy," Molly said in a blasé voice. "Can I go home now?"

Jonas joined Bridget by the side of the rolling bed. "The ER doctor has to look at your CAT scan first. Then your mom wants to talk to him, so she can ask any questions she might have, and then you can go home."

"But I'm bored," Molly said.

Audrey opened the door and helped the orderly put the bed back in the examining room. "That happens," the nurse said. "I brought you some magazines you can read while you're waiting." She got Molly settled and gave her *Highlights For Children* and *Tiger Beat*.

"What-do-you-say," Bridget murmured, on mom autopilot.

Molly remembered her manners. "Thanks, Audrey. Thanks very much." She chose *Tiger Beat* and flipped eagerly through the pages, choosing an article on her favorite boy band.

"Ready for that coffee yet?" Jonas asked Bridget.

She exhaled a relieved sigh. "Sure. What else is there to do?"

"You know how it is. It may be an emergency room, but everything takes forever."

Bridget laughed, looking over at her daughter. "Okay with you, Molly?"

"Sure," the little girl said absently, glued to the article.

Jonas and Bridget left the room and walked the short distance to the vending machines. He pulled a handful of coins out of his pocket, indicating the push buttons for powdered creamer and sugar. "Have it your way. It's awful no matter what you put in it, but it is hot."

She grinned as she made her selection, feeling better about life in general and Molly in particular. The coffee trickled into the cup, joined by shots of her additions, and the machine wheezed and stopped.

"There you go."

Bridget reached down to get the cup. "Thanks." She took a sip and made a face. "Gah. But it's comforting."

They sat down on a bench in the hall as she drank, looking at him over the paper rim. He seemed so at home in this setting, but that was to be expected.

"So what kind of doctor are you, Jonas?" she said at last. "I never did ask."

"Family practitioner. I do basic medicine. I rotated through them all—pediatrics, geriatrics, orthopedics, OB-GYN, you name it. I'm a generalist, not a specialist, if you know what I mean."

Bridget nodded. She got the idea.

"I'll tell you what appeals to me. An old-fashioned family practice that incorporates all of what I've learned. Settling in a community and making a lifelong commitment to the health of the people in it." He gave her a rueful smile. "I guess I'm an idealist too."

"Isn't—" Bridget hesitated. "Isn't that something you can do in New York?"

He nodded. "I am doing that in New York. But a big-city clinic is overwhelming. It's a struggle for a lot of people there just to get basic health care, and we see too many problems that could have been prevented. Everything from grandmothers with uncontrolled diabetes to teenagers with at-risk babies. And the tough cases too—drug abusers, HIV/AIDS patients, victims of domestic abuse . . ." He shook his head. "Yeah, you get all that in a rural setting. But there's a better quality of life up here. More breathing room. People look out for each other more. I want that, Bridget. And I think I can do some good."

Holy cow. The work he did, his plans for the future, were the exact opposite of what she'd imagined about his life in New York.

"I'm sure you will," she said softly.

After Bridget had conferred with the ER physician, who said that there was no evidence of a skull fracture or other underlying injury and explained what to watch out for, Molly was released. Audrey helped her into a wheelchair despite the little girl's protests.

"I can walk," Molly said.

"Regulations, honey, sorry," Audrey said. "Now you take it easy when you get home, you hear? And listen to your mother." She reached into the back pocket of the wheelchair and pulled out the *Tiger Beat* Molly had been reading. "You can keep this. I know you weren't finished with that article."

Molly sighed. "Thanks. I wish I didn't have to wear these torn-up clothes."

"You can shower and change when you get home. Your mom will help you."

Bridget handed her car keys to Jonas. "You go ahead and bring it around in front."

She walked next to Audrey, thanking her for caring for her daughter, words that Audrey waved away.

"Just doing my job. I'm glad there was nothing seriously wrong with her."

Jonas pulled up just as they went through the automatic doors. Audrey assisted Molly to rise from the wheelchair. Bridget noticed that she moved slowly, a little unsteady on her feet, a stiffness having already set in to add its discomfort to her bruised body. What with one thing and another, they had been in the ER a long time.

Bridget checked her watch. Hours, in fact.

Fiercely independent, Molly shrugged away Bridget's attempt to help her as if she had something to prove to Jonas. Gritting her teeth, she made it to the car, smiling at Audrey, who opened the door for her and helped her into the back seat.

"Buckle up."

"I will." Bridget heard the painful sigh of relief her daughter made when she relaxed against the upholstery and fumbled for the seat belt. Two clicks and she was buckled in. Bridget got into the front seat and did the same. Jonas made no comment as he put the car in drive.

They were all tired. There was only silence as they began the drive back until they reached the Y in the road. A left turn would take them to the chalet, and a right would lead them to town. Jonas slowed the car nearly to a stop.

In the driveway of the chalet he walked around to the passenger side as Bridget helped Molly slide out of the car. Getting out was proving more painful than getting in, as her stiff and sore body was not coordinating properly.

Jonas gave Bridget a questioning look. "Should I carry her in?"

"No!" Molly cried in protest.

"I think it's a good idea, Molly," Bridget said. The ER doctor had made it clear that they could expect to see irritable and irrational behavior from Molly, a typical after-effect of even a mild concussion.

They hadn't reached the chalet steps when her mother's voice halted them. "Bridget! My God, what happened? We just got your note, but—oh, Molly!"

Turning, Bridget saw her mother rushing across the road, running while still maintaining a ladylike air. Glancing at Molly in the bright light of day and not under hospital fluorescents, she realized how bad her daughter looked.

There was a goose-egg-size lump on her forehead and a red graze on her cheek. The checked blouse was dirty, the cut sleeve hanging loosely to reveal the gauze-wrapped abrasion—and a faint trace of blood that had seeped through the gauze. Her jeans were cut away from her leg, the white bandage around the knee showing plainly against the blue. They'd had to bring her home in those clothes but she looked much more seriously hurt than she was.

"Oh, no," Jonas murmured, his lips barely moving. "Your mother looks like she's ready to give me hell."

"Molly, baby, what happened?" Margaret Harrison demanded in alarm when she saw her granddaughter's tattered state.

"She fell off her horse," Jonas answered. "She has a few cuts, some abrasions, and probably a lot of bruises, but no serious injuries."

"You look terrible, Molly," Margaret wailed. Hardly a remark that would make her little granddaughter feel better, Bridget thought with annoyance. "Will she be scarred?"

"No, Mrs. Harrison," Jonas answered with veiled impatience. "Everything will be fine. Molly received excellent care. They'll all fade in time." He slid a help-me look at Bridget. "If you'll open the front door, I'll take your daughter inside."

Quickly, Bridget stepped forward to open the door and hold it for him. When she would have followed him inside, her mother caught at her arm.

Whispering, Margaret Harrison accused, "You didn't let him treat Molly, did you?"

"He is a doctor," Bridget said defensively. "He was out riding and he happened to be close by when she fell, and he went with us to the hospital. But no, he didn't treat her. The ER staff took care of Molly."

"I know he's a doctor—" her mother began, sounding peevish.

"But you don't know much else about him," Bridget declared, shaking her head in faint exasperation. "Nothing new anyway—oh, never mind." It was no use sharing what Jonas had told her with her mother, who was determined not to like him. Turning, she walked into the house with her mother following.

Margaret Harrison glanced around the empty living room. "Where has he taken her?"

"To her bedroom. Where else," Bridget replied crossly.

"But how would he know where it is?"

"I would guess Molly told him, wouldn't you?" she retorted. She didn't feel like explaining the rapport Jonas had established with Molly at the hospital.

Molly would be proud to show off her loft bedroom anyway. The walls were a patchwork of posters of whoever happened to be Molly's idol at the moment, and Bridget was sure that the squeaky-clean star of the *Tiger Beat* issue Audrey had given her would be pinned up next.

"Yes, of course you're right," her mother agreed with the plausible explanation.

Bridget started toward the open stairwell leading to the loft. At that moment Jonas appeared at the top of the steps, hesitating for a fraction of a second as he looked at her before descending.

"She wants to change into some clean clothes," he stated.

"She'll need help. I'll go up," Margaret Harrison declared, hurrying quickly up the steps Jonas had just come down.

Jonas watched her disappear, then turned and spoke softly. "She means well, I guess."

Bridget stiffened, slightly indignant that he should voice a double-edged comment like that when it was possible her mother could overhear.

The last thing any of them needed was to revive old conflicts that were best left buried. Of course, that also meant they were left unresolved, but there was nothing Bridget could do about that. It simply wasn't possible to fix the past. She reminded herself that he had walked away ten years ago. There was a limit to how much she was able to trust him, even if he had helped her so much today just by being there.

It didn't really prove anything. She and Molly had managed pretty much on their own for all this time, and done pretty well, all things considered. Just the thought of that balance being upset in any way was enough to make Bridget want to proceed with caution.

"I have to let her help, Jonas." She started to walk past him to the stairs.

"Okay. I understand. Let's go over what you need to know one more time. If Molly's head begins to ache . . ." His tone was cool and professional again. He went through the warning signs of head injury complications once more and Bridget didn't mind. He meant well, she thought with a faint smile. ". . . give her a couple of non-aspirin pain reliever tablets," he was saying.

"Okay." She didn't ask who she should call. Obviously Jonas was closest if she needed him—and he was right about the shortage of doctors in rural communities. Doc Winston wasn't the only one who planned to retire, and he was well into his seventies. Again she started up the steps.

"You're not exactly listening," he said curtly.

"Yes, I am." With one foot on the stairs, Bridget paused, feeling a little guilty. "And hey, I haven't thanked you for all—" Belatedly she began to express her appreciation, but he interrupted her.

"Forget it. I'll bring the horses back later."

As she turned, she discovered she was talking to no one but herself. The front door was closing behind Jonas. She trembled weakly. He seemed to have taken some of her strength with him when he left.

Chapter Six

After dinner, near sundown, Bridget looked out the kitchen window and noticed the light shining in the window of the horse shed. She guessed that it had to be Jonas returning their two horses. She hesitated at the sink, then quickly wiped her hands on a dishtowel.

There was the tack to be cleaned and put away and the horses to be fed. She couldn't let Jonas do that. She was already in his debt because of Molly. And that was another thing she wanted to clear up.

Glancing over the breakfast bar into the living room, Bridget could see Molly lying on the sofa in front of the television. She was wearing a loose-fitting cotton robe of Bridget's to keep from irritating the abrasions on her arm and leg.

"Molly, Jonas has brought the horses back. I'm going out to take care of them," she called to her daughter, but didn't receive an answer. She walked partway into the living room and saw that Molly had fallen asleep.

Bridget debated whether or not to wake her, then decided against it. She would probably be back in the house before Molly woke to find her gone. Quietly, she slipped out the back door of the house and hurried to the stables.

The golden shadows of sunset were coloring the green hills rising from the valley meadow.

Unlatching the door, she swung it open and stepped inside. A breathy excitement gripped her lungs, a sensation she always experienced on meeting Jonas. She was greeted by the pungent odor of horse liniment burning her nose, and the nicker of a horse.

The sorrel mare, Flash, was in her stall, the well-formed head turned, ears pricked at Bridget's entrance. But it was the adjoining stall where the gleaming hindquarters of Molly's bay were visible that drew Bridget's gaze. She could hear the rustle of straw and the low, soft crooning of a masculine voice.

Bridget walked to the end of the stall and stopped as Jonas straightened from his crouch beside the bay's front legs. In the shadowy glow of the overhead lightbulb, his hair was rumpled and gold lights glistened in the brown thickness.

He was tall and lean and rugged, the way she liked to remember him, with a faded denim jacket hanging open, a worn cotton shirt opened at the throat, and snug-fitting Levi's that molded the muscular length of his thighs and legs.

There was a veiled intensity in the way his eyes returned her look. Temporarily, Bridget forgot why she had come to the shed, her voice forgetting how to work.

"How's Molly?" Jonas turned slightly, picking up the bottle of liniment from the manger to cap it.

"Fine," she nodded jerkily.

"I fed and watered the horses, cleaned the tack, and put it away." He ran a stroking hand over the bay's flank, pushing the horse aside to walk from the stall.

"There was no need for you to do that," Bridget protested. Her poise returned along with her common sense. She had to heed the inner voice warning her not to let his sensual attraction overwhelm her. "I didn't expect it."

His gaze briefly swept her figure, an unnervingly thorough study despite its swiftness. "It was no trouble." He shrugged indifferently and walked by her to replace the liniment in the metal cabinet on the far wall.

"Maybe not, but I—"

Jonas interrupted as if he didn't care what else she had to say. "The mare's right fetlock is slightly swollen. You might have your father look at it or call a vet."

"I—I'll do that," Bridget replied, momentarily non-plussed.

"I'd like to see Molly before I leave," he stated.

"She really is fine," she assured him quickly, not wanting to invite him into the house.

A mocking light entered his eyes and his mouth quirked slightly. "Do you object if I see that for myself?"

He was a doctor, Bridget reminded herself, and she should treat him as such. She had to school herself to be indifferent to his presence. It wasn't as if she would be alone with him. Molly was in the house, albeit sleeping, but she was there.

"Of course not." Bridget started for the stable door. "She was sleeping when I left."

Jonas followed, switching off the light and making no comment. Bridget hadn't expected that her last remark would change his mind, although there had been the possibility it might have.

The twilight sky was suffused with purple as they walked to the house in silence. The evening star shimmered above the darkening green hills, the pale white of a crescent moon waiting also for night. But the air was still warm from the afternoon's sun. The Vermont dusk was peaceful and serene, but Bridget couldn't match its mood.

"Molly is in the living room lying on the sofa," Bridget said as she walked through the back door of the house ahead of Jonas.

Her over-the-shoulder glance saw his nod of under-standing, but he said nothing. Bridget led the way through the kitchen into the living room where Molly lay still sleeping on the sofa. Jonas stood above her, but made no attempt to wake her.

"Has she complained of anything?" he asked.

"A slight headache. I gave her two pain reliever tablets a few hours ago," Bridget admitted.

"Any complaints other than that?" he persisted.

"Like what?" she frowned."

"Dizziness, sharp pains, difficulty focusing her eyes." Absently, Jonas listed the by-now-familiar possibilities, his attention absorbed in its study of Molly's sleeping face.

"Nothing like that." Bridget shook her head with certainty but felt faintly alarmed.

"Good," he nodded. "I didn't expect she would."

"Should I . . . wake her?"

"There's no need." He ran a hand through his hair, a gesture that implied weariness, and slid a disinterested sideways glance at Bridget. "You wouldn't happen to have any coffee made, would you?"

"I think there's still some from this afternoon—I had to get the taste of the vending machine coffee out of my mouth. But the pot I made is probably too strong by now," she answered. Maybe she shouldn't have said that. She didn't quite want him to think that she'd been keeping some hot just in case he came over. Their closeness in the hospital had been fleeting, and their mutual wariness had returned. As far as she was concerned, they were back where they started from.

"I don't mind. The stronger the better." His mouth curved fleetingly into a smile. "I'd like a cup, if it's no trouble."

"It isn't," Bridget said. All these mixed emotions over a cup of coffee—she didn't know what was the matter with her.

He followed her into the kitchen, taking a chair at the dinette table while she poured coffee into a stoneware mug. "Cream and sugar?" she offered, carrying the cup to the table.

"Both. Will you join me?"

How could she refuse? The only other alternative would be to stand around waiting for him to drink it, and that would only add to the vague sense of unease she was fighting.

"I think I will," Bridget agreed with a stiff smile.

Filling a matching stoneware mug with black coffee, she took a chair opposite him at the table. She cupped her hands around the mug in an attempt to ward off the chill pervading her limbs.

Jonas sat motionless in his chair, an arm hooked over the back. He seemed withdrawn and distant, but she was going to wait for him to do the talking.

"I owe you an apology, Bridget," he said at last.

His words caught Bridget by surprise. She looked at him, startled, but she couldn't catch his eye. A faint furrow of concentration drew his brows together.

"Why?" she asked with a trace of confusion.

"Well, before the ambulance arrived, I was giving the orders." He paused. "Am I wrong in saying that you didn't like it?"

"It's all right," Bridget dismissed the need to apologize. "I didn't know what to do. Believe it or not, that was the first time Molly ever fell off a horse. Considering how fearless she is, she's been lucky. Anyway, I'm glad you were there." So he wanted to know what was on her mind—well and good—but she suddenly didn't want to have that kind of conversation.

"I could have been"—Jonas hemmed and hawed, searching for the right words—"more personal and less professional. I could have handled it differently." He ran a hand through his already rumpled hair. "You know, when residents do rounds, our handling of different cases is critiqued—"

"You don't have to second-guess yourself on this one. You did the right thing." Bridget fell silent. There was no way she was going to explain the irrational resentment she felt during the agonizing minutes after Molly's fall. As a single mother, she'd had to be everything to her daughter, but she couldn't do it all the time. It wasn't wise or healthy.

"Okay." He let out a deep sigh. "I guess I'm worrying about something I don't need to worry about." Despite his words, his look at her was searching and worried.

She was grateful to him. He obviously needed a little reassurance and it was no big deal to give him that.

"Jonas, maybe you were brusque at first but you had to follow medical protocol or whatever it's called at the scene of an accident." Bridget attempted a shrug of indifference, knowing that he was likely to see right through it. He was incredibly perceptive to have picked up on what she'd felt at the time.

"So long as you're okay with it," Jonas refused to drop the subject.

"You put Molly first. I respect that," she said levelly. "Could we talk about something else?"

"Sure we can. I just want to make sure that we understand each other. I mean, for a little while there it was like we were a family. Do you know what I mean?"

We. Family. Simple words that held poignant meaning. She wasn't remotely ready to think of herself and Jonas as linked in any way. They were entirely separate individuals and she wasn't at all sure they would ever understand each other.

Immediately Bridget broke away from his compelling gaze. "Does it matter all that much? I'm not exactly sure of what you're getting at—and I have a headache myself." Trying to conceal that his remark had disturbed her, she picked up the mug, her hand blessedly steady. "So, do you really plan to open an office here in Randolph?"

The grooves around his mouth deepened in a slight frown at her introduction of a different subject. His gaze focused on her lips as she lifted the cup to her mouth. She tried to sip the coffee with an air of nonchalance, denying that his look had any effect on her, and nearly scalded her tongue on the hot liquid.

"I'll be opening a practice, yes," he answered finally. "That was one of the things I was talking to the resident about when you and Molly went off for her CAT scan. There's a building available with a long lease, and he knew where I could get medical equipment and furniture at a reasonable price. He even recommended a nurse—a gem, he called her, named Schultzy."

"That was fast," Bridget said.

"Not really. I have to hire a lawyer, do due diligence, obtain a Vermont medical license—there's a lot of work to be done. But it is what I want."

"Then you are definitely staying?" Bridget asked. She shook her head. "Sorry, dumb question. You bought a house." Why would he stop there? Funny. At the hospital, she'd been touched by, had even admired, his determined idealism. But the reality of Jonas setting up a practice in the town she and Molly lived in was different. She fought a sinking sensation.

"Yes, I am definitely staying," Jonas stated quietly as if he guessed her unspoken reaction to the news. "I made up my mind about that after I saw you in March and Bob told me later that your husband had died."

Whoa. Where was he going with that remark? "You shouldn't have let that influence you," she replied curtly. All of a sudden Bridget was on the verge of panic.

"Probably not," he conceded.

"Won't you miss New York? Don't you want a Park Avenue office?" Unwittingly, Bridget put a sarcastic edge on her words.

"I told you I worked in a clinic, Bridget," he said patiently. "I was on staff, on salary. Yes, I can get start-up loans based on my earning potential, but most of my patients couldn't even afford to be sick. What do you take me for? Not every doctor is obsessed with making money."

Bridget avoided that subject even though she had brought it up, if only by implication. It would ultimately lead to a discussion of the past and arguments and bitterness and all the old hurt. It was difficult enough to deal with Jonas's presence without all the old emotions resurfacing.

"Good health care is expensive," she said blandly. Bridget changed the subject again. "I suppose the clinic will be sorry to see you leave. Had you worked there long?"

"Since qualifying. The administrator will have to replace me sooner than she expected but that's how it goes. As far as I'm concerned, I'm out of there as of now. I made some good friends and I think I really helped a lot of people, but I was just about burned out. They knew my ultimate goal was to start my own practice and get away from the city."

There was a glitter of impatience in his gray-green eyes as if he was aware she was trying to sidetrack him. His hand, large and well shaped, wrapped itself around the side of his coffee mug.

Bridget searched for a noncommittal response. "There isn't any place quite like Vermont." An inane comment under the circumstances. The air was crackling around her, charged with emotional undercurrents she tried desperately to ignore.

"I didn't come back for the scenery and you know it," Jonas muttered. "I came back because of you." His hand reached out for hers and she wasn't quick enough to dodge it. "I had to come back to see if we still had a chance together."

The enveloping warmth of his grip coursed through her entire body. It took all of her self-control and resolve not to be swayed by his nearness.

"You're a doctor, Jonas. You save lives," Bridget answered evenly. "But not even you can breathe life into something that died ten years ago." Gently but firmly she drew her hand free of his hold. Rising, she smiled politely. "Would you like some more coffee?"

There was a brooding fire in his eyes as he stared at her silently. Then he pushed his mug toward her. "Please." The acceptance of her request was issued tautly. "I let it get cold."

Picking up his mug, Bridget walked to the counter where the coffeemaker was plugged in. Heat was rising from his cup, but she poured out the contents and added more from the pot.

"It isn't dead for me, Bridget." With cat-soft footsteps, Jonas had approached her from behind. "Is what you once felt for me really dead?" he demanded huskily.

His fingers brushed the chestnut hair away from her neck, their touch against her skin thrilling her, no matter how much she wanted to resist him. His hard mouth re-stamped its brand on the curve of her neck, nibbling at the sensitive cord.

The floor seemed to roll beneath her feet, but it was only the trembling of her knees. She swayed for a second against the solid wall of his muscular chest, feeling the promised strength of his arms.

The sensual weakness was momentary. Straightening, she turned, wedging a space between them, and forced the hot mug into his hands. Jonas had no alternative but to take it.

"Your coffee," she declared shakily and took a hasty step away from him.

Her heart was beating so fast it frightened her. Her fingers nervously raked a path through the chestnut hair above her ear. She was being torn apart by the physical and mental conflict going on within. Jonas was still standing by the counter, not moving, watching her intently, gauging her reaction.

"Bridget . . ." His voice was low and insistent.

She had to divert him. "I, er—" She couldn't think of anything to say. His next move was sudden and unexpected: his hand captured her wrist.

Her startled gasp was wasted as he pulled her smoothly into his arms. She was caught, his muscular thighs burning their imprint on her own, his virility all too obvious and his lips too close to hers.

"Let me go!" She was angry—angry and frightened because part of her didn't want him to let her go.

Determinedly she kept her face averted from his. The strong odor of horse liniment was clinging to his jacket. Bridget couldn't avoid inhaling it as his arms made a smaller circle to draw her closer. The warmth of his breath caressed her skin an instant before his mouth brushed against her temple. Jonas made no attempt to capture her lips, content to explore the winged arch of her brow and her curling eyelashes.

Taking his time, he remapped the familiar territory of her nose and cheek and the lobe of her ear. By the time he was ready to seek her lips, Bridget was trembling with the need to feel the languid passion of his kiss.

Her defenses had crumbled under the slow and steady assault. His mouth closed over hers, tasting the sweetness of her lips. As before, his kiss made no demands of her, but when she responded to deepen the kiss, Jonas answered hungrily. The molding pressure of his hands arched her closer to him, crushing her breasts against the hard metal snaps of his jacket.

The flames of love leaped and spiraled inside her, seeming to join with his to blaze brighter and stronger until she was blinded to all but the rekindled desires that drove both of them. His hands slid beneath her blouse to trace her spine and she didn't try to fight her immediate arousal.

When his fingers began tugging impatiently at the

buttons of her blouse, she knew a momentary gladness that so slight an obstacle could be so quickly removed. With a flash of soberness, she also realized where that abandonment would lead. She knew she couldn't do it. She couldn't let Jonas hurt her again and ultimately she would suffer if she gave in to her physical desires, because then she would love him as fully and completely as she had done ten years ago.

Hadn't she learned anything? Hadn't she learned that he couldn't be trusted? She heard her mother's voice in her head: *he took what he wanted, used it, and when something better came along, he walked away.* No, no, she wouldn't fall under his spell again, not again.

"No!" Her surrender had been so complete that Jonas hadn't expected resistance at this late stage.

Bridget twisted out of his embrace, taking three quaking steps before his hands closed around her waist to draw her back. The tormenting need to know his possession was agony. She closed her eyes in an attempt to shut it out, her shoulder blades rigid against his chest.

"You keep saying no while every other part of you says yes," Jonas muttered hoarsely, his mouth moving against her hair.

His hands were spread flat over her churning stomach. Bridget tried to tug them away, without success. His seductive mouth was trailing over the curve of her neck to her shoulder, raising more havoc with her senses.

"The answer is no," she insisted with a choked sob, "I'm not going to let you get to me again. Now let me go!"

Somehow she managed to find the leverage to pry her way out of his arms. This time Jonas didn't attempt to bring her back but stood staring at her. He was breathing heavily, the frustration of anger and desire blazing in his eyes.

Bridget took a wary step backward in retreat, brushing

the loose tangle of chestnut hair from her cheek. A fine mist glistened in her eyes from the torment of pain and love.

"Do you enjoy turning me inside out?" Jonas asked in a low voice.

"No!" she cried. "You started this!"

"Does it make you feel better to blame me?"

She stiffened. "No. But you have no right to walk back into my life and expect to take up where we left off, just like that."

"Don't put words in my mouth," Jonas taunted savagely. "Maybe that isn't what I want. You're not the only woman I ever made love to, you know!"

Something snapped inside her and the palm of her hand struck his lean cheek with a vicious slap, the hard contact shooting needle-sharp pains all the way up her arm.

"Get out!" she hissed.

His gaze narrowed. The livid outline of her hand marked his cheek; but his fists remained clenched at his side. For a long moment, Jonas stared at the fury in Bridget's expression, then his long strides carried him to the back door. She closed her eyes as it slammed behind him, the violent action rattling the windows in their frames.

In some way, the slamming door released her own pent-up hostility, but the aftereffect was not pleasant. She felt weak and sick to her stomach. A pain more agonizing than she had ever known was filling her heart. Love-hate, love-hate—she wished she hadn't heard those words in her life.

"Mom?" Molly's drowsy but alarmed voice called out to her.

"I'm—in the kitchen," she answered in a brittle voice, fighting for self-control, her fingers clutching the counter for support.

"What was that noise?"

Bridget glanced at the back door, Momentarily silent, unable to explain to Molly. "What noise?"

"That loud bang like something exploding."

"Maybe it was the TV. How do you feel?"

"Awful," was the grumbling response, "I hurt all over. I'm one big ache!"

That makes two of us, Bridget thought briefly. "What about your head? How does it feel?"

There was a second's hesitation before Molly answered. "It's sore, but my headache's gone away." Bridget knew a measure of relief at that announcement. "Can I have something cold to drink? My mouth feels like the dentist forgot to take the cotton out of it."

"Iced tea?" Bridget suggested.

"Have we got any lemon?"

"Yes."

"Iced tea with lemon, then," Molly requested.

Bridget attempted a laugh, forced and unnatural. "You can't be feeling too badly if you're still particular about what you are drinking and how it's fixed."

As she walked to the refrigerator to get the pitcher of tea and a lemon, Molly asked curiously, "Was somebody here?"

With the refrigerator door open, Bridget paused, tensing. "Why do you ask?"

"I thought I remembered hearing you talk to someone in the kitchen while I was sleeping."

A small "Oh?" was all Bridget could manage, fearing her daughter might have overheard some part of the argument with Jonas.

"Maybe I was dreaming," Molly sighed, not quite convinced.

"It could have been Jonas." Bridget filled a glass with tea and sliced a wedge of lemon to add to it.

"Why was he here?" Molly demanded.

Bridget walked into the living room with the tea. "He brought back the horses."

"Did you feed and water them for me?" Molly struggled

into a sitting position, wincing and gasping at the pain of moving.

"They're all taken care of," Bridget assured her, without identifying who had done it.

"I should go see Satin. She'll wonder what's happened to me." Molly tried to get to her feet, but fell back. "I hurt all over!" she moaned dramatically. "I bet I'll be one big black and blue bruise tomorrow morning!"

"You probably will." Bridget smiled, but her heart wasn't in it.

"Will you help me, Mom?" Molly pleaded. "I want to see Satin and make sure she's all right."

"You lie still. Satin is fine."

Instantly Bridget remembered Jonas's comment about a swelling and his suggestion to have her father look at it. She handed the glass of iced tea to her daughter and walked to the phone.

"Who are you calling?" Molly wanted to know.

"Your grandfather."

"Why? Something is the matter with Satin, isn't it?" Molly concluded immediately, her eyes widening in alarm.

"Jonas noticed a slight swelling around her fetlock," Bridget admitted. "He didn't think it was serious, but he suggested your grandfather should look at it."

"What does he know about horses?" Molly's rude question only betrayed her concern for her beloved horse.

"He's been around them," Bridget answered coolly, dialing her parent's telephone number.

"If anything happens to Satin," Molly wailed mournfully. "I'll just die!"

Bridget could have told her that when you lose someone you love, you don't die. You keep on living, even if the living is sometimes worse than death. She had firsthand experience, and the sensation was beginning to close around her again.

Chapter Seven

Jonas stood beneath a spreading maple tree on the rock-strewn hillside, an arm braced against the trunk. A haunted look in his gray-green eyes, he gazed silently at the steeply sloping roof of the chalet across the meadow below him.

It was the end of summer, and the mountain air was noticeably cooler these days. Leaf season was just around the corner and that meant a fresh influx of tourists. All to the good. Bridget's shop would do more business. He wanted her to do well but he felt a little silly for caring so much when she was so skillful at keeping her distance. His New York buddies would laugh if they knew and tell him to give it up, that there were other women he could have just for the asking, without the heartache.

The few happy times he'd shared with Bridget—so far, the photo shoot in her shop had been the high point of his return—had been outnumbered by the tense ones. There was a volatility just under the surface every time they met that exploded all too readily, fueled by passion and self-protective frustration that was driving both of them a little crazy.

Underneath all the drama—perhaps that was inevitable, he thought ruefully—he sensed something essential that she was reluctant to share with him. He didn't have to know every detail of their ten years apart and he sure as hell didn't have the right to be jealous of whatever happiness she might have found in that time. Jonas hadn't asked many questions but he knew she was holding back, emotionally speaking.

It made sense, looking at it from her point of view. She had a young daughter and they were very close. The last thing Jonas wanted to do was come between them. He'd been through psychology rotation, studied family dynamics, and he could make an educated guess: Molly was likely to see him as competition for her mother's attention.

The kid was smart and—thanks to her grandmother, not Bridget—a little spoiled. Maybe headstrong would be a better word. But he intended to keep those opinions to himself. It wasn't his place to tell Bridget how to raise her daughter.

The depths of his feelings where she was concerned made him uneasy. He was a doctor—he was supposed to have some control over his emotions.

Of course, he had to admit to some good old-fashioned jealousy: Molly was another man's child. A man Bridget had probably loved. The thought bothered him more than he wanted to think about. He loved her more now than he had ten years ago, and he wanted to make her love him. It didn't do any good to remind himself that he couldn't make Bridget love him. Without knowing quite how, he had pushed her the opposite way.

Jonas saw Bridget come out to the clothesline in the yard behind the chalet and begin to take in the wash. Like a lot of Vermonters, she believed in going green and not using a dryer if she didn't have to. She reached up to pop off the clothespins one by one, her slender body arching with each motion. A tormenting knot twisted his stomach, a hollow ache to touch her and hold her and physically prove that he loved her. Except that wasn't the way.

Damn. He shouldn't be watching, even though he'd just happened to see her. She was totally unaware of his distant presence.

Jonas tore his gaze away from her. What had possessed him to buy the land adjoining her parents' farm? He must have been out of his mind. That was as good a way as any to describe his mental state since seeing her again. Nothing he'd done had been rational, from up and leaving the New York clinic to buying the Hanson place.

He stared at the ground beneath his feet, realizing that he could wear a path to this tree if he wasn't careful. The protectiveness he felt for her didn't give him the right to watch her, even if this vantage point was only a few hundred yards from his house and provided an unlimited view of what went on around the chalet.

Of course, since their last encounter at her house just after Molly's accident, Jonas had seen her often in town, but mostly when it had been impossible for Bridget to avoid him. The fierceness of their rekindled passion probably scared her—it almost scared him. The feeling was intense, both emotionally and physically. Alone with each other, it could get out of control fast. Paradoxically, the photo shoot at her shop had been one of the times he'd felt closest to her, even though there'd been so many people around.

Maybe she felt more relaxed in the company of others. Their renewed relationship—if he could call it that, it was difficult for him to define—could benefit from a few mutual friends. He wished he had someone to talk to about what was going on, for Bridget's sake and also for Molly's. But what with renovating the old farmhouse and following through with his plans to start his own practice, he didn't have much time to cultivate new friendships.

As if drawn by a magnet, his gaze was pulled back to the chalet. He saw Bridget pausing at the door with a basket of clothes in her hands. She lifted a hand and waved.

For a leaping instant, he thought she had seen him and his pulse soared.

But no, not at this distance. She didn't have any idea that he kept this lonely vigil beneath the maple tree and it was unlikely that she could see him. He searched the rolling landscape for the recipient of that wave and saw a child cantering a bay mare across the pasture through the dairy herd.

He recognized Molly. The girl and the gold band on Bridget's finger were ever-present reminders of her past life—ten long years that he hadn't been a part of. In time, there might be something he could do about replacing that wedding ring on her finger. But Molly might not like that at all.

She might very well resent him if things got serious between him and Bridget. Of course, Molly was too bright not to figure out that Jonas was something more than a casual acquaintance of her mother's, but he had no real way of knowing what the little girl thought of him. He and Bridget seemed to have come to an unspoken agreement to be polite when they met and let it go at that. He didn't even try to date anyone else and always got himself home by ten. Alone.

At his age, it was ridiculous. But he had to admit that Bridget was worth it. Some day, if he was patient enough, Bridget just might love him again.

If only there was someone he could talk to, someone who knew both of them, who could help him think things through. Loving Bridget was making him desperate.

Jonas went down the sloping hill and back to his house. He entered his kitchen, peering into the vintage refrigerator that wasn't working well. Not much in it and what there was, was past its shelf date. He slapped together a sandwich out of iffy cold cuts, a spoonful of mustard, and a stale roll. The Lonely Bachelor Blue Plate Special, he thought grimly. Jonas took a few bites and tossed it in the trash. He could get a decent lunch in town and pick up a few things at the hardware store for a project he had in mind. He needed something to do besides brood, and physical labor always made him feel better.

One juicy burger, two cups of coffee, and a slice of pie went a long way to making a man feel better. Jonas left a healthy tip for the waitress and headed out of the diner, whistling.

An older woman going by looked up at the cheerful sound and fixed her gaze on his face.

"Jonas? Is that you? Oh, for heaven's sake—it's so nice to see you! It's me, Bunny Fremont!"

His high school guidance counselor. The one person who'd believed in his potential back in the day. The one person he'd truly been able to talk to after his parents died. White-haired now, Bunny didn't look all that different otherwise. She was laughing at his puzzlement, dimples flashing in her cheeks. Her sunny personality hadn't changed, that was for sure. Jonas ran down the steps and gave her a hug.

"Bunny, can I take you out to lunch? I mean, I already ate, but I'd love to talk to you if you have the time."

"Of course, Jonas. But I had lunch too, about an hour ago, thanks all the same. I just stopped in Randolph to do a little shopping on my way home. How about a cup of coffee and pie at To Go?"

"Fine with me." A second slice of pie wouldn't kill him. If Bunny still lived two towns over, he didn't know when he would see her again. Running into her was a stroke of good luck.

Warmed by the late afternoon sunlight coming in the window of To Go, he and Bunny lingered over their coffee and pie. She took a final bite and pushed her plate away, all her attention on Jonas.

"You're probably right about Molly," she began. "She is headstrong. I had her in my Sunday school class for a while. Bridget used to bring her but not anymore."

Jonas nodded. "No offense, but I think Molly would rather ride her horse on the weekends."

"Well, I was the same way at her age," Bunny said indulgently. "She's a lovely child and very bright."

"Yeah. She takes after her mother. Not that I knew her fath—the guy Bridget married," he said hesitantly. "When I came back to Randolph last March, all I was thinking about was the time when Bridget and I were together. But that was ten years ago."

"I heard about that," Bunny replied. "But not the details. Just that you were very much in love with a Randolph girl."

"I guess people talked."

She considered her answer for a minute. "Not that much," she said at last. "Do you want to tell me more?"

Jonas took a calming breath before beginning again. "I think I do."

"You know I won't breathe a word of it, Jonas. You go right ahead and talk. I have a feeling there's a lot on your mind."

He looked into her warm blue eyes. Bunny had been the soul of discretion and kindness back then, almost like a mother to him. "I loved Bridget. I wanted to marry her."

Bunny nodded thoughtfully. "But you didn't."

"I'm sure that Molly's glad about that. I get the feeling she wouldn't want me for a father. And she hasn't exactly warmed up to me. She and Bridget are close—like the *Gilmore Girls*. Maybe I shouldn't come between them."

"I wouldn't think of it that way. Now, I don't know Bridget, but I would guess she's being cautious. You shouldn't take it that personally, Jonas," Bunny said, "but I do think you've done right to go slowly. You have to think about what you want too. Are you ready for fatherhood?"

Jonas shrugged. "I might not be half bad at the job."

"Glad to hear it. I personally think you would make a wonderful dad. I just wanted to know what you thought before I said so, though."

Jonas gave a rueful chuckle. "You still believe in me, huh?"

"Yes," Bunny said firmly. "I do."

"Anyway," he went on, "I really loved Bridget and as I was saying, I wanted to marry her. At the time she wanted to marry me. But she was young, barely eighteen, and I still had the rough years of medical school ahead of me."

"I knew you could do it," Bunny said with quiet pride.

"Well, it wasn't easy. Not that anyone said it would be." Jonas hesitated, considering his next words. "My family didn't have much money, you know that. And my mom died less than a year after my dad, when I was seventeen. I always had to work for everything I wanted, including college. I'm still paying off my medical school loans."

Bunny looked a little sad. She'd helped him fill out applications for the scholarships he'd won, and paperwork for supplementary financial aid.

By the time he'd graduated from college and applied to medical school, he'd done that for himself. Without rich parents, getting a degree meant going into debt. "So that's another issue. Her parents are fairly wealthy. Bridget had always had just about everything she had ever wanted."

Bunny's voice was gentle when she replied. "Is that why you didn't marry her?"

"It was a combination of reasons." He tried to explain. "Bridget said she loved me, but I wasn't sure what she felt was real and how much was simply romantic dreams because she was so young."

"So were you, Jonas," Bunny said gently.

"Yeah. Older than her, though."

"Not by much."

"Well, the money thing was a problem. It isn't easy to watch every penny you spend when you've never done it in your life. Bridget had never had to do that and I doubted that she could."

"Well, people change. Doesn't she work at that wonderful yarn store?" Bunny asked.

"Actually, she owns it." He explained Bridget's business as best he could. He felt the warmth of Bunny's approving look.

"Then she is doing well. Don't underestimate her, Jonas. You have to remember that she's ten years older now. She has been married, as much as you might not like that fact—"

Good old Bunny was pretty shrewd. Jonas hoped his former guidance counselor didn't notice his involuntary flinch when she mentioned Bridget's marriage to another man. He disliked admitting that it bothered him.

"—and she's obviously learned a great deal about budgeting and managing," Bunny was saying. "Maybe it's her independence that worries you, Jonas." The older woman gave a mischievous little laugh. "Have you ever thought of that?"

Embarrassed, he only shrugged.

Bunny reached over and patted his hand. "Perhaps I shouldn't speak so frankly when I really don't know everything that happened. Forgive me, Jonas."

He shook his head. "Well, you could be right. I'll have to think about it."

"Good. You do that."

Jonas had to laugh a little. "Bunny, you're too much. Talking to you is helping me puzzle this out. Are you sure you want to hear the rest, though?"

"Yes indeed."

He folded his hands together and heaved a sigh. "Her

parents didn't approve of our getting married. They knew it would be several years before I could even make a living, not until I'd qualified as a doctor and set up a practice. And I don't think her mother believed I would finish my training. The Harrisons didn't want her working to put me through school."

He and Margaret Harrison had never got along, but Jonas didn't feel it was necessary to go into the psychological reasons behind all that. Bridget's mother had said outright at the time that he was hopelessly immature, which was ironic, considering what she was like. Starring in her own personal soap opera would be his description of Margaret, but he wasn't going to share that with Bunny. Just before the break-up, he'd gotten wind of her mother's ridiculous fears of him running away with a sexy nurse and abandoning her daughter. Margaret loved to talk to anyone who would listen.

"Margaret Harrison just plain didn't like me," Jonas said. "And she still doesn't. I get the impression she wishes there was a way to make me go away again."

"She may be out of luck this time," Bunny replied dryly. "You seem to be as determined as ever to me."

"Maybe so," he sighed. "But getting back to what we were just talking about . . ."

He fell silent when the waitress came over and refilled Bunny's cup, then his. Jonas frowned thoughtfully. "This is the part that's going to be difficult to explain."

Bunny sipped her fresh coffee, giving him an encouraging look over the cup.

"If Bridget and I had married ten years ago, we might have had a little girl like Molly." He met Bunny's look squarely. "Instead I went away and she married another man."

"Maybe she loved him." Kind as she was at heart, Bunny could be blunt.

"I know," Jonas snapped. He glanced away, agitatedly

running a hand through his hair. "So I have to admit I'm jealous. I know it's not rational. But Bridget found someone else to love instead of me, and she had his child instead of mine. Do you understand what I'm saying, Bunny?"

"I . . . think so," she nodded hesitantly, her eyes wide, as if sensing the unfathomable depth of his emotion.

"Really?" His laugh had an ironic edge. "Then can you explain it to me?"

"I can try." Bunny hesitated as she searched for the right words. "Okay . . . you still love Bridget and you hope she'll love you again. You still want to marry her."

"Right so far," he said ruefully.

"But you're afraid she doesn't want to marry you, for several reasons—her mother's misgivings, her daughter not wanting it—all that could change, you know."

"Maybe," Jonas said hopefully. "Maybe it won't always be that way."

"That little girl is always going to remind you that Bridget married someone else—Molly's father. You don't want to admit how much that bothers you, but it does."

He let out the breath he'd been holding. "That about sums it up. So now what do I do?"

"Be patient, Jonas. That's all you can do. Bridget has to figure out what she wants to do. If she loves you—"

Jonas scowled. "Big if."

"Not necessarily. Give her time to think things through. And do the same for yourself. You've waited ten years."

"So I have," he said quietly. "So I have."

Bunny looked at him thoughtfully before she spoke again. "Let's come up with a strategy."

"Okay." He grinned at her. Bunny liked nothing better than helping someone realize their dreams.

"Bridget O'Shea and Molly are inseparable, as you say. That means you'll have to work twice as hard to win them both."

Jonas groaned. "How?"

Bunny smiled brightly. "I'm teasing you. Just be the same great guy you always have been, Jonas Concannon. And have patience. It's not going to happen overnight."

"True. I moved back to Randolph in April. We're not even at the six-month mark."

"Exactly my point."

He drummed his fingers on the table, wondering what she would say next. Bunny leaned forward and her voice dropped to a conspiratorial level. "Love ain't easy."

"Amen to that. I'm losing sleep."

She winked at him. "Don't worry so much and don't try so hard. And don't get too emotional. You may be coming on too strong."

He gave her a rueful look. "Bingo. You're right about that."

"Relax a little. Most likely Bridget will too. And one last thing, Jonas . . . don't forget to have fun."

Jonas raised an eyebrow. "Is that the deep, dark secret of life?"

Bunny flashed a dimpled smile at him. "Yes, it is. One of them, anyway. And I'm old enough to know so."

He'd decided to take Bunny's advice and go with the flow. In Randolph often to get his medical office furnished, staffed, and ready to open its doors, he ran into Bridget now and then, and did his damnedest to seem easygoing and unthreateningly friendly.

It worked. It didn't take all that long before she seemed to become more relaxed in his presence, just as Bunny had predicted. And wonder of wonders, she'd even accepted his invitation to go fishing. He planned a family-style outing with Molly, catered by To Go, which would provide the box lunches, so she didn't even have to do make sandwiches.

Casual as he wanted to seem, he'd planned that down

to the last detail too. He'd borrowed inner tubes in case they wanted to do some lazy drifting on the section of the little river where it was deep enough. He'd bought fishing rods with line spools guaranteed not to tangle, and he'd stocked up on fishing flies, reasoning that Molly was likely to be squeamish about worms.

Saturday dawned bright and sunny, and he was up at six, already packing everything in the back of his SUV, checking the spare, and fixing the wobbly mirror on the driver's side. He caught a glimpse of himself in it and had to chuckle. He had the air of a nervous teenager getting ready for a major date—except for the thick stubble he'd woken up with.

Jonas rubbed his bristly chin and grinned, glad he was a grown man. When he got done with the packing, he'd go back in and shave. With Molly around, he wasn't likely to be able to steal a kiss, but it wouldn't hurt to be prepared.

Somewhat later, shaved, dressed, and looking as good as he could without looking too eager to impress, Jonas got behind the wheel and headed for Randolph to pick up the box lunches. He drove down the back road for about a mile, spotting Dotty Pomfret on the shoulder, walking with a woman he guessed was her sister—they looked alike, even from the back—and her black-and-white dog Kiwi. He honked before he slowed down beside them.

"Good morning, ladies. Need a ride to town?"

"No, but thank you. Elizabeth and I were just taking our constitutional."

At her side, Kiwi wagged his tail, looking at Jonas with intelligent eyes.

"Okay. Let me know when you do. See you around, Kiwi. You stay on top of those sheep, pal."

He waved and continued on, accelerating slowly and watching the trio in his rearview mirror. The leisurely pace of summertime in the Green Mountains was doing him good. Little by little, the mental tension of living in New York was ebbing away.

There wasn't much doing in Randolph, but he knew To Go would be open. They did a brisk business on Saturdays. He parked, and went in through the double glass doors, informing the girl at the counter about the order he'd placed yesterday. She went to check on it as he got some serve-yourself coffee, sipping from the paper cup and reading the notices on the community bulletin board.

The Bread and Puppets Theater, a hippie holdover that was wildly popular, was putting on a show up in Glover in the Northeast Kingdom. The beads-and-flowers crowd was sure to turn out for that, Jonas thought. He ought to buy tickets for Dotty and Elizabeth, and drive up with them for the day. He'd bet anything the old sisters would be tickled to pieces if he did. Jonas set down his coffee and jotted down the phone number on the flyer.

He perused the other thumbtacked papers on the board, realizing that it would be an excellent place to publicize his new practice with a flyer of his own. It didn't have to be anything fancy—just a notice of their hours and that it was a family practice, plus a picture of himself, and Schulzy, the nurse, and whoever he hired to run the office. Jonas liked the idea of a medical office with a human touch.

The girl at the counter came back with three box lunches, stacking them on the counter. "Will that be all?"

"Nope." Jonas went to the beverage cooler, and took out several lemonades and an assortment of sodas, just barely making it back to the counter without dropping them. He peered into the glass-fronted bakery cabinet and requested three sugar-dusted apple turnovers oozing delicious-looking filling, a pound of assorted cookies and a peach pie. The key to keeping a kid happy was keeping a kid fed, he knew that much. Especially a rambunctious kid like Molly. And Bridget's womanly figure meant she didn't pick at her food. One more thing he loved about her. He had never met a woman in New York who didn't obsess over her size and her clothes and what she ate.

"There are cookies in the box lunches, you know," the girl said with a laugh.

"Might not be enough." He took out his wallet and put two twenties on the counter.

She rang up everything. "You must be feeding an army."

"No. Just my best girls. Sweets for the sweet."

Molly and Bridget were waiting on the porch of the A-frame when he pulled up, backpacks at their sides. He leaned out the window to say a quick hi, but they didn't give him time to get out and open the doors for them.

Molly clambered into the back and Bridget took the front seat, looking great with her chestnut hair pulled up in a flyaway ponytail. She wore a frayed plaid shirt tied in a knot around her middle, and cutoff jeans shorts that revealed firm, well-rounded thighs. Jonas had to take a deep, self-disciplining breath before he looked in the rearview mirror to back out onto the road.

What she had on was what everyone around here would wear for a day on the river, but on her . . . the outfit was fit for a centerfold.

He kept his eyes on the road and they made small talk about lucking out on the weather and things like that for the first few miles.

Bored with listening to them and looking out the window, Molly gave him a detailed update on Satin's injury, which had healed nicely. Jonas was glad to hear it.

He was even more glad just to be with them on a perfect day. No stress. No drama. Just the three of them, heading down a country road with tall trees arching overhead, their leafy tops moving slightly in the late summer breeze. Here and there a solitary leaf had turned scarlet or gold, a brilliant harbinger of the season to come, but the overall effect was dappled green, shot through with sunlight.

They reached the parking area by the river, but Bridget told him to go another half-mile. There was a turnout where they could park under trees, and have a more secluded part of the river to themselves, where it widened and the water slowed.

Sounded good to Jonas. He pulled in where she pointed and they began to unload, leaving the food in the cooler and bouncing the inner tubes out of the back.

"I wanna go tubing!" Molly said excitedly. She wore a bathing suit under her shorts and T-shirt and was ready to get in the water in under a minute.

Jonas watched Bridget slip off her ragged shorts, kicking them over unlaced sneakers with a hole in one toe. She had a bathing suit underneath, of course, but the sight of a small-town goddess getting ready to go tubing was sexier than any striptease. Her sneakers came off next.

She and Molly tossed the tubes into the water and wriggled into them, managing to end up with their butts in the water, and their arms and legs over the sides. They splashed and moved in lazy circles as he watched, grinning.

So far, so good.

He went around the other side of the car, under the low trees where no one could see him, and changed into swim trunks. Then he rolled his own tube down to the river, getting into it more awkwardly than the lithe O'Sheas. They laughed at him and Bridget kicked her feet to splash him when he drifted by.

Okay, he was ready to kiss his dignity good-bye. And his troubles. The peaceful river was slow here, eddying around the three of them as they rotated. Molly bumped gently against her mother's tube, then floated off, letting her head loll back on the warm rubber.

"I'm going to check around these rocks, ladies," he called to them. "See if there's trout."

"They're going to see you first," Molly called.

"Can't be helped." He reached into the water and paddled with his hands to an outcropping of rocks that extended into the water. There was no direct sunlight on the surface and he could see several feet down.

Aha. A flicker of movement at the base of a big rock half-in, half-out of the water caught his eye. Could be a trout. The problem was how to get the gear over to this side. He suspected the fish avoided the bank where they had unloaded, preferring this side for that very reason.

He heard light splashing as Molly paddled over.

"Do you see a fish?"

"I think so."

"Want me to go get the poles?"

Jonas shook his head, looking down under the rock again. There it was: a silvery, speckled flash. Definitely a trout. "I'll do it."

"Let's do it together."

Jonas looked up with surprise. That was a start. "Okay, Molly. I could use your help."

They paddled back, parting to go around Bridget, who was blissfully lazy, her eyes closed and her arms and legs flung out.

"Mom! Wake up!"

"Why?" Bridget murmured dreamily.

"Because there are fish!"

She yawned hugely. "Let me know if you catch one."

"You're no fun."

Jonas wagged a finger at Molly. "Let your mother catch a few z's. She works hard."

The little girl scowled at him, then thought better of it. Jonas could see Bridget's quirked-up smile.

"Thanks, Jonas," she said, her eyes still closed.

Score one for him. Jonas and Molly continued to paddle and soon they were at the bank where they'd parked the car. They scrambled out of the tubes in the shallow water, dragging them up onto the bank. Butts dripping water, they got the fishing gear ready and Jonas tied flies on two rods.

"Ever been fly-fishing?" he asked Molly.

"Yup. With my grandpa. He said I was pretty good. We were in a boat, though, on Lake Memphremagog."

"That's way up north."

"Grandpa says you can catch three-foot-long trout up there."

Jonas laughed. "I think he's pulling your leg. Now how are we going to get these rods back to where we were?"

Molly reached and flipped open the lid of a cooler to look inside. "This one's empty. Let's float everything in it. The rods are light. It won't sink."

He ruffled her hair. "Smart kid."

She found a bungee cord and hooked it around one handle of the cooler so they could hang on to it. Molly carried it to the water while Jonas set the tubes back in, and they were off.

Bridget was still floating in blissful circles as they went by.

"Toot-toot!" Molly said, gently bumping her mother's tube with her own.

Bridget opened her eyes to watch the flotilla go by, smiling at Jonas and her daughter. Then she settled back, content to daydream.

An hour or so of casting from the rocks got a few rises from the lurking trout but no hits. Molly really did know how to cast, Jonas was pleased to see. Her feathery fly landed lightly on the water each time, and she never snagged one of the overhanging branches.

He did. Twice.

With small, nimble fingers, Molly helped him untangle his line when he pulled the branch down in a graceful arc the first time, but she was having trouble with it now. Her earnest expression and determined air made him want to smile—her grandpa had taught her well. She was going to keep at it until they caught something. Quite a kid. He wouldn't mind being her dad, not at all. In fact, it would be an honor.

Jonas remembered what Bunny had told him about being patient. He was going to take this one step at a time.

Molly glanced down into the water. "There's one," she whispered.

He actually didn't want to catch it. He wanted her to catch it. Jonas left his snagged line where it was and reached out for her rod and reel. "Go get him."

Walking carefully and noiselessly over the rocks, Molly found a spot where her shadow wouldn't fall on the water and made a perfect cast, sending line and fly sailing over the water. Just as the fly touched the calm surface, the trout rose—and swallowed it whole. Molly lifted her catch with a shout, calling to Jonas to come help her. It was a good-size fish but the hook held.

"Mom, look!"

Bridget rotated and opened her eyes. "Wow! Honey, that's great!"

Jonas got close enough to reach for it, but the wildly flopping fish was too slippery to hang on to. He whipped off his T-shirt and used it to get a grip on it, bringing the catch to Molly, who looked at her gasping catch with pride. "That was fun. Okay, let it go," she said.

"You sure?"

She nodded. With a quick twist, Jonas removed the hook and slipped the trout back in the river. It disappeared in less than a second.

"Bye-bye, fish." She waved to it. "Your T-shirt is going to be stinky."

"Not a problem. I brought another one." He stuck it in the

waistband of his trunks, and, balancing on the big rocks, they went back to the branch where Jonas's line had tangled.

"I think I can get this loose." Molly picked at the nylon filament until it suddenly sprang loose and he could undo the rest.

"Great work. Thanks, kiddo."

Molly nodded. "You're welcome. It's your turn to fish."

"I think that one learned his lesson."

The little girl shrugged. "Maybe he has a stupid friend under the other rock. You never know. You have to try."

"You're right, Molly." He fished for another half-hour, with her watching, giving him a few pointers on his casting.

Yes, sir, he thought. One day at a time. And one trout at a time.

They picnicked on the bank by the car, devouring the box lunches and starting in on the sweets. Molly swigged lemonade when she was finished, curling up in a nest of sun-warmed towels. She reached into her backpack and pulled out a magazine.

"Let me guess," Jonas joked. "*Field and Stream*."

"Nope," Molly said. "This is the back-to-school issue of *Teen Vogue*. I'm planning my wardrobe."

Bridget snorted. "Aren't you a little early?"

"Mo-om," Molly said indignantly. "School starts in only two weeks."

"I meant for *Vogue*. Excuse me, *Teen Vogue*."

Molly shook her head but otherwise didn't answer the question.

She flipped the pages, dog-earing a few, then lay back with the open magazine over her face. "I'm sleepy."

"So take a nap," Bridget said.

Molly mumbled her agreement from underneath the magazine, and Jonas drew Bridget against him.

"Having fun?"

"Yes," she admitted. She rested her head on his chest for a few seconds. "Is this part of a nefarious plan to get me to calm down?"

Jonas laughed, pushing back the damp tendrils of chestnut hair that had escaped from her ponytail. "Uh-huh."

"Careful. If I get too relaxed, we might end up . . ."

"What?" Jonas asked softly.

She put a finger to her lips as the magazine pages rustled.

"You might end up smooching. That's disgusting," Molly said. "Also sickening. And repulsive."

"Open your eyes and look," her mother said indignantly, straightening away from Jonas. "We aren't doing anything."

Molly lifted the magazine and looked. "Good."

He got up and put away the fishing gear, not wanting to push his luck. Later, on the ride home, with Bridget and Molly dozing together in the back seat, Jonas felt a little lonely. He glanced in the rearview mirror at mother and daughter, swaddled in towels, with faintly pink noses and damp hair. The car smelled fishy, although he hadn't caught anything. Must be the river water they'd mopped off their tired bodies at the end of the long day. The tubes bounced in the back, getting in the way of his view of the traffic behind them.

There were lots of other vehicles on the road, from new SUVs with expensive mountain bikes on roof racks, to ancient station wagons filled with happy kids and disreputable mutts who also looked happy, and every other kind of car imaginable. The drivers looked like dads for the most part, nominally in charge behind the wheel. Some families were just tooling along, some were singing or squabbling, but they all had the same look: like the people in them were connected to each other.

Something he wanted very much to happen for him and Bridget and Molly.

In the west, the setting sun was splintering pink and gold rays over the green mountains. A serene hush had settled over the valley. The air was still, the temperature cooling. Bridget felt the quiet peace close around her, but it brought no comfort to her troubled mind.

As much as she had tried to keep Jonas at a distance she thought was healthy for her and for Molly, he was always in her thoughts. She hadn't been able to say no to his occasional invitations for family outings—they'd been on several. He'd kept things between them low-key and a lot less intense, for which she was grateful. But even so . . .

Bridget wandered to the pasture fence. In the stable, she could hear the rustle of the horses moving around in their stalls, the scent of hay drifting faintly in the air. Black-and-white Holsteins were grazing in the pasture meadow.

Her gaze swung to the hill rising on the far side of the pasture, Jonas's land. For an instant Bridget thought she saw a flicker of movement near the top. Her heart did a crazy leap as she stared intently, but she could make out nothing. A sigh quivered through her.

Bridget hugged her arms around her middle to contain the lonely ache she felt inside. "Why did I have to fall in love with you again, Jonas?" She sighed.

Chapter Eight

"Molly," Bridget sighed in exasperation, "I thought I told you to wear your blue pants."

"But the white sweats with the side stripe look cooler," Molly argued, her mouth curving downward in a rebellious pout.

"You're growing up too fast."

"You keep saying that."

"Don't talk back. They won't look so cool when they're all grass-stained. Go up to your room and change before Jim gets here," she ordered.

"Aw, Mom!" was the grumbling response. Molly turned to leave the kitchen, then stopped. "How come Jim is taking us to the picnic?"

"Because he asked us to go with him." Bridget added the silverware to the picnic basket.

"Yeah, but he's asked you out a lot lately and you haven't gone with him. How come you decided to go with him this time?"

"Because Jim is leaving," she explained. "He was offered a position at his former college."

"I thought he was teaching at Technical." Molly frowned.

"He was, but he persuaded them to release him from his

contract so he could take this other job. In fact, he's already moved. The picnic today is a kind of farewell party for him."

"I thought we were having the picnic because it's Labor Day."

"Wow, are you whiny. Okay, Molly, that's enough," Bridget declared, giving her daughter a warning look. "You can talk until Jim comes if you want, but you're still going to have to change your pants before we leave."

Molly flashed her an angry look and flounced from the room. The half-smile curving Bridget's lips didn't last long as she thought about the coming afternoon picnic. Her first instinct had been to refuse when she learned Jonas had been invited. The two men hadn't gotten along at Bob and Evelyn's party back in April, to say the least.

But Jonas was old friends with the others. He couldn't very well have been left out. Still, it was one thing to go out with him for an occasional date or meet him on the street or in her store and quite another to see him at an informal gathering like this picnic. Yet she didn't want to make a big deal out of nothing—the antagonism between Jim and Jonas had died down, as far as she knew—and she'd decided to attend.

There had been another reason for her acceptance. All summer—actually, pretty much since Jonas's return— she'd kept turning down Jim's invitations to go out. It hadn't seemed right to accept them when it was Jonas she secretly wanted to be with.

Bridget knew Jim had been confused by her sudden reversal, but she couldn't explain her reasons to him. She couldn't explain her reasons to anyone. But Jim was leaving and she wasn't going to turn down his last invitation.

Bridget had stopped kidding herself about Jonas. The ten-year separation hadn't ended her love for him. But it seemed the better part of wisdom to take it as slowly as possible from here. There were hard questions to be asked on both sides—and when they got around to doing that and dealing with the honest answers, both of them might find it difficult to trust each other the way they once had.

A car pulled into the driveway, a horn honking. "Molly!" Bridget called. "It's Jim. Are you ready?"

"Coming!"

The scarlet leaves of the sumac set fire to the roadside. The rusty, cone-shaped seed clusters were thrusting upward to the gold sun. Hills and mountainsides were beginning to don their autumn coat of many colors, the red hues of the sugar maple predominant.

It was a scenic drive to Brookfield. The white of a church spire gleamed brilliantly against the background of russet reds and golds of a distant hillside. The closer they came to Allis State Park, the quieter Bridget grew, pretending to admire the colorful scenery. Jim pretended not to notice her silence as he responded to Molly's steady stream of talk from her seat in back.

Jim slowed the car as they entered the small community of Brookfield with its cluster of old houses, beautifully preserved. Bridget's tension increased while Molly leaned eagerly forward.

"Are we really going to cross the floating bridge?" she asked.

"We are unless you want to get out and swim across Colt's Pond," Jim teased.

They turned a corner and the floating bridge was at the bottom of the small incline. Buoyed by barrels, it offered passage over the narrow pond.

"We haven't been over this in ages." Molly squeaked with excitement.

"Don't wriggle around or you'll capsize us," Jim teased.

The car rolled slowly onto the wooden planks atop the barrels. The bridge took its weight, dipping slightly, permitting water to flow over the boards. The tires made a soft splashing sound as Jim drove slowly across.

At the top of the hill on the opposite side of the pond was the fire tower in Allis State Park. They were among the first of their party to arrive at the picnic area, but the rest soon followed. Bridget kept bracing herself to see Jonas's wagon drive up. Everyone had arrived and there was still no sign of him.

"Where's Jonas?" Evelyn looked around with a frown. "Isn't he here yet?"

"I haven't seen him," someone else replied.

"You talked to him, didn't you, Bob?" Evelyn turned to her husband. "He was coming, wasn't he?"

He shrugged. "That's what he said when I saw him in town the other day."

"I wonder if we should wait for him," Evelyn murmured absently.

"I'm hungry, Mom," her youngest complained.

"Let's fix the children's plates," Mary Chapman suggested. "If Jonas isn't here by then, I think the rest of us should go ahead and eat."

"We can save something for Jonas," Evelyn agreed.

The children were called and Molly came rushing up to Bridget. "Do we have to eat with the kids?"

Bridget glanced at the Chapman girl hovering beside her daughter. Both were in fifth grade and positive they were too old to be mixing with younger children.

"You and Patty fix your plates now, but I think it will be all right if you and she find some place by yourselves to eat away from the smaller children." She checked the breathless rush of thanks from the pair by adding, "Check with Patty's mother first. She might want her to watch Tommy."

"We will," Molly promised before they went dashing off.

A few minutes later, Bridget saw the pair stealing quietly away to another picnic table beneath a tree, some distance from the other tables. When all the children had their plates filled and were seated at a table, there was still no sign of Jonas and the adults sat down to eat.

An hour later they were all sitting around the tables, the bulk of the food gone. A car door slammed. Bridget didn't turn around to see who it was. She guessed it was Jonas before the first greeting was called out to him.

"We were beginning to give up on you, Jonas. What kept you?"

He walked to the table. "Sorry I'm late."

"We saved some food for you," Evelyn smiled.

"Thanks." Jonas sounded tired.

Bridget couldn't help noticing his crumpled appearance. His print shirt and chino pants both looked as though they'd been slept in. His hair looked as if it had been combed with his fingers. His features seemed leaner, darkened by a shadowy stubble. There were haggard lines etched around his mouth.

"From the looks of you, you must have been at one helluva party last night," Bob observed jokingly.

"It was no party," Jonas replied, sliding his long legs under the picnic table and sitting down with obvious weariness. "A maternity case."

"Who had a baby?" Mary Chapman asked.

"No one from around here." He shook his head. "A young couple from Massachusetts came up to spend the holiday weekend at Lake Champlain. She went into labor about one in the morning. I was on call at the hospital. Temporary gig. They were short-handed and the hospital director called me in."

"Got it," Bob said. "You're a good guy, Jonas."

"What did she have?" Evelyn asked. "Boy or girl?"

"A girl." He made an effort to smile, but it couldn't reach his eyes. He glanced at Bob. "You don't happen to have any beer left?"

"I think there's a couple of cans left in the cooler." Bob winked.

"What would you like to eat?" Evelyn asked. "We have—"

"I'll take a couple of those hot dogs. That's good enough," Jonas insisted.

His gaze slid to Bridget, then skipped to Jim sitting beside her, but there was no outward reaction, except a kind of resignation. Bob sat a can of beer in front of him and Evelyn passed him some hot dogs and chips. The conversation became general again.

Jonas had finished the first hot dog and picked up the second when a loud ringtone sounded, coming from where the cars were parked. He breathed in deeply and set the sandwich on the paper plate.

"Excuse me," he said, rising tiredly to his feet and stepping over the bench.

He walked to his car as the ringtone blared a second time. Bridget watched him discreetly, her heart aching oddly at his lack of vitality, something that had always been so much a part of him. Leaving the car door open, he sat sideways in the driver's seat. A second later she saw him flip open a cell phone and listen intently to whoever was talking.

"Let's start clearing up this mess," Connie suggested as she pushed up the sleeves of her sweater.

"We'll get out of your way," Bob laughed.

"You could help," Evelyn told him.

"We could," he admitted and grinned as he and the rest of his buddies hastily did the right thing, not caveman enough to leave the women with the dirty work.

Jonas returned a few minutes later, wearily rubbing his forehead. The plate with his food had been left on the table, but he didn't walk back to it. Instead he wandered to where the men had gathered and leaned a shoulder against a tree a few feet away, a part of the group yet aloof.

"Bridget," Evelyn spoke quietly, looking at Jonas with

faint concern, "why don't you take his plate over to him? He doesn't look as if he's had a decent meal in days."

Bridget agreed, but she hardly wanted to be the one to point it out to him. She hesitated for a second, unable to find an adequate reason to refuse. Finally she nodded and picked up the plate, walking quietly over to where he stood.

"Jonas," she murmured his name, and he turned. His gray-green eyes looked at her, yet his gaze was unfocused. It was as if he was looking right through her. She held out the plate. "You didn't finish."

He glanced at it and looked away. "I'm not hungry."

"I admit it doesn't look too appetizing now. The meat is cold, but you really should eat something," Bridget persisted in a calm tone.

"Probably," he agreed indifferently and rubbed a hand over the stubble on his jaw and chin. "I forgot to shave," he said absently.

"You also forgot to eat. Please, Jonas." She offered the plate to him.

His gaze shifted to meet her, held it for a second, then looked at the plate. Straightening from the tree, he took the plate from her hand. Bridget waited, guessing that the moment she turned her back he would set it down or dump it in the nearest garbage can. He eyed the hot dog, then unexpectedly and roughly shoved the plate back in her hands.

"Jonas—" Bridget started to protest.

"I lost the baby," he declared in a low, angry voice.

"Oh!" she breathed in sharply.

"She was premature, an ounce over two pounds," he explained gruffly. "We did everything we could. The hospital didn't have a neonatal ICU and there wasn't time to fly the mother to a hospital that did. We couldn't save her baby."

Bridget could sense his frustration, his feeling of helplessness when he felt he should have been able to do something. She wanted desperately to offer him some kind of comfort.

"I'm sure you did everything you could, Jonas." The trite phrase came automatically to her lips.

"Yes." His mouth twisted as he continued staring off into space. "But it wasn't enough, was it?" he murmured rhetorically. Breathing in deeply, he closed his eyes for a second. When they opened, the brilliant fire in his gaze was focused on her. "I had to tell someone. I don't know, for the life of me, why I chose you. You don't care."

"What?" His words were like a stinging slap, the pain intensified by the step he took away from her. Her fingers touched his forearm to stop him.

"That isn't true, Jonas," she denied tightly. "I do care."

He studied her upturned face. "Yes, but not the way I mean. Excuse me." And he walked away from her light hold.

Bridget watched him join the men and saw him refuse Bob's offer of another can of beer. There was a lump in her throat as she walked back to the picnic tables. She swallowed it hurriedly at Evelyn's frowning look.

"He wouldn't eat?" she asked.

Bridget shook her head. "He said he wasn't hungry and I couldn't persuade him he should eat anyway." She guessed that Jonas didn't want the party spirit dampened with the explanation for his brooding mood. She would have to keep silent about the loss of the baby.

Bridget helped the women with the rest of the clearing up, but her gaze kept straying to Jonas. He looked utterly exhausted but he didn't sit down, just kept standing or wandering around. Bridget was certain it wasn't restlessness that drove him but a fear that to relax would bring sleep. She knew intuitively that Jonas was denying himself the luxury of rest.

The impulse was strong to seek him out again and persuade him to go and get the sleep he so obviously needed. She understood his bleak mood, but he would only feel worse if he took it out on her a second time. Maybe it was best to keep her distance.

When the picnic tables were cleared and the baskets returned to the cars, the women began to join the group of men. It was as if Jonas sensed the exact moment that Bridget started toward them. At her approach, he strolled with seemingly aimless intent away from them. Automatically, Bridget slowed her steps to see where he went, stopping when she saw him heading for the tree where Molly was sitting with Patty Chapman, scrolling through the song list on Patty's iPod. Engrossed in their happy chatter, they didn't see or hear his approach. He didn't talk to the girls, but turned away once more.

Bridget suddenly thought of the name for his behavior and knew what she was seeing: he was in shock. All of her senses were attuned to him and she gravitated closer. Jonas stopped, his gaze slicing to where Bridget had stopped. A hard mask stole immediately over his rugged features, concealing the emotions that had shone through only moments ago. She had never seen him in such a state and had no idea what to do.

Stay with him, her heart whispered. That's all you can do.

His troubled gaze swung to the picnic group and Bridget's did likewise. No one seemed to have noticed them together or were even looking in their direction.

"Let's walk," Jonas suggested.

"Okay," Bridget agreed. She, too, preferred that their conversation should be private without the risk of someone overhearing.

Jointly they turned and walked away from the others. Looking up from the iPod screen, Molly watched them go, her eyes round and innocent. A thin layer of fallen leaves carpeted the grass beneath their feet, making a soft rustling sound as they walked.

He inhaled deeply and the action seemed to accent the

tired, strained lines etched around his mouth and eyes. Bridget felt nothing but compassion for him. As the seconds stretched, so did her nerves.

Finally Jonas said, "We need to talk."

"Jonas, I know you just went through a traumatic experience, but . . ." Bridget hesitated. "Now might not be the best time to talk. Maybe later."

"Later? Let me tell you something, Bridget. There isn't always a later. That young couple—" He took a ragged breath and a tear streaked down his cheek. "The social worker who was filling out their paperwork casually told them they could try again. Like they hadn't just lost their first baby. Like they didn't need time to grieve. Like anything could be forgotten, so long as you wanted to forget it."

"Oh, Jonas." Her heart was breaking for him but she couldn't tell him that. "You need to get home and lie down and—and—give yourself time. What happened wasn't your fault."

"No. But seeing that young couple hold each other and cry like they did made me realize something."

She willed herself to be calm. "Go on."

He took a deep breath. "That . . . that love is real. They had each other. They didn't let go, Bridget. Do you know what I'm talking about?"

"No," she whispered.

He reached out to her and took her gently by the shoulders. The touch of his hands made Bridget suddenly and very acutely conscious of him. Her skipping heart was blinding her to all the reasons she shouldn't respond to him. She stood unresisting beneath his light hold.

"You've let me get a little closer, Bridget," Jonas continued, his darkening gaze roaming over her upturned face, "I'm grateful for that. I'm not going to give up, you know. Not easily. I still want you and I still love you. Maybe some things have changed, but that hasn't. There are some things you just can't forget."

His head bent to lightly claim her lips, seeking nothing more. He gently drew Bridget into the circle of his arms. All she wanted to do was lie with him for just one night in a room somewhere, comfort him as best she could, let the pain they both were feeling ebb away until the sun rose once more. If time could stand still, Bridget would have been content to let that night stretch for an eternity.

When he raised his head, the satisfying warmth of his kiss fled. Bridget felt chilled. The strangely emotional state they found themselves in would vanish when he came to his senses. She forced her mind to take over control from her heart.

"I think what happened at the hospital—" she broke off, uncertain of how to continue. "It really affected you. But—"

He breathed in deeply and let go of her. "Sorry. Am I coming on too strong? Getting too emotional? Someone told me that wasn't a good idea."

Who would say that to him? "You're in shock, Jonas," she blurted out. "You're so tired you can't think straight. I can't respond to what you're saying—it wouldn't be right."

He held her gaze for several more seconds before glancing at his watch. "Excuse me"—his tone was withdrawn and indifferent—"I have to be back at the hospital at four."

Chapter Nine

Autumn's fire had begun to spread through the hills with more leaves changing to the brilliant fall colors. Only the evergreens remained immune to change, staying darkly green, nature's accent for the others.

From the kitchen window, Bridget stared at the hills, not seeing their steady change to autumn's glory. She was thinking of the man who lived in the farmhouse hidden by the nearest hill. She was thinking of Jonas.

Since their conversation at the picnic almost three weeks ago, he had occupied her thoughts almost exclusively. His achingly tender words haunted her, shaded as they were by the tragedy he'd had to witness and the unknown young couple whose misfortune had brought her and Jonas heart to heart at last.

He'd slept for eighteen hours once he'd gotten home, or so he'd told her. After that, he'd returned to being his usual self, and he hadn't mentioned what had happened between them on that day. She had seen him half a dozen times in the last three weeks, talked to him on each of the occasions, but there had always been others around. Jonas hadn't suggested, invited, or asked to speak to her alone. And Bridget had been hesitant to take the initiative.

Despite the awkwardness of their reunion, despite their mutual reluctance to really open up to each other, their feelings for each other had begun to grow again. The passion was still there, no doubt about that. But, ten years older now, she knew that was only part of a truly loving relationship. The long-ago issues between them remained unresolved. All the goodwill and silent patience in the world weren't going to clear the air. She was beginning to realize that waiting and wondering would drive her crazy. She would have to forget her pride or her reluctance, whichever it was that stopped her, and make the first move.

Bridget glanced at the telephone mounted on the kitchen wall and immediately dismissed its use as the way. She wanted to see Jonas. She wanted to see him now. Bridget didn't want to wait another second.

Taking her coat from the closet, she slipped it on as she hurried out to the car and drove out of the driveway onto the road.

The tires spun uselessly in the gravel for a second before finding traction. The small car shot forward. After weeks of waiting, Bridget was overcome by the need for haste. Within minutes, she had covered the semicircular route to the Hanson farmhouse.

It was Jonas's house now, she told herself. He was here to stay.

The engine had barely died when Bridget stepped out of the car and walked swiftly toward the back door of the old place. Her knock didn't bring any answer and she knocked louder, with the same results.

There was always the possibility that Jonas was up a ladder or something like that and couldn't come to the door. He liked to fix things. She felt a pang of wistfulness, thinking that their relationship was probably one of the very few things he hadn't managed to fix right away. Didn't stop him from trying, though. Nothing stopped Jonas.

His SUV was parked in the driveway, so he had to be here. She tested the doorknob and found the door unlocked, then pushed it open and walked into a silent house. She hesitated in the kitchen, listening and looking at the empty rooms—empty of Jonas, anyway.

"Jonas?" she called. "Jonas?"

The back door of the house opened behind her and Bridget turned with a jerk, her heart leaping at the sight of Jonas striding toward her. A frown tightened the angular planes of his face.

"Bridget," he said her name as if he couldn't believe his eyes. "What are you are doing here? What's wrong?"

Relief washed through her at finding him. She hoped he would be willing to listen to all her questions—and answer them. She might finally know if she had been misjudging him for ten long years.

"Oh, Jonas, I'm so glad to see you," she declared weakly.

He misinterpreted the reason for her statement. His expression grew worried as his gray-green eyes bored into her.

"Is it Molly? Has something happened to her?" he demanded.

"No, no, Molly's fine," she assured him with a tremulous laugh of relief.

"Then why—" He gave her a wary once-over.

"I had to see you," Bridget explained. There was a husky catch in her voice that seemed to do something to him.

"Why? What about?" Jonas demanded, then groaned. "Uh-oh. Don't give me that look."

She knew exactly what he meant. Her emotions were revealed in her eyes. He knew her too well not to read them.

He had. Suddenly Jonas's fingers curled into her chestnut hair, lifting her head to meet his descending mouth. There was an explosion, flames leaping within Bridget at the searing fire in his kiss. Her hands curved inside his fleece-lined parka and around his waist, feeling his muscles straining to press her closer.

Gladly, she tried to oblige. Her toes barely touched the floor as she arched against him, his length taking her weight and the hard circle of his arms providing support. The male scent of him was an aphrodisiac to her senses, drugging them with an erotic nectar.

His driving hunger was insatiable. Sensually he devoured her lips, nibbling, tasting, exploring, never getting his fill. The furious hammering of his heart was as loud as her own, thudding in her ears with a wild tempo.

Slowly he let her feet touch the floor, bending her slightly backward over his arm. He began diversionary tactics to completely undermine her self-control, exploring the curve of her cheek, the delicate and sensitive lobe of her ear and the pulsing vein in her neck.

His searching, caressing hands pushed at her coat, its bulk interfering with his desire to touch her. Bridget aided his attempt to remove it, letting it slip to the floor. Then she tugged at his parka until Jonas shucked it quickly.

It was done in one fluid movement that ended with Bridget being lifted off her feet into his arms. Automatically she wrapped her arms around his neck, glorying in the male strength that carried her weight so easily. His gaze burned over her love-soft face before his mouth sought her eager lips again.

The living room sofa was his objective, sitting on it with Bridget across his lap. His hands caressed her waist and hips, arousing her, gliding down her thighs and back again. Every inch of her felt on fire, a molten mass of desire, her flesh yielding to his unspoken demands. She wound her fingers into the luxurious thickness of his golden brown hair.

"My God, I've waited so long," Jonas declared in a throaty murmur against her cheek, pressing hard kisses on her smooth skin. "To hold you like this again."

He lifted his head to look at her, desire blazing in his half-closed eyes. What breath she had was stolen by that searing look.

"I know," she softly echoed his sentiment.

Her fingers began a tactile exploration of the lean, ruggedly hewn features she loved. They traced the jutting curve of his cheekbone and lightly stroked the hard angle of his jawline to his chin. From there, her fingertips outlined the firm male curves of his mouth, trembling slightly as he kissed them.

Then his head was bending her toward her again, seeking the hollow of her throat. "All the waiting and watching was worth it," he said huskily. As he spoke, the warmth of his breath sent dancing shivers over the skin of her neck.

"Huh? You were watching me?" Bridget murmured with absent curiosity.

Her hands slid down the tanned column of his neck to the open collar of his shirt. She fingered the buttons, loosening them from the material to splay her hands over his rough-haired chest, warming them with the body heat radiating from his hard flesh.

"Now and then. From the hill behind the house," Jonas admitted, nuzzling her collarbone. "Like a lovesick puppy."

"I didn't know that."

His mouth trailed slowly up her neck to her soft lips, closing moistly over them, forcing them apart, although they needed little persuasion. He kissed her long and lovingly, and stopped only to whisper an explanation of sorts. "I didn't want you to know that. I didn't do it often. But seeing you now and then was never enough."

"Oh, Jonas . . ."

"Shhh." His weight pressed her backward onto the seat cushion of the sofa. Jonas shifted so that he was half lying beside her and half above her, their legs entwining.

There was seductive mastery in his deepening kisses,

yet their passion was languorous, building slowly, as if each wanted to savor the soaring joy of the moment. Bridget trembled as he unfastened the buttons of her blouse and slid his hand inside to cup the fullness of her breast enclosed in a lacy bra.

Moving his lips from her mouth, Jonas directed his attention to the exposed swell of her breasts and the tantalizing cleft between them. Bridget shuddered at the intimate contact, her desire leaping at the dizzying caress.

"Where's Molly?" Jonas asked huskily.

"Molly?" She felt completely disoriented by his heady nearness.

"Yes. Is she home? With your mother? God, I hope she doesn't expect you back soon," he groaned achingly and buried his mouth along the curve of her neck, becoming entangled in her silken chestnut hair.

"No, she's at a . . . party." Bridget caught at her breath as he located the sensual pleasure point near the nape of her neck. "A—a birthday party for one of her friends."

"What time do you have to pick her up?" Jonas asked.

"I don't," she answered and felt the rigidity leave his muscles.

"Is someone bringing her home?" he asked with almost absent-minded interest, concentrating again on arousing a sensual excitement in her.

"No, she's—" Bridget paused as he succeeded in sidetracking her thoughts.

"She's what?"

"She's spending the night with Vicki," she finally managed to answer.

"Then you're spending the night here," Jonas declared huskily, "with me."

The blunt statement acted as a brake to Bridget's previously unchecked desire. When he would have again claimed possession of her lips, her fingers lightly pressed themselves against his mouth to stop him. "Jonas, wait," she begged.

"That's all I've done since I came back." He pulled back a little and looked into her eyes, trying to fathom her sudden hesitation. "I love you, Bridget."

"I believe that," she said and had to swallow the sob in her voice. "I love you, too, but—" She admitted what she hadn't been able to deny to herself.

"But what?" Jonas frowned, his compellingly handsome face only inches above her own.

"There are some questions I wanted to ask before—" Bridget faltered and left the rest unsaid. "That's why I came over tonight."

Jonas looked away, his eyes closing as he exhaled a long breath. With suppressed emotion, her levered himself upright, away from her, and savagely rubbed the back of his neck.

She watched silently, knowing he was upset and frustrated. She was upset with herself for letting his embrace make her forget the reason for her visit. Unexpectedly he rose from the sofa and started to walk from the room.

"Where are you going?" Bridget frowned in confusion.

"To get some coffee," Jonas snapped, not hiding his irritation. "If this is going to be another one of our typical exchanges, I'll need to pay attention."

His disappearance into the kitchen was followed by the slamming of cupboard doors and the clink of cups on saucers. Shakily, Bridget pushed herself into a sitting position on the sofa as the impatient tread of footsteps signaled his return.

A glance at the hard set of his features made Bridget regret again that she had allowed his incredibly sensual kisses to sidetrack her from her purpose. The small tray in his hands held two cups of coffee. He set it on the low table in front of the sofa and took one of the cups.

"Here you go." With the clipped announcement, Jonas sat down in an armchair opposite the sofa as if needing distance between them.

Bridget picked up the remaining cup, hoping the black coffee would steady her nerves. She held it with both hands, trying to ward off the pervading chill that had suddenly enveloped the room.

"All right, what are your questions?" he demanded, breathing out heavily in an attempt for patience and control.

"Look, we got off to an awkward start and I'll be honest, Jonas—I wasn't thrilled to see you back in March."

"I noticed."

"And when you bought the Hanson place and announced you were opening a medical office in Randolph, I didn't know what to do or say. And then there was Molly to be considered. It's always been just me and her—almost always," she amended quickly, glancing at him. "Anyway, every time I saw you or we happened to be alone . . ." She trailed off. "Okay. You can finish that sentence as well as I can. We can't keep our hands off each other, but that doesn't mean we can fool around like kids. We're not kids."

Jonas nodded wearily. "Right now I feel about a thousand years old."

She laughed a little. "You look good for your age."

"Thanks. Okay, bring it on. I can feel the gray hair you're about to give me growing."

"Don't say things like that, Jonas," she pleaded. "I'm not doing this to be mean. You've been so nice to me and to Molly this summer—Jonas, I can't tell you how awful it feels to have to dredge up this old stuff and hash it out. But I—" she hesitated, "I think I want this relationship to go somewhere. So we have to resolve some things and clear the air and then—and then—I don't know."

Jonas shook his head. "You know something? That's the one sentence that really scares a man."

"What?"

"*We have to talk.* Eve must have said it to Adam when they got kicked out of paradise. And it was all downhill from there."

"We do have to talk. And we might as well begin with the tough stuff—the money." Bridget stared at her coffee, unable to meet his piercing regard.

"Oh, yeah. Scene One, Line One. Margaret Harrison offers Jonas Concannon, her innocent daughter's boyfriend, big bucks to get out of town and not come back. Cut to detergent commercial and tune in tomorrow."

His flip retort irked her. "Skip the sarcasm, Jonas. It actually did happen and it should be obvious to you why it's so important."

"Ten years later? No, damnit, it isn't!" His cup was returned to its saucer with a decided clink. "Let's get one thing straight right now: your mother is nuts."

"She is not!" Bridget set her cup aside and rose in agitation. "She said you took the money she offered you and you left."

"And you believed her."

Bridget gave a tiny nod.

"Mind if I quote from my psych textbook? I still remember a diagnosis that fit your mother perfectly. Narcissistic Personality Disorder. She'll do anything to be the center of attention. Including lie."

"That's not true," Bridget insisted.

"Yes, she offered me money, but if she told you I took it, she was lying. I didn't know what to think. I wanted you but I wasn't brave enough to take on a potential mother-in-law from hell. I walked out. You didn't call me. I didn't call you. Once I was gone, I decided not to come back. I figured you knew." Jonas would have gone on, but Bridget interrupted him.

"I knew what she told me. You were nowhere to be

found all of a sudden. Not like I could ask you, could I?" she accused.

"Bridget, I told you I loved you a thousand times before any of that happened, but when it did, you never spoke to me again." His voice was low and tightly controlled, as if he was determined not to turn it into a shouting match.

"Yes, you loved me." Bridget laughed bitterly in disbelief. "That's why I received so many letters and e-mails from you, I suppose," she taunted. "I didn't get one, Jonas, in case your memory has failed you on this point, too. Not a single, solitary one! You left Randolph ten years ago. Seems to me like you had plenty of time to cool off, make some effort to see me—something. You never did. Why should I have assumed that you were coming back?"

"Did it ever occur to you that your mother had something to do with that? You're so used to Margaret Harrison's random insanity that you think it's normal!"

"Watch what you say," Bridget said icily. "I know my mother is self-absorbed and she sure as hell is a drama queen, but insane is a strong word."

"She asked me to leave you and leave town! And your father just sat there and didn't say a thing. Do you want the whole truth?"

"Go for it."

His gaze narrowed sharply, a sudden angry watchfulness to his expression. "I wasn't that much of a hero at eighteen. If you expected me to stand up to your parents, you didn't tell me that. In the long run, you would've had to do it yourself."

Bridget flinched. He was right, much as she hated to admit it. She never really had. Door-slamming and bickering with her mother was about as far as she'd gone. She'd needed her parents too much, especially when Molly was little.

"Has anything changed all that much?"

She didn't want to answer that, wasn't ready to answer that.

"You live across the road from them, your mother marches in and out of your house whenever she wants—I think you're afraid of growing up, if you really want to know!"

"Oh, please," she challenged with a toss of her head, clasping her arms in front of her. "You haven't got a clue as to what goes on in my head. Not one clue."

"Oh, yes I do." Jonas nodded with certainty, a harsh glitter in his look. "There's more. Your mother is amazingly manipulative. She said over and over that you were too young for marriage, and she had me half convinced. Hell, I wasn't much older than you and I was intimidated. Me, a poor kid from two towns over, up against the high and mighty Harrisons, pillars of the freakin' community."

"I never cared whether you had money!" Bridget almost shrieked the words. "I only cared that you would take it from them!" But he hadn't. She understood now, a sinking feeling in her gut, just how far her mother had gone.

"It was her idea that there be six mouths of absolutely no contact between us. Supposedly after six months if we still felt the same, she wouldn't stand in our way."

"She said that?" she breathed.

"And you didn't know about it?" An eyebrow quirked in a suggestion of mockery.

"I didn't."

"That's possible," Jonas conceded with a disgruntled sigh.

"But after the six months, why didn't you try to see me? Why did you wait for so many years?" Bridget ran a hand through her chestnut hair in confusion, believing him yet not fully understanding.

"You're forgetting something this time. Or maybe you're deliberately ignoring it," he said cynically. "Maybe I wasn't in direct contact with you, but I did stay in touch with some of our friends. Within a couple of months after I left Vermont, you did, too. By the end of six months, there were rumors that you'd married or were marrying someone else. Which you did, didn't you, Mrs. O'Shea?"

"Jonas, I—" she began.

"So what was the point of my trying to get in touch with you? Your mother had proven her point. You couldn't have loved me or you would have waited. Anyway, you were too young to make that kind of commitment," he stated in a hard, flat voice.

"No," she whispered.

"That probably applied to your late husband, too, but he conveniently died before that could be proved."

"That isn't true." But Bridget didn't want to explain about Brian yet. "Everything you say sounds so reasonable, but there is one thing you haven't explained to me."

Jonas leaned back in his chair, although there was no way his body was relaxed. He seemed ready to spring, alive with a powerful energy that the argument had released. Bridget wished there was no more to talk about. She wished she could be in his arms.

But, until these questions were out of the way, she knew that no matter how much she loved him, she would never be able to completely trust him. The doubts had to be eliminated or confirmed.

"What is that?" he asked with forced patience.

She faced him. "Why didn't you at least tell me that she'd offered you money?"

He exhaled a short, silent laugh and shook his head. "And risk you believing your mommy if she denied it? It was her word against mine. I figured I didn't stand a chance and it didn't matter what I said. I felt so powerless then."

"I did too," Bridget replied in a low, hurt voice. "As far as I knew, you sold me out. You sold our love out. I had no reason to wait for you." She was trembling all over. There had been a reason and she should have waited. But she still wasn't ready to tell him that.

For ten long years Bridget had believed she knew all the details surrounding his leaving. Now she realized that she hadn't—only what her parents had told her. There were a lot of things they had failed to tell her, it seemed.

A cold chill ran down her spine. "You are telling the truth." It was a statement.

"Don't take my word for it." Jonas gave her a look that made her feel even colder.

"I—" Bridget was about to deny the need for that.

But Jonas interrupted, "I mean it, Bridget. Don't accept what I say. Ask your parents. As a suggestion, if I were you, I'd ask your father: I'm not certain your mother would be capable of giving you an unbiased answer."

"But I—"

"Go home," he said firmly. "Go home and ask them."

Bridget stared at his wide shoulders. Her heart was filled with an aching love that was boundless. She wanted to touch him, to somehow show him how deeply she cared.

"I believe you, Jonas," she said in a soft, throbbing whisper. "I don't need my parents to confirm your story."

"I want them to confirm it." He pivoted to face her. The line of his jaw revealed his unyielding stand. "When you come to me, Bridget, when you marry me, I don't want there to be any room in your heart for doubts. None. Not about you and not about me."

She wanted to protest, to argue, but his hard, short kiss silenced the attempt. She swayed toward him. He broke it off, but he held her firmly at arm's length.

"Go home, Bridget," he ordered and gave her a little push toward the back door.

Bridget left, not because Jonas had ordered her to leave, but because he was right. And because he had said *when you marry me*. Not *if*. *When*.

The instant she walked into the chalet, she went straight to the phone and dialed her parents' number. Jonas had been right about another thing: her father was more likely to give her an unvarnished account, although he had a few things to answer for himself.

If she had stopped at the house, the chances were that she would not have been able to speak to her father in private. On the phone, she could persuade him to come to the chalet under one pretext or another.

Her mother answered the telephone. "Is Dad there?" Bridget asked.

"No, he's gone to an auction. He probably won't be home until late. Why? Is something wrong?"

"No, nothing," she assured her mother quickly.

"Why are you calling?"

"I heard about a used horse van that was for sale," Bridget lied. "The price sounded reasonable and I was going to ask Dad if he would mind looking at it for me. I'll talk to him tomorrow about it."

"I'll mention it to him. Molly does have her heart set on one, doesn't she?" her mother commented.

"Yes, she does," she agreed.

It was nearly twenty minutes later before Bridget was able to end the conversation with her talkative mother.

With getting Molly off to school in the mornings, working at the shop all day herself, and trying to elude both her daughter and her mother in the evenings, it was four days later before Bridget had a chance to speak to her father. He confirmed everything Jonas had told her, as she had guessed.

To his credit, he offered an explanation of sorts. Something about agreeing with Margaret being easier than arguing with Margaret.

After trying three times unsuccessfully to reach Jonas at home or on his cell, Bridget finally gave up and waited until the following day to call him at his office from her shop. The phone rang several times before his receptionist answered.

"I'd like to speak to Dr. Concannon," Bridget requested.

"Did you wish to make an appointment?" was the crisply professional reply.

"No, I would just like to speak to the doctor."

"Regarding what? Are you one of our patients?"

"No. It's a personal matter," Bridget explained.

"He's with a patient. Let me see if he can take your call now. Who's calling, please?"

"Bridget O'Shea."

"Oh!" The woman's voice immediately became bright and cheerful. "Of course he'll take your call. Just give me a minute to pull the stethoscope out of his ear and hand him the phone. He'll be right with you. Hold, please."

Bridget waited, anxiously watching the shop door, hoping she would have no customers until she had spoken to Jonas. There was a vague fluttering of her heart as she realized that nothing stood between her and Jonas any longer. They could be together.

"Hello, Bridget."

His voice, when he answered the phone, was calm and level, as though he saw nothing momentous in the occasion, while Bridget was suddenly all nervous and jittery.

"Jonas!" she spoke his name in glad relief. "I called to tell you I talked to my father last night in private."

"And?"

"And he told me exactly what you had."

"Good," Jonas said decisively.

"When I think of the things I said to you and what I thought all these years, I—"

"There's no need to apologize," he interrupted smoothly. "You didn't have all the facts. I should have put you straight in the beginning. You misunderstood, and you were scared."

"Maybe, but I—" But that wasn't important anymore. "When will I see you, Jonas?" she asked boldly.

"I'll be attending a convention this weekend, so I'll be

out of town." He sounded so distant. "Let's make it a week from Saturday."

"So long?" Bridget frowned. "Jonas, what's wrong?"

"Nothing is wrong." Then he hesitated. "Bridget, I want to have time to think very seriously about us. We've waited more than ten years. We can wait more than a week."

"I love you, Jonas," she said.

Those three little words seemed to stop him cold. She waited anxiously for a reply.

"Tell you what," he said after a long pause. "What with one thing and another—okay, let's leave out the passionate kisses and runaway horses and crazy arguments for now— we've been doing pretty well at getting to know each other. Agreed?"

She thought it over. "I guess so—I mean, yes. It's been an amazing, um, almost a year."

She heard him chuckle. "Yup. But the acid test of any relationship is—drum roll, please—the holidays."

Bridget glanced at her calendar. Thanksgiving. Christmas. Fooling around in summer and looking at fall foliage just didn't have the emotional weight of those two occasions. Her parents would expect her to—

She set down the receiver.

"Bridget?" she heard him say. "You there? Wait just a sec—" He didn't hang up. Someone in his office was talking to him and he'd probably slung the receiver over his shoulder, judging by the muffled tone of the exchanged words.

She twisted her hands in her lap, her last thought echoing in her mind. *Her parents would expect her to . . . her parents would expect her to . . .* do what? And what if she didn't? Her life had been all about their expectations for too long. Maybe it took someone who'd been away as long as Jonas had to make her see that clearly.

Bridget had never left Vermont, never been to college,

never let herself fall in love again . . . but she had to admit that Jonas was the only man she had ever loved.

She couldn't change that. But as far as the rest, it was time to do something—anything—different. The holidays were as good a time as any. She didn't have to be mean, didn't have to pitch a fit. She just had to make it clear that she was going to jump the highest fence she'd ever jumped and do things her own way. Not her mother's way.

"Bridget?"

She picked up the receiver again. "I'm here. Sorry, I dropped the phone."

"That's okay, I was talking to Schulzy. So, should we try celebrating the holidays together? Let's start with Thanksgiving. I'm up for a little good old-fashioned certifiable insanity with all the fixings, how about you?"

"Sure," she said.

"I just don't see how you can do this on your own, Bridget."

Bridget counted to ten, reminding herself that arguing with her mother was an exercise in futility. She settled for a rhetorical question instead. "Mom, how hard can it be to cook a turkey?"

"You'll find out," her mother said darkly.

Maybe so, but Bridget was still happy to be on her own at Thanksgiving for the first time ever. Her lips curved in a serene smile. Just knowing that her parents were flying to Florida tomorrow for an extended vacation was a liberating feeling. She hadn't even had to argue with them.

An old friend of the Harrisons offered them a week at her time-share apartment in Orlando, and Margaret had persuaded Bridget's dad to go. Bill Harrison was a stickler for routine when it came to family holidays, but after an early November ice storm that had done more damage than anticipated and kept everyone indoors to brood about the weather, he'd given in, eager to just sit in the sunshine somewhere and let his wife shop in the tourist traps to her heart's content.

Bridget had put in her two cents, reassuring him that she and Molly would be fine, and it was high time she learned how to cook the traditional feast from scratch. Nonetheless, fearing the worst, her mother had gone out and bought jars of gravy, cans of cranberry sauce and candied yams, and frozen side dishes of creamed onions, stuffing, green beans almondine, and five pies. Right now she was unpacking a giant frozen turkey that was much too big for two or three people and would take up most of the space in the refrigerator. Margaret had warned Bridget that it would take at least two days to defrost and she would be long gone by then. But she'd had to buy it just in case, she'd said.

Just in case the fresh, free-range bird Bridget planned to roast wasn't good enough.

Bridget kept that thought to herself. All of this unexpected bounty was going to be donated to the church's food pantry for their Thanksgiving, and kept in the church's basement freezer until then—she was just waiting until her mother left town. She really did want to make everything from scratch. Mrs. Dutton, who usually celebrated the holiday with her sister's family, had volunteered to hold down the fort at the shop the day before, so Bridget could get a head start with the preparations on Wednesday. She would do the actual cooking on Thursday, with Molly at her side. It was going to be just the two of them . . . and Jonas.

She hadn't told her mother she was inviting him, sidestepping her mother's inevitable disapproval. Margaret wouldn't think it was the neighborly thing to do. Bridget wasn't as brave as she wanted to be when it came to him. Some day. Not now.

"Bridget," her mother was saying. "Can you help me

with the turkey?" She'd managed to wrestle it out of the plastic shopping bag but she was barely hanging onto it. The turkey looked heavy enough, if dropped, to go right through the kitchen floor or break Margaret's toe at the very least. Bridget rushed over to grab it and set it back on the table.

"Wait a sec," she said. "I haven't cleared a shelf in the refrigerator yet." Make that two shelves. "I'll do it right now." She opened the refrigerator door and Margaret tsk-tsked.

"Look at all those takeout containers," her mother said.

"They're mostly empty," Bridget pointed out.

"Then I'm glad I shopped for you. I don't want you to starve while I'm gone."

Bridget ignored that comment and made quick work of reorganizing the refrigerator, tossing the takeout and neatly stacking the rest. Her mother held the door open while the mega-bird was transferred from the table to the shelf with the most room. *Where it will stay until I rush it over to the church under cover of darkness*, Bridget thought with a secret smile.

The rest of the food was put away and she walked her mother to the front door, only half-listening to her last-minute instructions and not replying.

"Are you coming over for breakfast tomorrow, honey? We're leaving for the airport around two. I want to see you before we go. I'll miss you, you know."

The wistful tone in her mother's voice got Bridget's attention. "Sure, Mom. I'd love to." She was surprised to see that Margaret's eyes were a little misty. "Hey, we'll miss you too. And thanks for all the food. It was really nice of you to buy it and bring it over. We're going to have a great Thanksgiving."

Margaret permitted herself a tiny frown, as if she wasn't too sure about that. "Dad and I will be celebrating in a restaurant, I'm afraid."

Bridget patted her on the back. "No dishes to wash. No out-of-town relatives coming in. No leftovers. No aggravation. You'll like that."

Her mother sighed. "I'm not so sure. It just won't feel like a family holiday without the aggravation."

Bridget laughed. "Oh yes it will. Don't worry. You're going to enjoy yourself and so will we."

A few hours later, she'd dropped off the frozen turkey—wrestling it back into a plastic bag hadn't been easy—and all the rest at the church.

"Thank you, dear." Mrs. Mildred Barnes, the tiny old lady who ran the program, was delighted to see so much food arrive, bustling around the basement kitchen in an apron and directing her volunteer staff. Even though Thanksgiving was two days off, their preparations were underway.

Mrs. Barnes issued immediate instructions as to proper defrosting procedure, and the turkey was put into the church refrigerator to do just that. It had company, Bridget noticed. There were two other frozen turkeys, not quite as big. Whoever was in need would be well-fed.

"Hello, Bridget." The quiet, familiar voice of Jonas came from behind her. Bridget whirled around, clutching the empty plastic bags she'd brought the food in to her chest.

"Jonas? What are you doing here?"

"Same as you. Dropping off donations."

"But you—" He didn't have a mom who brought over a week's worth of un-asked-for food. He must have gone out and bought the six bags of groceries that he held, three in each of his big hands. Bridget couldn't help but notice how easily he lifted them when he set them on the long table that the church used for socials and the weekly suppers they provided.

"Here you go, Mildred," he called to the tiny old lady in the apron. "Got the fresh stuff you asked for. Hope it's enough. Are you going to let me help cook?"

"Be there in a jiffy," the old lady called back. She was busy stacking canned goods on the other side of the room.

"You know Mrs. Barnes?" Bridget asked, somewhat taken aback. It hadn't occurred to her that he'd become involved in community projects like the food pantry, let alone that he would volunteer as a cook.

"Sure. She insists I call her Mildred, by the way. She likes to flirt a little."

"No harm in that." Having a great-looking guy like Jonas show up to help probably tickled Mrs. Barnes no end.

"So, what did you bring?"

"Oh, just a turkey and some other stuff."

One of the middle-aged women helping Mrs. Barnes opened the refrigerator and exclaimed over the size of the bird on the top shelf. "Thanks, Bridget!" she turned to say. "What a big one. Just what we needed."

Jonas gave her an approving nod. "Nice of you."

Bridget shook her head hastily. "I can't take credit. My mother gave it to me, plus a truckload of side dishes, but I wanted a smaller bird—a fresh one. Not that I didn't appreciate it, but it's going to be just me and you and Molly this year . . ." She hesitated. "You are coming over, right?"

"Of course." He bent down and brushed a gentle kiss over her lips.

"Wow. Mmm. Anyway, I was going to make everything from scratch. Turkey, gravy, pies—I don't know how we'll eat it all."

He looked at her curiously. "Where are your parents going to be? You didn't tell me they were leaving."

"In Florida."

"Oh." His expression was noncommittal, as if he didn't

want to ask a whole lot of questions that she probably didn't want to answer.

Bridget winced inwardly. She should have told him they would be gone; she should have told her parents she'd invited him. But her mother wouldn't find out until after she and Dad had returned from Florida—oh, Lord, why she was she still so afraid of her mother? Maybe it wasn't fear anymore, she told herself quickly. The habit of placating her overly dramatic, overbearing mother for too many years wasn't easy to break overnight. There hadn't been a reason to stand up to her until Jonas had given her one.

The realization startled her. Bridget exhaled a small sigh, bothered by her conflicting emotions. Maybe she was obsessing over relatively small things because she still hadn't dealt with a big thing: the secret she had yet to tell to Jonas.

How would he take it? She had no idea. All he'd asked was to celebrate the holidays with her. And Molly, of course. That he was working on making himself a part of their little family of two was not lost on her.

The thought touched her—and scared her more than a little. Maybe it was best to concentrate on the cooking and all that and set her other worries aside. It didn't seem quite fair, though. Just when she thought she'd be able to celebrate a major holiday in her own way, along came the Doubt Fairy, who waved her little wand and knocked holes in Bridget's self-confidence.

She looked up at Jonas, who generally seemed to have confidence to spare. He wore a rough-side-out suede jacket that looked like he'd been chopping firewood in it— there were a few raw white slivers on the sleeves. Thick work gloves had been stuck in one pocket and his plaid shirt did something really nice for the brawny chest it covered. All of a sudden, she wanted to slide her arms around his waist and get hugged up by him. Not here, of course.

But the thought was tempting. His downward look at her

held evident desire and it wasn't all that far under the surface. She wanted nothing more than to bury her nose in his shirt and enjoy that great outdoorsy smell of big, strong man and warm leather.

"Want to help me chop celery?" she asked in her most seductive voice. "I have to get started on the stuffing."

"You make it sound so sexy. Okay. Where's Molly?"

"At a friend's. She finds my company unbelievably boring these days."

Jonas grinned. "I don't."

"C'mon over, big boy. You can peel the chestnuts too."

He leaned down and growled in her ear, then nipped the lobe. Bridget giggled.

The next morning, Molly came home to find the two of them in the kitchen, busy with preparations for the feast. Bridget was humming as she stirred dry bread cubes into the sautéed chopped onions and celery, adding a handful of fresh sage leaves and a big dash of salt.

Jonas, wearing an apron, came over to investigate. "How about adding some browned sausage to that?"

"I was thinking of oysters, actually."

"Sausage."

"Oysters."

"Sausage."

"Oysters."

Molly looked at them wide-eyed. "Are you actually having an argument over something that dumb?"

Bridget shook her head, hiding a smile. "No."

"I'm calling Dr. Phil," Molly teased. "You two need a relationship rescue."

Hmm. Interesting. Her daughter didn't seem to think twice about referring to what was going on between Jonas and herself as a relationship. Very interesting, Bridget thought.

"How do feel about peeling sweet potatoes, Molly?" Jonas pointed to a toppling pyramid of them.

"Okay. Show me how."

Jonas took a peeler and demonstrated. "Peel away from yourself."

"Yes, Dr. Concannon."

He smoothed out a paper bag for the peels to land on. "You wouldn't believe how many people end up in the ER with cut hands on Thanksgiving."

"I don't ever want to go there again. Okay." Molly picked up a potato and brandished it at both of them. "This is the first potato I've ever peeled. Mom, don't you want to take a picture?"

Bridget continued stirring. "You have a point. I captured your first steps and your first day at school. We might as well record this for posterity. Jonas"—she pointed with the spoon in the general direction of the living room—"the camera's on the mantel. Would you mind?"

Jonas strode over and got the digital camera, standing far back enough to get them both in the shot. "Smile, you two. Say oysters."

"Oysters!" they both yelled.

"Does this mean I win?" Bridget asked. "Can I put them in the stuffing?"

"No. It means you look surprised in the picture," Jonas said. "You can't say oysters without looking surprised."

Molly tried it a few more times, looking at herself in the shiny surface of the toaster. "Hey, he's right. It makes your eyebrows go way up."

"You two are crazy," Bridget said, laughing. She turned the heat off under the large sauté pan. "Okay, I don't want this cubed bread to get too soft. I'm going to leave it here until it's time to stuff the turkey. There's nothing in it that can spoil."

Jonas sat down by Molly, another peeler in his hand. He

was fast, finishing three potatoes while she did one. Competitive to a fault, Molly went faster, scraping short strips onto the paper bag. Bridget watched fondly as she noticed Jonas slowing down just enough to let Molly get ahead, but not so slowly that her daughter would notice that he was letting her catch up.

The two of them finished the last two potatoes with a flurry of swift strokes. Jonas held up his to show the little strip of peel still on it and Molly held up hers, perfectly smooth and orange. "And the winnah is . . . Molly O'Shea!" he said in a track announcer's booming voice.

Molly beamed. "Take another picture."

Bridget did the honors this time, capturing both of them in the silly, wonderful pose. She felt a pang. Why had she waited so long to bring Molly and Jonas together? The question was essentially unanswerable. She had, that was all. The other times the three of them had been together, it had just sort of happened, or Jonas had invited them both—but she had never taken the initiative.

Stop beating yourself up, Bridget told herself fiercely. You did it when you were ready. And that's that.

She was really too busy to obsess over anything but the cooking. Cookbook open on her lap, she studied the recipe for giblet gravy.

Molly had already made a disgusted face when the giblets were pulled out of the turkey, and Bridget couldn't say she blamed her. She got them out of the fridge and let them slither out of the wrapping into the broth simmering on the stove, wondering how her mother magically transformed such ugly little things into delicious gravy. Well, if they didn't turn out right or she overcooked them, they were going to go straight into the garbage. She hadn't given all the jars of gravy to the church food pantry.

Speaking of that, they were due to arrive there by seven in the evening to help serve. That is, she and Molly would serve; Jonas was going to don an apron and cook. Mrs. Barnes had explained that the meals were offered to all comers in the afternoon and again in the evening. There would be plenty for him to do.

Volunteering there would be a first. Margaret Harrison was generally unsympathetic to the less fortunate and she had certainly never offered to help or donate food.

Bridget was beginning to realize that her mother had cast a long, cold shadow over her life. But she didn't want to fight with her, and she wasn't going to blame her mother for everything that had ever gone wrong in her life. What she was after—and the process was going to be slow—was understanding.

It would have to do.

She gave the simmering giblets a poke with a long-handled spoon. Were they done? They still looked disgusting. She decided to let them simmer some more.

Bridget went back to the cookbook. Steam this, skim that, baste this, poach that. The cumulative effect of so many instructions in so many different recipes was confusion. She began to chop yet another onion, and a large tear rolled down her cheek.

Jonas, who had been playing a raucous game of poker with Molly in the living room, came into the kitchen. "Haven't seen you for a while. What's up?" He put his arms around her waist.

She heard Molly go up the stairs to her loft bedroom. Bridget wiped away the tear with her sleeve, and another one followed it.

"Uh-oh. Put down the knife and step away from the onion," Jonas said. "You need to sit down with a glass of wine."

"I can't do that. It's not even noon. And I'm not finished cooking."

He kissed the top of her head and moved his hands up to

cup her breasts. Bridget remembered all the wonders of the night they'd spent together. Her whole body trembled with sensual pleasure and she leaned back against him.

"Screw the cooking. I want a kiss, Bridget."

She turned in his embrace and put her arms—her oniony, floury, oily arms—around his neck. "I'm a mess," she said.

"I don't care." He bent his head down and claimed her lips with real passion, giving her a good, long, hot kiss.

"Mmm," she whispered when he stopped to breathe.

He reached out an arm to turn off the stove without looking into the pan. "Whatever was in there is dead now. Boiled dry."

"Oh, shoot. The giblets. We might have to use gravy from a jar."

Jonas sighed. "I think it's time I took over, little lady."

She went to the sink to wash up. "Fine with me. Where'd you learn how to cook, anyway?"

"My first roommate in New York was an apprentice chef."

She looked him up and down. Tall and brawny as he was, it was hard to imagine him living in a small New York apartment, let alone sharing one with a roommate.

"I didn't know that."

Jonas smiled slightly as he stuck a fork in the giblets. "You know, I think these are salvageable. Just give me that little cutting board and a knife, and I'll show you what to do with giblets."

In another couple of minutes, he'd minced them and strained the broth they'd cooked in, putting both into a saucepan and putting it in the fridge. "You add the dark drippings from the turkey pan after it's roasted—skim the fat first—and some cream if you like, and season to taste. That's how you make giblet gravy."

"I'm impressed. The more I know about you, the more I find to like, Jonas Concannon."

He poured her a half glass of wine. "You sit down and sip that. I'm going to get the turkey in the oven."

"I preheated it."

"Great. Good thing it's a small bird. It'll be done in time. I figure we can eat by three. Does that work for you?"

Bridget grinned. "Of course it does. Especially since you're now doing all the work."

At exactly three o'clock, the three of them sat down for dinner. Molly had insisted that Bridget get out of her kitchen-grungewear and put on something presentable.

She'd gone through her mother's closet and found a dark green dress in a matte jersey fabric that she insisted was perfect. Bridget had tried it on and she'd had to agree, wondering why she'd forgotten about it. The low, scooped neck was flattering, especially with her antique chain necklace strung with tiny enameled flowers.

"You look so pretty, Mom," Molly looked at her mother from across the dining room table and nodded her approval.

"Thanks, honey."

Jonas studied her for a moment. "Yes. You do. Although I kind of miss the flour on your hands and the streak of cooking oil on your cheek."

Bridget laughed as she unrolled her napkin and flicked it at him. "Tough luck. Now you're the messy one."

Jonas's shirt revealed his efforts to get the meal on the table. "S'okay. Gravy goes with everything."

He had carried that out of the kitchen last, holding up the Victorian gravy boat like a ceremonial chalice. A flea market find, the thing had four little feet and a huge handle, as if it had been designed by a committee.

Bridget would have just as soon used something plain and serviceable, but Molly insisted that the gravy boat come down from the high shelf it had been relegated to. She thought it was very grand.

She looked at her daughter, then at Jonas, and smiled. "Okay, who would like to say grace?"

Jonas shook his head. "I'm no good at that. Molly, how about you?"

Molly clasped her hands and bent her head. "Thank-youGodforeverythingweareabouttoreceiveincluding-sweetpotatoeswithbrownsugarandmarshmallows. Amen."

Jonas cracked up. He had put in the last two ingredients at Molly's request, despite Bridget's protests that it would make the traditional side dish too sweet, especially since there were three different kinds of dessert.

Molly and Jonas were getting along well. Her daughter had set the table under his watchful eye, not arguing with him the way she often did with Bridget.

Oh well. Jonas was someone new to her daughter, and she wasn't inclined to talk back to him. Yet.

Bridget smiled at both of them, smoothing her hair. Much as she'd wanted to make the whole meal herself, letting Jonas take over had given her an hour to relax and have some mother-daughter time before dinner was ready.

Jonas, his hands clasped by his chin and his elbows on the table, smiled back. He'd eased her out of the kitchen and kept her from getting overwhelmed as if it was the most natural thing in the world for a man to help the way he had.

Hardworking as her father was, he would never have set foot into her mother's domain—their family traditions meant much more formal affairs, with a lot of fussing over the snowy purity of the tablecloth and possible spots on the crystal stemware and family silver, things it had been

Bridget's job to polish. Margaret Harrison's Thanksgivings had been picture-perfect in every detail—and rather tense.

There was a lot to be said for a more relaxed celebration. She and Molly had dusted; stuffed a big pile of unread mail, magazines, and catalogs into a basket by the side of the sofa; vacuumed; and let it go at that. She had only dressed up at Molly's insistence. The little girl had settled for a bright pink sweatshirt adorned with a silk rose pin— the odd combination somehow worked, Bridget thought. And Jonas looked even more masculine and sexy than usual with his sleeves rolled halfway up his biceps and his thick hair a little messy and damp from the kitchen's heat.

Molly tapped her fork lightly against her glass. "Mom, look at me. I'm about to do the second part of the blessing."

"What—oh!" Bridget blushed and nodded her head at her daughter. "Sorry. I didn't know there was going to be a second part."

Molly cleared her throat and clasped her hands together on the edge of the table. "For family and friends and food. And anybody who doesn't have them, we ask that they will."

"Amen," Jonas and Bridget said simultaneously.

Later, dishes done and the Harrisons called in Florida and wished a happy Thanksgiving, the three of them sprawled on the living room furniture to digest a little, deciding to eat dessert later. Bridget and Molly had the sofa, and Jonas, the large armchair. He was dozing, much to Molly's amusement.

"Shh," Bridget whispered when the little girl giggled too loudly.

"But he's snoring."

"Just a little. He's entitled. He worked hard, doing all that cooking."

"So did you, Mom."

"Well, I'd say it was about even. And you sure helped, honey. Thanks again."

Successfully distracted, Molly leaned over and hauled up the basket they'd filled with mail when they were cleaning up before dinner. "You're welcome. Want me to sort the mail?"

"Sure." Bridget was content to sit with her stockinged feet curled under her while her daughter went through the basket. Molly the Mail Girl had been a favorite game of hers when she was really little, and she'd loved to put each item into the right pile and then watch her mother open it all.

Bridget rested her head on the back of the sofa, feeling drowsy and content.

"Bleaggh. This is mostly junk mail." Molly had learned to tell the difference pretty early. She flipped through it, setting envelopes and catalogs against her mother's side. "For you, for you, for you. For me. For you, for you," she said softly. "Okay. Big fat envelope for you, Mom." She passed it over.

Bridget yawned. "I'll look at it later."

Molly poked her side. "No, now."

"If you insist." Bridget ran a fingernail along the edge of the manila envelope and slid out the contents: two copies of *Good Living*, with a note from Gil Bland saying thanks. "Oh, my! Look at that!"

"Let me see, let me see!" Molly scrambled over and nabbed one of the copies. "Wow!"

For the cover, the art director had chosen a close-up of Dotty's yarns arranged on a shelf. The handspun skeins looked almost like an abstract painting in swirls, with that one strand of yarn he'd pulled hanging down like a bright little wiggle of color.

They each flipped quickly to the article.

The first picture, a double-page spread, was of Dotty

posed with her flock. Kiwi was by her side, looking very much in charge.

"Check out that dog," Bridget laughed. "I swear he's smarter than all of us."

Grinning photogenically, Kiwi sat proudly, his black-and-white coat brushed to perfection. The sheep were another matter. Their heavy, densely curled wool was matted and muddy, but the springtime setting made up for that. Dotted with tiny flowers and thick with clover, the meadow was idyllic. Dotty's face, wise and wrinkled, was framed by her long gray braids, and Harry, the photographer, had captured her intelligent, slightly amused expression perfectly.

"He's a star," Molly said, excitement making her voice rise a little. "He could be famous."

Bridget shook her head, smiling. "I think he'd rather herd sheep, honey." She turned the page. "Oh!"

She and Jonas most certainly did have . . . chemistry. She remembered exactly how it had felt to have his hands around her waist that day when he'd pulled her close under the fake mistletoe. There had been absolutely nothing fake about that glorious kiss.

"Huh," Molly said noncommittally. She was studying the picture of her mother and Jonas with an expression on her face that Bridget couldn't quite read. "Smoochy-woochy."

"Gil and Harry wanted us to pose that way," Bridget said hastily. "I—I didn't realize that Jonas and I were going to look quite that, uh, enthusiastic."

"It's okay," said Molly, not seeming overly concerned. "You're a lot prettier than that model, Mom."

Bridget flipped to the photograph her daughter was looking at, one of Mara alone in the nubby sweater the model hadn't liked. All the same, Mara's expertise at striking a pose made the sweater look great—and Bridget was very pleased to note that its knitter was mentioned by name in the accompanying text.

The shop looked great too. The custom cabinetry, finished in honey tones, made the yarns and fabrics glow with warmth against the white walls. The Christmas decorations she'd put up with Albert struck just the right quaint note as well. No one would ever know that the shoot had taken place on a warm day in May.

"Where am I?" Molly asked no one in particular, flipping ahead until she yelped with horror. "Oh no! There's me and that icky boy!"

"Mrs. Dutton's nephew is a nice kid," Bridget said, fighting back a giggle. "And you look very pretty."

"It doesn't matter!" Molly wailed. "I made sure my lips didn't touch his face but it looks like they did in the photo! That is so disgusting!"

Jonas cracked an eye. "Okay, I'm awake. What's all the commotion about?"

Bridget held up her copy of *Good Living*. "Fame comes at a price. Molly isn't happy with her picture."

Molly flopped back on the sofa, hiding her face behind the magazine. "Help me! I will never live this down, not ever! The kids are going to tease me so much, Mom!"

"I wouldn't worry about it," Bridget said, trying to sound reasonable when all she wanted to do was laugh out loud. "More likely they'll think it's great. And you really do look pretty. That taffeta dress with the velvet bodice was just perfect—"

A long groan from Molly drowned out the rest of Bridget's reassurances, eventually subsiding as Jonas and Bridget exchanged smiles. Molly lifted the magazine off her face and squinted at her picture. "Do you really think so?"

"Uh-huh." Bridget turned her copy around so Jonas could see the photo. "Don't you think so, Jonas?"

"You look cute, Molly," he said right away. "It's a funny photo. You two could be in a comedy together."

"You mean like a movie?" Molly asked doubtfully.

The trace of confidence in her daughter's voice let Bridget know that she was getting used to it. Seeing your own face in a national publication was a little disconcerting. Without saying anything besides a fast "Yes," Bridget flipped back to the photo of her and Jonas.

Holy cow. They were kissing so happily they looked like an ad for mistletoe.

"So, uh, how did the photos of us look?" Jonas asked Bridget nonchalantly.

"They only used one."

He sat up a little straighter in the armchair he had been dozing in. "Mind if I see it?"

"Not at all." Bridget opened the magazine to it and handed it over, watching his neutral expression change to one of masculine pride when he looked down at the photo.

"Very nice," was all he said, glancing at Molly, who was still obsessing over her own photo with Mrs. Dutton's nephew. Jonas favored Bridget with a very suggestive wink once he was sure her daughter wasn't looking.

Bridget cleared her throat. "So . . . everybody ready for dessert?"

Much later, when Molly was in bed and they could get as close as they liked on the sofa, Jonas gave Bridget a lingering, warmly sensual kiss. His body was to the side of hers, his weight and strength a pleasure to have so near. She reached up a hand and stroked his cheek. "Thanks for everything. That was a wonderful Thanksgiving."

"I'm thinking we could do that every year," he said casually.

"Oh? I'm not sure how my mother would react." She sensed him stiffen slightly.

"Maybe it's time that . . . never mind."

Bridget frowned, knowing she'd said the wrong thing. "Mmm. Sorry I mentioned her."

"It's all right." Jonas began to kiss her again, almost as if he wanted her to not think about anything but him. As distractions went, it was quite effective.

"So," she breathed, when he decided to take a rest, "what are you doing for the rest of the four-day weekend?"

"Hmm," he said into her hair. "This would be nice."

"Molly's going to be around," she reminded him. "And I have to open up the shop early tomorrow to get everything ready for the Christmas shoppers."

Jonas growled and grumbled into her ear. "I can take a hint," he said finally. "Okay, I have things to do too."

Laughing, Bridget put a hand on his muscular chest and gave an ineffective little push. He stayed right where he was. "Such as?" she asked.

"I have to drive back to New York and get the last of my stuff out of storage. See some people at the clinic. Things like that."

She pouted. "I wanted to see the Christmas windows on Fifth Avenue."

Jonas shrugged but he drew her closer. "You're too busy."

With one hand, she managed to roll up the copy of *Good Living* wedged into the sofa, and swatted him with it. "We got national publicity. I'd like to take advantage of it and do really special Christmas windows right here in Randolph. I need some inspiration."

"I see," he said. "Tell you what. Let's go down in early December. We don't even have to drive—we can take the Vermonter train all the way to Penn Station."

Satisfied with that idea, Bridget nestled into his chest

again. "Okay. My mother will be back by then to take care of Molly."

Jonas stroked her hair, not answering right away. "Well, I know how excited she'd be to see the city at Christmas, but we can bring her another time. This is going to be just you and me, babe. We'll do the town together. How does that sound?"

"Sounds good to me." She lifted her face and he gave her the best kiss of the day.

Chapter Ten

December . . .

"Not so bad, huh?"

"Oh, my! I'm getting a crick in my neck." Bridget had to tip her head all the way back just to take in the tallest building of Rockefeller Center and the towering Christmas tree that sparkled in front of it.

"You look like a tourist," Jonas teased.

"I don't care," she laughed. "I am a tourist. New York at Christmastime is amazing." The plaza was thronged with people who felt the same way, happily taking pictures of each other in front of the world-famous tree, the NBC storefront, New York police cars—in short, everything.

"Want to go skating?" He nodded toward the rink below the tree, crowded with skaters of every age going around at a stately pace.

"Uh—okay. It's been a while, though." She thought back to the pristine lake where she and Jonas had once gone skating, years ago. There hadn't been a mark on the thick, snow-swept ice until they'd ventured out onto it together, hand in hand. The hush of woods in winter had been broken only by their voices, echoing back from the surrounding hills.

The recorded music, a waltz, came to an end and the skaters left. From its place in the corner, the Zamboni machine rumbled forth to scrape and smooth the ice. Bridget watched the process, thinking how much Molly would enjoy skating here. The rink had plenty of kids her age waiting in line for their turn to skate.

"Let's do it." Jonas took her hand, giving it a squeeze. She could feel the warmth through her gloves and his. They descended the stairs on the Fifth Avenue side of the plaza, pausing to admire the Christmas angels in facing rows, made of white wire that looked like spun sugar, their trumpets raised in silent joy.

The line moved quickly as people rented skates and put them on, clomping the short distance from the rental counter to the ice, laughing and talking. The novices grabbed the rails of the clear encircling wall to get there, bravely stepping out, knees wobbling.

Jonas took care of the rental while Bridget just enjoyed the show. Red-cheeked, bundled-up children went by, clinging to the hands of adults, some of whom were pretty good skaters, she noted with surprise. Like almost everywhere in New York, the rink was crowded, but the people on it maneuvered around each other with an expertise only acquired in big cities.

It wasn't Vermont but it sure was fun. The flags of Rockefeller Center fluttered above, streaming out from black-enameled poles, their bright colors picked up by the scarves and winter coats of the tourists. She'd noticed that even black-clad New Yorkers allowed themselves a dash of color around the neck—the street vendors of scarves and shawls made that kind of impulse buy too easy and too inexpensive to resist.

She felt Jonas's hand pat her on the back and they sat down on a cold bench to put on their skates, as giddy as they had been all that time ago.

In another few minutes, they were gliding around in a stately circle of their own, big smiles on their faces.

"I feel like I'm in a Christmas card," Bridget said.

"You are," Jonas said.

She let go of Jonas and skated a little ahead, then turned around to look at him, going backwards. "I can still do it!" she cried gleefully. She skated back to his side in a few seconds, not wanting to be reprimanded by the rink monitor, who was fortunately looking elsewhere.

"Good for you," Jonas chuckled. He nodded to a guy who cast an appreciative glance at Bridget, his silent message obvious. *Forget it, pal. She's with me.*

Yes, I am, Bridget thought. And do I ever like it.

They tired of going in circles eventually and returned their skates, watched by a line of people that had grown even longer during their time on the ice.

"Okay, we can cross that off the list," Bridget said. "Now I want to see the windows at Saks Fifth Avenue."

"It means another line," Jonas warned her with a laugh.

"Let's get cocoa to go. At least we'll be warm while we wait."

The strategy worked well, although Bridget would have to say that New York was nowhere as cold as Vermont. The crowds that bustled by, the constant flow of heavy traffic, even the tall buildings, seemed to create a warmth of their own—and an excitement that was contagious.

Their cups of cocoa were empty before they turned the final corner on the temporary ropes in front of the holiday windows. Jonas took hers and stacked it inside his own, slipping the empty cups inside his pocket.

"Thanks," she said, then peered into the windows, close enough to see the detail of each fantasy setting at last. Winter fairies were up to delightful mischief in the first, and each subsequent window had its own tale to tell, using animated figures and design wizardry that was far beyond anything she could possibly do in Randolph. But what she saw was so magical that Bridget was determined to bring at least a little of it to her own holiday decorating, at home and at her shop.

She sighed with admiration over each window, reluctant to leave. But there were other people waiting patiently in line and they couldn't linger. She let Jonas take her arm as they crossed the street, heading south on Fifth Avenue. "Where are we going?" she asked.

"To see a couple of friends of mine."

She looked up at him, a little worried. "Oh. Who?"

"You'll see."

They walked on, just another couple in the surging crowd, until they'd gone almost ten blocks. Bridget looked up at the green-and-white street sign. They were at 42nd Street.

Letting go of Jonas, she stepped off the curb. An oncoming taxi swerved into the next lane over, horn blaring.

He grabbed her and pulled her back. "Careful. Those guys drive like maniacs."

"No kidding," she said wryly. "So where are your friends? Nobody actually lives right around here, do they? This doesn't look like a residential area."

With a new skyscraper going up on one corner, an old building wrapped in scaffolding on the diagonal from that, a magnificent public building backed up by a big park of some kind across the street, and a retail establishment behind her, Bridget didn't see anything that looked like it might contain apartments.

"They've been here for years," he reassured her. "Okay, we have the light. Let's go."

A little more cautiously, she crossed the wide intersection, aware that Jonas, a head taller than she was, was keeping a wary eye out for taxis this time. She let him take the lead, too jostled to do anything but follow, looking into the faces of people who seldom looked back. When they were halfway down the next block, he stopped. "Look up. Meet my friends."

Bridget laughed. Two magnificent stone lions gazed out over the stream of shoppers and office workers, resting nobly on pedestals that flanked wide, wide stairs.

"Ta-da. The New York Public Library lions," he said. "All decked out for the holidays."

Each lion wore an enormous green wreath made of metal around its neck, adorned with a red metal bow.

"Wow," she said. "They're wonderful. Introduce me."

"Huh?"

"Do they have names?" she said patiently.

"Hmm." Jonas rubbed his chin with a gloved hand. "I think they do. Oh, I remember. One is Patience and one is Fortitude. But I can't remember which is which."

Bridget took his arm and leaned into him, looking up at the lions. A few tiny flakes of white drifted down as she did, and she caught one in her palm. "It's snowing a little."

Jonas held out his hand and caught a few more. "Want to take the bus downtown?"

"Well, it doesn't look like we're in for a blizzard," she laughed. "But okay."

They got off downtown where Fifth Avenue ended, and walked through Washington Square, beneath the fine old triumphal arch and under bare trees that surprised her by their size and age. The lightly falling snow outlined the bends and twists of massive branches arching overhead.

"I didn't know there were trees this big in New York," she murmured.

"Yes, that surprised me too, when I was first here. Of course, this is one of the oldest parts of Manhattan. The streets down here have names instead of numbers."

"Hmm." The thought of him once being as new as she was to this city was somehow comforting. "Hey, I'm hungry."

"Me too. What would you like to eat? Take your pick."

They had exited the park and come out onto a narrow street that ran through small, old buildings with intriguing stores on the ground floors and a daunting variety of exotic restaurants.

Bridget didn't really feel like eating Thai or Russian or Senegalese food. "Can I be unsophisticated and just have a burger?"

"Sure. If you don't mind walking some more, we can go to one of my favorite places for that."

"Okay. I'm not tired."

As the snow continued to fall lightly but steadily, they went through Greenwich Village and Little Italy, into a neighborhood of big loft buildings that made the old streets seem even narrower.

"Are we there yet?" Bridget asked. "Oh gosh, I sound like Molly."

"Almost. Gotta go two more blocks to the right."

She took a deep breath and kept on.

"There it is. The Moondance diner."

"Oh my goodness." There was something improbable about the place: it was a tiny, railroad-car-style diner that had been plunked down on the corner decades ago and topped with a fanciful sign that was larger than it was.

A huge crescent moon, the color of cheddar cheese, revolved over the bottom part of the sign. The blue letters that spelled out Moondance were outlined with metal sequins that shone brightly under the street lamps. Next to that was a giant blue coffee cup with stars rising from it instead of steam. The crescent moon motif was repeated on the little windows, and a warm glow came from inside. Despite the snow—or maybe because of it—there were quite a few customers.

"Molly would love this place," Bridget said. "It doesn't look all that real."

"It is though," Jonas said. "Brrr. I'm freezing. Let's go in."

She stood on the sidewalk, resisting the pull of his hand, admiring the funny little diner for a few more seconds.

"Come on," he coaxed. "Before they knock it down and build a condo tower in its place."

"I hope not," she said, laughing.

They were shown to a table by an ancient waiter, who handed them rather grubby menus and left them to make up their minds.

"Not exactly five-star food," he whispered. "But you're pretty safe with a burger."

She ordered one and so did he, with Cokes and fries. When they'd eaten and Jonas eased out from behind the table to pay the bill at the cash register, she noticed the old-timer who had been sitting at the table behind theirs. He smiled at her in a friendly way, dawdling over a cup of coffee and a piece of pie.

The diner was so small that they could talk to each other without having to speak loudly. And he looked old enough to have been a customer when the place was new. He might know something about it. Bridget figured she'd ask. "Cool place, isn't it?"

"Yes, it is," he replied. "Always has been."

"Have you been coming here a long time?"

The old man nodded. "Since I don't know when."

"Could I ask you a few questions?"

"Go ahead."

Jonas had returned and he seemed amused by her interest. He stood by her and waited for the other man to reply.

"Would you happen to know who made that sign? An artist? It's really unusual."

"Now let me think." He took a bite of pie and chewed thoughtfully, as if nourishment would help him remember. "He was a young fella. Ingenious. That's a complicated sign, what with that revolving moon. It's been in a few movies and television shows." He sighed. "But he put it together more'n twenty years ago. He wasn't from around here, I don't think."

"Oh," Bridget said eagerly. "I wonder where he was from."

The old man blinked. "You need a sign made that bad?"

"Well, no. But it would be fun to talk to him."

Jonas shook his head and smiled.

The old man was still mulling it over. "He could have been from upstate New York. I'm not sure. Where are you from?"

"Vermont."

He nodded. "Well, maybe the sign guy was from there," he said diplomatically.

Jonas picked up her coat and held it out. "It's snowing harder. We should get going."

She stood and slipped her arms into the sleeves. "Thanks so much," she said to the old man. At the rate he was going, the piece of pie would be finished by sometime tomorrow.

"Wish I knew more," he said. "You two take care now."

They said their good-byes and left, walking carefully on a sidewalk that was slippery with uncleared snow. She waited, flipping up her coat collar and wishing she'd worn a hat as Jonas stepped from the curb to hail a taxi.

One pulled over in record time and he bustled her into the back. He gave directions to the driver and closed the panel between the back and the front of the taxicab. "I can't wait to get back to the hotel and get you into bed," he murmured into her ear.

Bridget leaned her head back on the warm vinyl and let him kiss her silly. She didn't think too much during the ride uptown, looking out only when they went through Time Square, awed by the gigantic electronic signs, flashing in giddy glory. There were so many that it was hard to tell there were buildings behind them all. Gorgeous as the sight was, it unnerved her. Bridget enjoyed New York and its tremendous energy, but she felt a pang of longing for her quiet little home town.

* * *

Winter hit Vermont in earnest a week after they got back. The temperature dropped well below freezing and stayed there. Bridget was busy with the Christmas rush at the store all the same, and grateful she had Mrs. Dutton to help. Jonas was just as busy at his office, treating a bumper crop of sprains and simple fractures caused by falls on snow and ice. He was doing his damnedest to take care of all the patients who came in. If it wasn't for Schulzy, the nurse he'd hired, he would have been completely overwhelmed.

When a night of unexpectedly heavy snow closed schools throughout the county the next day, Bridget brought Molly to the store and let her do her homework on the computer. She took a few minutes to go online herself, holding Molly in her lap to show her a few of the sights they'd seen in New York: the Rockefeller Center skating rink, the public library lions, and the Moondance diner. As Bridget had thought, Molly loved the diner and begged to go to New York so she could see it.

Bridget kissed her daughter's silky hair. "Maybe in summer."

"But you and Jonas had so much fun. I need a vacation, you know."

"Christmas break is almost here, honey. You get two weeks off and you can see your friends in Randolph."

"I have an idea," Molly said eagerly. "Take me and Vicki to New York."

"That might not be a vacation for me," Bridget laughed.

"Oh, Mo-om. We'd be good."

"I'm sure you would be. But there's a right time for everything and right now . . ." She hesitated. "We're going to stay in Vermont for Christmas like we always do."

"But you got to go."

Bridget winked at her daughter. "That's because I'm a grown-up and sometimes grown-ups get to go first. Ever think of that?"

"No." Molly stuck out her lower lip.

"Stop sulking. I'm not going to give in."

Molly snapped out of it, and tried asking for something else she was a little more likely to get. "Can I sleep over at Vicki's tonight? After we make the Christmas cookies?"

Bridget thought about it. If Molly was gone, then Jonas could come over later. She missed him. More than that, they had to talk. The question-and-answer session that had ended with her father's explanation wasn't enough. She couldn't stall indefinitely. Bridget didn't want to start a new year without *really* talking to Jonas at last. There were still things he didn't know . . . and it was never going to get any easier to explain.

"Mom? You're a million miles away."

"Huh? Oh—sorry. Sure, you can sleep over at Vicki's."

Molly slid off her mother's lap. "Yay!"

"*If* your homework is finished."

"The cookies are going to be beautiful, Mom!" Molly declared in a loud stage whisper as she bent over the counter to get a better look.

"They won't be if you don't get out of my light," Bridget warned.

Dutifully, Molly leaned back as Bridget added the finishing touches, outlining the gingerbread men and women with white icing. There was only one man left. Bridget paused to add more white icing to the decorator tube.

"Can I put candy buttons on them now?" Molly asked.

"Wait until I'm through," Bridget answered, hiding a smile at her daughter's impatience. Molly always got like this around Christmas. Bridget had taken all the wrapped presents over to her parents' house, otherwise Molly would have poked and shaken every single one a thousand times—and guessed what most of them were. Patience was not Molly's strong point and never had been.

Bridget had barely begun squeezing from the tube when there was a loud knock at the door. The suddenness of it made Bridget squeeze too hard and squirt a glob of icing onto the gingerbread man's face. She cursed beneath her breath and reached for the knife.

"See who it is, Molly," Bridget ordered and started to repair the damage to the cookie.

"It might be Vicki. She was going to come over and make sure we have everything we need for the party." Molly skipped to the kitchen door.

"What party?" Bridget frowned. "What are you two up to?"

"We were planning a Come As Your Secret Self party at her house. She invited Kathy too. I have to bring dress-ups. Can I raid your closet?"

"No, you can't—"

"I already did," Molly informed her as she opened the back door. "Jonas!" she cried in delight.

Bridget pivoted sharply as he walked in. He looked rugged and sexy, like he'd finally gotten out of the office and up to the mountains for several hours of much-needed R&R. He was wearing a dark suede parka lined with fleece. Bridget wanted nothing more than to burrow into it and get a huge hug from him.

Her stomach somersaulted and she felt weak at the knees. Then she became conscious of Molly eyeing her curiously. It wouldn't do to let Molly catch on about Jonas coming over. Bridget nibbled uncertainly at her lower lip.

"It's going to snow again," Jonas declared, shutting the door behind him.

Bridget's gaze flickered to the gray sky outdoors. She

tried to respond calmly. "We're going to have a white Christmas. Global warming or not."

"I think we're going to be up to our ears in snow. Is that okay with you, Molly?" His gaze moved to her.

"I can't wait! But I better get going! Mom, I'm going to pack, okay?"

"Okay. I can handle the gingerbread gang. Thanks for helping."

Molly ran out of the kitchen.

"I didn't expect you so soon." Bridget became conscious of her appearance.

She had wanted to change and put on fresh makeup before he arrived. She brushed the hair away from her forehead with the back of her hand, forgetting about the icing-coated knife she held and smearing some on her cheek.

"You were expecting Jonas?" Molly breathed in surprise, poking her head around the frame of the kitchen door.

"Hey, I thought you went upstairs."

"I came back," Molly said innocently.

"So I see. Didn't I mention to you that he was coming over?" Bridget set the knife down, knowing very well she hadn't said anything to Molly because she hadn't wanted to make a lot of explanations yet. Taking a damp towel, she wiped the icing from her cheek, which was slightly tinged with embarrassed pink. "Although I had thought it would be later tonight." Oh geez. Molly and Vicki would have a field day with that snippet of information. "Sorry, Jonas. I haven't had a chance to clean up."

"You look fine," Jonas assured her.

"You always look great, Mom," Molly added her endorsement, but it didn't carry the same weight as his.

"I suppose I should apologize for coming early, but what with the snow and all, I wanted to make sure that Molly got this particular Christmas present. Do you mind if she opens one in advance?"

"Not at all. She might decide to stop driving me crazy," Bridget said wryly.

His arm moved to reveal a large, ribbon-wrapped box he had been holding behind his back.

"For me!" Molly shrieked.

"Do you know anybody else in this house named Molly?" Jonas teased and handed it to her.

"Can I really open it now?" Molly asked Bridget, clutching the package excitedly.

"Go ahead," Jonas said, and Bridget nodded her agreement with his answer.

With painstaking care, Molly slid the bright ribbons from around the gift-wrapped box, her hazel eyes sparkling. The paper was removed with equal care before Molly lifted the lid of the box to see what was inside.

"A saddle blanket!'" she cried with delight.

"Careful," Jonas warned when she started to lift it out. "There might be something else wrapped up in it."

Molly's eyes widened before she set about unfolding the bright blue blanket. The thick material kept Bridget from seeing what was inside, but she did see the frown that suddenly appeared on her daughter's face. Just as suddenly Molly started laughing.

"What is it?" Bridget asked, overcome with curiosity.

"A doll!" Molly declared, lifting a china doll from the blanket's folds.

"I thought every girl should have one whether she was too old to play with them or not," Jonas stated, his mouth twitching in a smile.

"It's terrific!" Molly grinned. "Both presents are terrific! Thank you, Jonas."

"You're welcome." He inclined his head briefly, smiling, the corners of his eyes crinkling.

The phone rang. "I'll get it!" said Molly.

"Answer it in the living room," Bridget told her and Molly darted into the other room.

A second later the ringing stopped and Molly called back, "It's for me!"

Slowly Jonas crossed the room to where Bridget stood. His gaze flicked briefly to the decorated gingerbread men and women. "Very nice," he observed.

"They taste pretty good too," Bridget said. "Here." She handed him the gloppy-faced one.

"You're kidding." Laughter gleamed in his eyes. "You mean you put in all that work and I can take a bite out of this guy?"

"No, I'm not kidding," Bridget smiled faintly. "I messed him up anyway."

He was standing close to her. She had to move only slightly to touch him, but somehow it didn't seem necessary. Bridget had the deliriously warm sensation that he was already holding her in his arms and loving her.

"Have you changed your mind?" he murmured, his compelling gray-green eyes holding her gaze.

"About what?" she asked, feeling the sensual pull of his attraction.

"About tonight," he answered. "You seem a little—oh, I don't know. Overwhelmed? Is that the right word?"

As usual, Jonas had made an astute guess. Between minding the store during the Christmas rush, keeping her daughter happy, and drawing faces on little gingerbread people with an icing tube, Bridget had just about had it. And all those stressful things, which were minor, didn't hold a candle to the one big thing that had been on her mind for months.

"Oh, you know—Christmas can get to anybody. Holidays are stressful."

He looked at her thoughtfully. "Is it just that? I haven't said anything but you've had a while to think about whether or not you want to marry me. Whether you really love me."

Bridget felt a sinking sensation and hoped her dismay didn't show on her face. "I've loved you for more than ten years, Jonas," Bridget answered with amazing calm. "Nothing has changed that."

His hands spanned the sides of her waist to draw her to him. Bridget melted willingly into his arms, lifting her head for his kiss. It was a searingly sweet promise of love, laced with passion and stamped with a hint of possession.

It was a good thing that she heard Molly hang up the phone to yell, "Vicki's mom is coming to get me!" and clatter upstairs for real this time.

Bridget got what she wanted: a chance to nestle inside his jacket and inhale the warm scent of him. Jonas rubbed her back lightly, giving her a thorough cuddling and murmuring affectionate nonsense into her hair. She didn't budge until Molly came racketing back down and headed out the front door. "Didn't you hear Vicki's mom honking outside?" she yelled to her mother.

"No," Bridget called as the front door banged behind her daughter. "Oh, well," she said to Jonas.

He grinned down at her. "I was just like that at her age. Did what I wanted, moved fast so no one could stop me, and—"

Bridget put a finger over his lips. "The word is headstrong. And yes, you two do share that quality."

He nodded. "You know, this may sound funny, but sometimes I think she could be my kid."

The casual remark made Bridget's heart skip a beat. She'd felt so close to him just then, accepting the tenderness he instinctively knew to offer. More than at any other time that Jonas had held her, Bridget felt safe and secure. He had come home. He loved and needed her as much as she did him.

"Have I told you today that I love you, Bridget?" Jonas made the declaration in a hoarsely fervent tone, lifting his head only inches above hers.

"No, I don't think so. Do you know I love you?" Her hands were resting on his shoulders. She was about to wind them around his neck when she noticed the decorating tube she still held and the swirling glob of white icing on the dark suede of his jacket. "Look what I've done to your coat!" she exclaimed with a rueful laugh. "I'll clean it off."

Twisting out of his arms, she set the decorating tube on the counter where it couldn't do any more damage and reached for the damp hand towel. Jonas watched her with a lazy smile as she vigorously wiped at the icing.

"That's enough," he stated after a few seconds and shrugged out of his coat to toss it on the nearest kitchen chair.

"I didn't get it all," Bridget protested.

"I don't care." Jonas shook his head briefly and curved his arms around her, locking them together at the small of her back.

The light in his eyes gave his next move away. He bent his head toward hers, brushing his lips over her cheek and temple. The musky fragrance of his aftershave lotion combined with his male scent to fill her senses with heady results. His body heat made her think she was standing in front of a roaring fire.

"What do you think about getting married next week?" he asked her, his mouth moving against her smooth skin as he spoke. "Before Christmas. As soon as I can arrange it with the minister. Is that all right?"

"Yes," she breathed.

"Will you have time to do everything? We can have a real wedding, Bridget, just as fancy as you want it to be. It ͏n't going to be any rushed, hole-in-the-corner ceremony. ͏e you and I want everyone to know it."

"I'll find the time. I'll enlist every friend I have in Randolph." Every second between now and her wedding day would be hectic and frantic, but Bridget knew she wouldn't want to change it. The smile faded from her lips as other, more serious thoughts crowded their way to the front. "Jonas, I want to tell you about Brian and my mar—"

"No." His hand covered her mouth to stop the words and stayed there. "This last week I've had time to do some soul-searching. During the ten years, nearly eleven, that we've been apart, a lot happened to each of us. I don't want you to explain anything to me about your late husband or your marriage. It's none of my business. Our life together starts from this moment, and that's all that counts."

"But, Jonas, there's—"

"I know," he interrupted. "There's Molly to be considered. I like her, Bridget. She's a great kid." Bridget noticed that he didn't make any more comparisons, or try to liken Molly to her or her father. "After we're married, I'd like to legally adopt her if you and Molly agree."

"I think both Molly and I would," Bridget nodded. "All the same, Jonas, I want to tell—"

"We aren't going to talk about the past any more, only our future," he insisted firmly.

She took a deep breath. If they were going to have a future together, she had to tell him the entire truth. Now.

"Jonas," she declared, "you have to listen to me."

His gaze narrowed on her serious face. "Okay. I'm listening."

Her voice was no more than a whisper when she finally found the courage to speak. "Molly is your daughter, Jonas."

"What?" He stared at her uncertainly.

"Do you remember"—her fingers began nervously smoothing the collar of his shirt, a caressing quality in their movement—"that Saturday we started out to go skiing cross country and happened across that abandoned logging camp? We went inside one of the huts to get warm and—"

His arms tightened fiercely around her. "Do you honestly think I've forgotten the first time we made love?" he demanded huskily. "We spent the whole day there. The sun was going down when we left. We barely got back before dark."

"Less than a month later, you left. A couple of weeks after you had gone, I realized I was going to have your baby."

"Why didn't you let me know?" he groaned.

"How?" Bridget reasoned without any bitterness. "You never told me where you were going or how I could reach you. I could have tried harder, but I—I was afraid."

"You shouldn't have been," he said softly.

"As far as I was concerned, you'd deserted me. My mother took over and she convinced me that you didn't have a right to know about our baby."

Jonas turned away from her in agitation, raking a hand through his hair. "I should have considered the possibilities," he growled in self-accusation. "I should have known."

"It wasn't easy, because I still loved you," she told him quietly. "My mother arranged for me to stay with her sister in Pennsylvania," Bridget explained.

Jonas was too upset to really listen. "This Brian, your late husband, I remember you told me that he was gentle and understanding. He must have been to marry you and be the father to another man's child. I understand why you cared for him so much," Jonas sighed heavily, rubbing the back of his neck.

"Brian—" she hesitated. "Brian O'Shea didn't exist."

"What?" Pivoting, Jonas confronted her with a piercing look.

"He was a figment of my mother's imagination. She wanted me to give the baby up for adoption once it was born, but I couldn't do it. And my mother—well, she didn't want it known that her only grandchild was born out of wedlock. So she came up with a plausible story and got everyone to believe it."

"Yeah, well, nobody wants to argue with Margaret Harrison," Jonas muttered.

"I went along with it because I felt a certain amount of shame, too." She breathed in deeply, staring at the gold wedding ring on her finger. It was a symbol of a self-protective lie that had gone on for far too long. A lie that no one had known how to stop telling.

"If I'd only known—I would have been there for you—I would have told your mother to stay the hell out of it."

"Jonas . . ." Bridget's voice was low with anguish. "I didn't want you to know about Molly. I wanted to be able to say she was another man's baby if you ever came back. I was afraid you would feel responsible or want to marry me because of her. I didn't want you that way."

"Bridget." His arms wrapped around her, hugging her close and rocking her gently as if to belatedly ease the pain and anguish she had gone through alone. "I love you. At least you know I wanted to marry you because I love you before I found out about Molly. If it's possible, I love you even more now that I know."

"I'm glad." But it was a small word to describe the wild elation throbbing inside her as she snuggled against him.

"I still can't believe it," Jonas breathed against her hair. "You know, ever since last summer, when that young couple . . ." He trailed off, unwilling to say more but she remembered how deeply affected he had been by the loss of the couple's premature baby. He'd been unable to maintain the professional, unemotional manner that doctors were supposed to have, were trained to have. She'd had a glimpse into his soul that day.

"Bridget, that made me realize just how precious a family

is. And in our own crazy way, that was beginning to happen with you and me and Molly. We were becoming a family."

"I know," she said, reaching up to stroke his cheek. "It surprised me, how natural the connection was. Seeing you and Molly together, I finally understood that there was nothing to be afraid of and that I had waited far too long. Molly needs you"—she swallowed hard—"she needs her real father."

"I missed so many years of her childhood," he said, his eyes troubled.

"I know that too," she replied. "And I have to hold myself responsible for letting that happen."

Jonas let out a heavy sigh. "Not entirely. Your mother— hell, I don't know what to say. You know what I think about her. She is who she is. But she can't control you the way she once did, Bridget. She can't control us. I won't let it happen."

"That's changing," she said in a small voice. "Slowly. But it is changing."

"I don't want to fight with her. But I don't think I'm ever going to call her mom. Sorry about that."

"Don't be. You have a right to be angry with her. With me."

"Nah. What good would that do? Nobody gets to rewrite the past, Bridget. Or relive it." Jonas drew her closer. "So I'm a dad. Damn. That is so amazing. Better late than never, huh? This may sound strange but I don't feel angry. I'm bursting with pride. I feel like passing out cigars. I have a child. We have a daughter!"

Bridget lifted her head to look up at him. Her breath caught at the sight of the wondrous smile illuminating his face. "Yes, we have a daughter," she agreed, her voice choked with emotion. "Molly doesn't know, of course, but we'll tell her."

"Together," Jonas promised. A flicker of concern crossed his features. "Do you think she'll mind?"

"We'll explain everything," Bridget said. "She's old

enough to understand. She likes you, too, Jonas. It might take her some time to adjust, but I know she'll love you eventually and be proud to be your daughter."

"Old enough?" He seemed to be thinking that over. "You told me she was eight years old going on nine. And I believed you. How old is she really?"

"Ten."

Jonas studied her face for a long moment. Bridget wanted desperately to look away but his gaze held hers. "From here on in, we tell each other the truth about everything. Agreed?"

"Yes," she whispered, scarcely daring to believe that he wanted to be with her . . . wanted to marry her.

Suddenly his mouth was teasing the corner of her lips. Bridget moved to return his kiss, happier than she'd ever been in her life.

They attended a service at the white-spired church on Christmas Eve, along with almost everybody else in Randolph. Bridget looked around at the filled pews, spotting the Pomfret sisters next to Mrs. Dutton, the mothers and fathers of Molly's playmates, her parents, old people and young, come together in fellowship on a night so cold that everyone kept their coats on. The church's boiler could be faintly heard, wheezing faithfully in the basement as it tried to heat the high-ceilinged interior of the church.

Then the choir lifted their music folders and began "O Little Town of Bethlehem." The beautiful song always reminded Bridget a little of her own little town somehow. The church windows, in keeping with traditional New England rectitude, were not stained glass but showed the dark sky above. The clarity of the wintry night made the stars twinkle with a piercing brilliance.

She looked at Jonas, over Molly's head, which was

bowed to follow the old carol in a hymnal. Even in profile, he radiated a serene strength that made her heart fill with love for him. She returned her attention to the choir, as they softly sang, ". . . the hopes and fears of all the years . . . are met in thee tonight . . ." drawing out the last note.

Bridget said a silent prayer for the three of them, a family at last, and looked down at the engagement ring Jonas had given her only a week ago—and the plain gold one next to it that he had slipped on in a ceremony in this church yesterday. The diamond shone with all the fire of the stars in the window, but it was the wedding band that mattered most to her.

She sighed and sat up straighter, then stretched out her arm along the back of the pew, behind Molly's head. Jonas did the same. He put his hand over hers and squeezed gently, looking at her with all the love she had ever wanted.

GREAT BOOKS,
GREAT SAVINGS!

When You Visit Our Website:
www.kensingtonbooks.com
You Can Save Money Off The Retail Price
Of Any Book You Purchase!

- **All Your Favorite Kensington Authors**
- **New Releases & Timeless Classics**
- **Overnight Shipping Available**
- **eBooks Available For Many Titles**
- **All Major Credit Cards Accepted**

Visit Us Today To Start Saving!
www.kensingtonbooks.com

All Orders Are Subject To Availability.
Shipping and Handling Charges Apply.
Offers and Prices Subject To Change Without Notice.

Unwrap a Holiday Romance
by
Janet Dailey

Eve's Christmas

0-8217-8017-4 $6.99US/$9.99CAN

Let's Be Jolly

0-8217-7919-2 $6.99US/$9.99CAN

Happy Holidays

0-8217-7749-1 $6.99US/$9.99CAN

Maybe This Christmas

0-8217-7611-8 $6.99US/$9.99CAN

Scrooge Wore Spurs

0-8217-7225-2 $6.99US/$9.99CAN

A Capital Holiday

0-8217-7224-4 $6.99US/$8.99CAN

Available Wherever Books Are Sold!

Check out our website at **www.kensingtonbooks.com**